G
SCARED

An absolutely addictive crime thriller with a huge twist

BILL KITSON

DI Mike Nash Book 10

JOFFE BOOKS

Revised edition 2020
Joffe Books, London
www.joffebooks.com

First published in Great Britain 2018

ISBN 978-1-78931-480-9

For Val
Wife, lover, best friend, critic, editor, and all-round superstar.

ACKNOWLEDGEMENTS

All the titles in the DI Mike Nash series involve research but *Running Scared* was a far more complex plot to put together and has taken several re-writes. I have to thank the following people for their contributions.

For nautical matters, Yachtmaster Tony Othick and Chief Officer Lorraine Gouland, without whose help the book might have sunk!

My readers, Wendy McPhee, Angela Gawthorp and Andy Wormald, for their feedback and confirming the logic of the storyline.

The real Sharon Meehan who wanted to be 'naughty'.

And my in-house editor, Val, I have to thank her for all her hard work in getting this book ready for publishing — and for being lovely.

CHAPTER ONE

"FORMER GAZETTE EMPLOYEE FEARED LOST IN YACHTING ACCIDENT". Detective Constable Viv Pearce glanced at the placards outside the newsagents; then stopped suddenly, causing another pedestrian to cannon into him. He muttered an apology then went inside and bought a copy of the *Netherdale Gazette*. He stared at the headline and accompanying photo in horrified disbelief.

It had been Pearce's turn to go for sandwiches. The tall Antiguan DC was on his way back when he passed the shop. He entered Helmsdale police station at a run, threw Jack Binns, the desk sergeant, his sandwich and sprinted upstairs, taking the flight two at a time to the CID suite. Binns stared after him, wondering what the panic was.

Pearce dumped the carrier bag on his desk and glanced towards DI Mike Nash's office. The door was open, the room unoccupied. 'Where's Mike? Is he back yet?' he demanded.

DS Clara Mironova looked up from the file she was studying. 'No, he's not arrived yet. He's still at HQ. What's wrong, Viv?'

Pearce held out the newspaper. Clara scanned the front page. 'Oh no!' she muttered.

The other occupant of the room, former superintendent Tom Pratt, now the civilian support officer, hurried over to see what was wrong. Together, they read the announcement beneath the headline that had attracted Viv's attention.

It is with deep regret that we have to announce that former Gazette staff member Rebecca Pollard is feared drowned following an accident in the Bay of Biscay. The yacht on which she was a passenger capsized during a freak storm. It is believed she was heading for Spain on a sailing holiday.

Miss Pollard, whose family has owned the Gazette for four generations, was an immensely popular member of staff. After leaving the paper, she worked in Fleet Street as an assistant editor and had built an outstanding reputation as an investigative journalist.

We extend our heartfelt sympathy to Becky's family and friends, both here and in London.

After scanning the article, the team members looked at one another.

'Clara, isn't Becky Pollard related to the chief constable?' Viv asked.

'The chief's Becky's godmother.'

'Maybe this is why Mike's not here,' Pratt said. 'I wonder what effect this will have on him.'

'I don't know, they used to be close, but that was a long time ago,' Clara replied.

The team knew the relationship had ended when Becky went to London to advance her career. At the time, Clara thought Nash would have tried to make her stay, but then again, perhaps that would have been useless. He had known Becky well enough to feel certain nothing would have persuaded her to change her mind. Although their relationship was over, she guessed he would be as shocked as they were at the news. Clara, who had come to regard Nash more as an older brother than a boss, was concerned for the effect this would have on him. Having recently suffered a huge personal loss, this fresh blow could be devastating for him.

* * *

Nash had been spending a leisurely Sunday afternoon off duty, catching up on some reading, when he'd received a phone call from Chief Constable Gloria O'Donnell requesting he should come to her home immediately. When he'd arrived at the house it was her husband, who opened the door.

'Mike, come on in. If you'd go through to the dining room' — he pointed to the right — 'I'll let Gloria know you've arrived.'

The chief, known by the affectionate title of God, from her initials rather than her position, was widely respected, not least by those serving under her.

She arrived with a tray of coffee. 'Mike, thank you for coming round, I wanted speak to you before tomorrow morning's newspapers are out.' She went on to explain the headlines she expected to appear in the press. 'I'm not going into the office tomorrow; the phone here is already ringing off the hook.'

'In the circumstances I'm not surprised.'

They talked for over an hour, at the end of which she stood up and looked at him, searchingly. 'Are you going to be OK?'

'I don't have much choice in the matter, do I?'

'Before you leave, I've someone I want you to meet.'

Nash followed Gloria into the sitting room. Her husband was seated in a comfy armchair, chatting over coffee with their visitor who, as they entered, stood up from the sofa. Nash smiled as he looked at the strikingly beautiful young woman; tall, with a superbly athletic figure. Her short lustrous dark hair, fine features, and her complexion like polished ebony, made her an absolute delight on the eye.

'Mike, I think you know Alisha Roberts. I believe you two have met before.'

Nash reached out to shake her hand. 'Alisha, it's been a long time; a very long time.'

* * *

Two days later, Clara walked into the CID suite at Helmsdale to find her boss already in his office. Nash called her through and gestured to the folders on the corner of his desk. 'These are outstanding cases. I've been through them and made notes for action.'

'You've done all that this morning? What time did you get in?'

'Six o'clock. Most of this is routine, although there is a lot of it. You might want to keep an eye on the figures, don't let them get out of hand.'

'Hang on, Mike, why are you telling me this?'

'I have meetings today and tomorrow, and as of Friday I'm on leave.'

Questions queued up in Mironova's mind. What meetings? she wondered. With whom? And why didn't she know about them? And what was this about leave? She hadn't been told, and Nash was usually meticulous in consulting her before even requesting leave. She ought to have been the first to know.

'On leave? For how long?'

Nash's reply provided a fresh shock. 'Six weeks. I'm collecting Daniel from school to spend summer in France with his aunt.'

'Yes, but six weeks, Mike. That's a long time to be off work.' Mironova tried a joke. 'I know you don't do much when you're here, but you do make good coffee.'

The joke failed miserably.

'Clara, I need a break.' He glanced at the photo frame on his desk, a reflex action that saddened Mironova. The photo was a painful reminder of the woman he had so recently loved — and lost.

'I know six weeks is a long time, that's why I wanted all the paperwork up to date before I go. Anyway, you'll have the superintendent to oversee operations. She's sending help over from Netherdale, so you'll be fine.'

And that was that.

As Mironova walked back into the general office, she wondered if the news of Becky's death had been instrumental in Nash's decision. Was he secretly grieving more than they imagined? He was certainly acting out of character. He hadn't been his usual self of late and now this. Perhaps hearing of the death of his old flame, a painful reminder, had been too much for him.

Although it would have been churlish to deny him leave, as a rule he had to be dragged away from work, such a long period was unheard of. And to take it without consultation or consideration for the others in their small team simply wasn't his style. They had managed before, short-term, but this was different. Clara felt the responsibility of long-term command a little daunting.

Nash watched Clara leave, aware that he had upset her. He stared ruefully at the door which she had closed with a quiet firmness that spoke volumes, more so than if she'd slammed it. He knew she was unhappy at the way she'd been told. Knew also that there was absolutely nothing he could do about it.

* * *

Ivan Kovac was sitting at his desk in the office of his meat processing plant in Leeds when Stanley entered the room. Kovac sensed his excitement.

'You've got to see this,' Stanley said as he thrust a two-day-old newspaper at his boss.

Kovac studied the news report with interest. He read the article describing the death of Becky Pollard in silence, and when he finished, looked up. His associate was visibly agitated, an excitement Kovac did not share. 'What do you make of it?' He asked the question quietly, because he saw no reason for celebration. Not yet, anyway.

Stanley shrugged. 'Saves me a job — and a lot of time and worry for all of us.'

'A slice of luck, you think?'

Stanley smiled, recognizing Kovac's humour. 'For us, certainly' — he indicated the paper — 'not for her though.

Although I guess drowning is less painful than what you wanted me to do to her.'

'The only variety of luck I've experienced has been bad. But I do believe in the sort of luck you make for yourself. This' — he tapped the paper — 'seems far too lucky to be true. When I first got word from London that she'd been snooping around my business interests, I ordered her watched. If the idiot you sent to grab her and bring her here hadn't botched things up and lost her, we would know we were lucky. Of course I could be wrong, but I think we should take this with, what's the English expression, a piece of salt?'

'A pinch of salt,' Stanley corrected him. Ivan's English was good, free from accent, but the idiom sometimes defeated him.

'Let me think about this. Then I'll decide what we do.'

Stanley paused at the door. 'It's a shame if that report is true. I was looking forward to meeting her.'

Kovac felt slightly sick at the man's final words. His voice had been calm, always was, but when he had spoken there had been no disguising his disappointment. Kovac had killed, but even he was repelled at the thought of what horrors Stanley would have inflicted on the reporter. Repelled even more by the obvious enjoyment it would have given him.

Few people knew Stanley's real name, or where he came from. And even fewer had the courage to enquire. Throughout the murky world in which they operated, he was known only by his nickname, Stanley, or to give the full one, Stanley Slicer. The long scar he carried down one side of his face was a souvenir of an early knife fight — he had never lost a fight since.

Ivan and Stanley shared a common bond, their true identities being shrouded in the past. Before he arrived in England, Todor Nikolic became Ivan Kovac, and the money he had laid out then had rewarded him with the paperwork as a Polish national to match his new identity.

His business empire was flourishing, Ivan, as he now thought of himself, had long wanted to expand his operations in England where demand and the rewards were high.

The drugs network he had set up both as a method of distributing illicit substances, and a channel for laundering the proceeds, ensured his continued and growing wealth. As he prospered, his fortune enabled him to diversify into a range of more legitimate businesses, granted, most of these were a cloak for his illegal activities.

In several areas, with the aid of the persuasive powers of Stanley, elimination of competition had left him with a monopoly in the drugs market. That had been the case until recently when Kovac's operation had been threatened from two angles. Firstly, from the investigative activities of Becky Pollard, and second, from a rival supplier who had entered the market and was undercutting him. There was no doubt this had cost him dearly and he was determined not only to regain his supremacy, but also eliminate the opposition. If circumstances had been different he would have resorted to strong-arm tactics, even to murder, but Kovac was reluctant to try that. The rival gang had a reputation for ruthlessness and a proven record as killers that surpassed anything either Kovac or Stanley could claim. Professional killers, trained in the art by the British Army, referred to by Kovac's team as the Soldiers.

A very real challenge awaited Kovac if he was to retain his position as market leader, but that would have to wait. His priority had to be the reporter. Although not one given to fear, the possible extent of her knowledge frightened him. He wasn't sure exactly how much she had discovered, which was why he had asked Stanley to take care of her. What worried Kovac most was that she might have uncovered his identity and origin. Ivan Kovac, respectable businessman, would fear little from even the most searching of probes. But Todor Nikolic, who had never actually been to Poland, but who had left Serbia one step ahead of the authorities and a large number of vengeful people, had every reason to be terrified of discovery. If people that had suffered from his past activities knew he was to return, he felt certain that his survival following his arrival at Nikola Tesla Airport would be measured in hours rather than days.

Becky Pollard might indeed have drowned, but that was a chance Kovac was unwilling to take. He called Stanley back into his office. 'That private investigator we've used before, get him to check on the Pollard woman's background. I want him to go right back to her childhood. Concentrate on where she came from before she went to London. Once we have his report, I want you to set our people checking all her old haunts, family, and acquaintances. My bet is that, if she is still alive, that will be where she's hiding.'

An hour later, Stanley came back. 'I spoke to the PI's office. The job's sorted.'

'Right, you'd better go to the park and make sure everything's OK there. Check to see if anyone's been snooping around. And see if you can get an angle on what the opposition are up to. If we can find out where and when they're operating, we might be able to hit them. If you can find that out, organize a couple of men to intercept one of their deliveries, we'll be able to see how they react to the loss of a valuable cargo.'

Kovac remained in his office, staring at the newspaper, pondering the report. A chilling thought struck him. Although they had no proof that she had left evidence behind that might incriminate him, what if there was a file waiting to be read? Or even worse, what if the information was already in the hands of someone who could act on it; police or immigration officials? Kovac broke out in a cold sweat. And that didn't happen very often.

CHAPTER TWO

The argument had been stupid. Even the farmer recognized that, and he'd been the one who started it. The row had been about money and was sparked by his wife mentioning that she wanted a new kitchen. It wasn't that she was particularly extravagant, or that he was mean, but her timing had been appalling. To make the suggestion first thing in the morning, after the traumas of the previous day, had been unfortunate.

The first of the traumas came courtesy of the postman, who delivered the winter feed bill. Then there had been the problem with the tractor and the expense involved in repairing it. Coming on top of those, her request had been like a red rag to a bull.

He had stormed out of the house and jumped into his Land Rover, pausing only to allow his dog to jump onto the passenger seat. The Border Collie sat bolt upright, tongue lolling out of the side of her mouth, eager for work.

As they drove towards Black Fell and the fields he rented on the lower slopes, his mind was full of the events of the previous day, a day that had been wasted trying to fix the tractor. He had worked on it until late afternoon, only to find that a vital component needed replacing. A call to the dealer provided more frustration as they didn't have one in stock and would have to get one from the continent. That meant airfreight, at a frightening cost.

As he pulled up alongside the hedge that shielded the pasture from the road, the farmer noticed that the gate had been left open. He muttered something extremely impolite about walkers who treated the countryside as their private playground without giving any thought to those who had to work the land and opened the car door. 'Come on, Gyp, let's see if the little buggers have strayed now someone's given them an escape route.'

The farmer glanced towards the field, but the hedge was too high to get a view of the land. It was only when he and the dog reached the entrance that they stopped, neither of them able to believe what they saw. Or rather what they couldn't see. Gyp looked up at her master, her expression one of puzzlement.

'Oh shit! Oh hell, no! The bastards!'

The dog didn't understand the words, but the tone of voice was sufficient to tell her that all was far from well. The field, which should have contained almost a hundred ewes and lambs, was now empty. Ramblers hadn't left the gate open.

Only a week earlier he had received an e-mail from the National Farmers' Union warning of the increased danger of sheep theft. The circular had cited some statistics that made for grim reading. He remembered the easy sympathy he had felt for those who had suffered such losses. The tyre tracks in the soft mud close to the entrance and the disappearance of his whole flock told him that the threat had been no idle one. He felt physically sick. The feed bill, the tractor repair, even the new kitchen, all paled into insignificance compared with the loss of stock with a value close to ten thousand pounds.

* * *

'Good morning, boss.' Sergeant Binns stood to attention and saluted Clara as she walked into the reception area of Helmsdale police station.

'Jack, if I didn't know you better, I'd swear you were taking the piss.'

Binns smiled and relaxed. 'In your capacity as leader of the CID team here, I have some work for you and your minions.'

'Go on, tell me the worst.'

'Let me see — what crime are you least expecting today?'

Clara sighed. 'It's a bit early in the morning for quiz questions, Jack.'

'How about rustling?'

'Rustling?'

'Yep, I've had a farmer from Drovers Halt on the phone a few minutes ago to report he's had ten thousand pounds worth of sheep stolen.'

Mironova stared at him in surprise. 'That sounds like a lot of sheep.'

'Around a hundred at today's prices, according to what he told me. He reckoned they were fetching over a hundred pounds apiece at last Thursday's mart.'

'That's not somebody killing for their own use.'

'Not unless they've an extremely large freezer,' Binns agreed. 'From what the farmer said, in between the swear words, there were tyre tracks leading into the field from the gate. The sheep were on summer pasture over at Black Fell, which is fairly remote and ideal — ideal for the thieves, I mean.'

'How would they do it though? That's a lot of animals. You were brought up around here; you know how these things work better than me.'

'I was thinking it over before you arrived. They'd need a big wagon for a flock that size. And they'd have to be experienced with sheep. Added to which they'd need a good dog. Even then it would be no simple matter, working on strange terrain at night.'

'Once they'd got them into the wagon, what would they do with them? I mean, where would they take them?'

'Good question. Wherever they went, they'd need paperwork.'

'You mean a bill of sale, something like that?'

Binns shook his head. 'They'd need passports.'

'Passports? For sheep?'

'I'm no expert, but I believe all livestock must have a passport these days. And if you want to move them from one location to another you must also have a valid movement order in place beforehand. That requirement was brought in after the foot-and-mouth epidemic, I think. You'd be better off checking the exact requirements with someone who knows more about it than me. A field officer from DEFRA or someone from the NFU for example.'

'I'll do that. First, though, I'd better send someone to talk to the farmer and have a look at the crime scene.'

Binns passed her the incident report form. 'One thing I will say. By now those lambs will have been slaughtered and hung in an abattoir somewhere.'

'Hung?'

'You have to hang them for a few days before butchering them otherwise the meat will be tough and tasteless. The bigger the beast, the longer it takes. Lambs need about a week, I believe. From memory, cattle could take anything up to three weeks.'

* * *

It was as if Nash's departure was a signal to the local criminal fraternity to spring into action. Clara and her colleagues found themselves investigating a string of incidents some petty, but some more serious.

Superintendent Jackie Fleming arrived from Netherdale HQ for a meeting with Clara. 'Is there anything we should be particularly concerned with? Given that all unsolved crimes are a worry, obviously.'

'Yes, there is something Viv Pearce discovered during a conversation he had with one of his informants. It seems there are now two suppliers of hard drugs operating in our area. That's bad enough in itself, but it may also be a contributory factor to the rash of petty thefts, as users steal to feed their addiction.'

'That is bad news. It tallies with something the chief constable mentioned this morning. There's a report due from the new Drugs Intelligence Unit, warning of an increase in class-A substances being brought into this part of the country. I don't suppose Viv's informant gave him anything really useful, such as names?'

Clara shook her head. 'No such luck. Apparently, whoever these pushers are, they've got the locals scared shitless. Nobody's talking and what little Viv did get had to be prised out of his contact.'

'Keep the pressure up for more details and I'll enlist uniform branch to keep a special lookout for transactions taking place. If we can catch someone in the act of dealing, or in possession with intent to supply, we might get them to talk and give us a lever on the operations that way. I'll have a word with the chief and see if she can get any background information, and as soon as that report is available, I'll let you have a copy.'

* * *

In the flagship restaurant of a large chain the head chef paused outside the door of the manager's office and looked over his notes. Only when he was completely satisfied did he raise his hand and knock on the glass panel of the door.

'I've prepared the draft for the next season's menus. There are quite a few changes, and the whole thing is subject to our suppliers being able to deliver the right stuff at the right price.'

He passed over a sheaf of papers. The manager skim-read the sheets, pausing when his eyes zeroed-in on one specific item. 'Venison?' he queried. 'That's a bit of a departure for us, isn't it?'

'Yes and no. We had a lot of success last winter with pheasant, partridge, and wild duck. If we add venison in the various guises I've listed there, it will hopefully enhance our reputation as a great venue for classic British food, the best of which is game.'

'Venison will be very expensive. What if it doesn't sell? What if everyone gets reminded of Bambi when they see it on our menu? It could have the wrong effect altogether.'

'They didn't think of Disney cartoon characters when we put duck on the menu,' the chef pointed out. 'And, you believed that lamb was going to be too expensive to serve regularly, but our supplier got it for us at a price that enabled us to make a healthy profit. Why not ask them?'

'OK, leave it with me. I'll give it some thought.'

It was all very well the head chef making bold statements such as those, but with five branches under his control the manager had to make sure they could all deliver to the same high standard. However, he had to admit that he had entertained similar doubts regarding the other game dishes and they had proved highly successful. Not only that, but venison wasn't a lot different from beef or lamb. His mind made up, the manager reached for the phone to check with their meat supplier. The next hurdle to overcome was the price. If it proved too expensive that would be a showstopper.

The meat factory manager was in the middle of dealing with a labelling machine that had been spewing tickets all over the floor when he was summoned to the phone to discuss a potential order. He spoke with the restaurant manager and was about to return to his repair but decided to place a call first. Inside his own office, he closed the door before speaking to his contact. At the end of the conversation he phoned the restaurant and reported he had successfully sourced the venison, quoted a price, and added his usual stipulation — the transaction would have to be cash with no paperwork involved. When his terms were accepted, only then did he return to the problem machine.

* * *

Two nights later, PC Geoff Riley was working the late shift. He'd been stationed at Netherdale HQ for five years and to some it might have seemed like the road to nowhere, but Riley didn't think so. The stress he saw on the faces of officers he met from big city beats, and the horror stories they told made him glad he'd opted for the quieter life of a rural posting. Even when the cutbacks hit, he knew there was less chance of his job being threatened than elsewhere, because they were already operating on the bare minimum staff levels.

It had its disadvantages, though. When someone was off sick, for example, there was frequently no cover available. That was the case at present. As he drove out through Kirk Bolton village, he passed the house of the colleague who should have been alongside him in the car. The previous week his colleague had struggled with a drunk, fallen and slipped a disc.

Not that he felt the need for backup or expected trouble this evening. The matter that was taking Riley out to Bishop's Cross was routine. Late-night drinking was now legal, but the complaint was to do with the noise generated by customers at the Red Lion and that couldn't be tolerated.

He dealt with the rowdy drinkers who had been indulging in an impromptu karaoke session and, shortly after one a.m., set off back towards Netherdale. It was a dark, moonless night and the woodland alongside the country road was like a black curtain, shielding the Winfield Estate from prying eyes.

As Riley steered the car round a right-handed bend he saw a brief flash of light in his peripheral vision. Instinctively, he braked, slowing the patrol car as he scanned the woodland. He was about to accelerate, convinced it had been his imagination or a distorted reflection from his own headlights when he saw it again. Whatever it was, Riley felt sure it had no right being there.

He slowed even further until the car was creeping along as he puzzled over what was going on and what he should do. He tried to remember the lie of the land. If he'd got his bearings right, there was a gate a few hundred yards ahead leading to a ride, cut through the woodland to act as a fire break.

As he turned the next bend Riley saw the gate and in front of it, parked nose out from the woods, was a Transit van. Of course, it might be a courting couple, but he didn't think so, not if they wanted any comfort. If it wasn't a courting couple, it had to be poachers. He pulled to a halt and contacted the Netherdale control room, thankful he had a signal. 'I'm on the Bishop's Cross to Kirk Bolton road, by Winfield Estate. There's a suspect vehicle parked in a gateway. A Ford Transit, I think, but I can't make out the registration number without getting out of my car. It's covered in mud. It could be somebody doing a spot of poaching, or it could just be someone having a bit of leg over. I'm going to take a look. I'll get back to you in a couple of minutes with the registration number.'

Approximately thirty seconds later, after Riley emerged from his vehicle, a hunting owl, disturbed by an unfamiliar loud crack of sound, abandoned her intended prey and swooped off into the distance uttering a loud screech of protest.

Riley also heard the sound, also heard the owl, but dimly, through the agonizing pain in his chest. Then both vision and hearing left him as he slumped to the ground.

'What the fuck did you do that for? You've killed a copper, you stupid bastard.'

'What did you want me to do? Wait for him to arrest us? In case you'd forgotten, those deer on the ground don't belong to us.'

'What if he's rung the number of the van in? We'll have to ditch it now.'

'Relax. Even if he did ring it in, it'll do them no good. That number belongs to a double-decker bus from Leeds. Now, help me get these deer in the van and let's get the hell out of here.'

Five minutes passed before the control room operator realized Riley hadn't called back. After several attempts to raise him, the operator contacted the nearest patrol car. By the time the officers pulled to a halt behind Riley's vehicle, the poachers were miles away, and PC Riley's body was already beginning to cool in the night air.

A couple of hours later, the Transit van pulled up at the back entrance of the meat processing plant in Leeds. Due to this being a different product to the ones they were used to dealing with, a fresh approach was needed. For one thing, previous deliveries were usually alive upon arrival at the plant. It was a novel experience for them to take delivery of a consignment that was already dead. More than that, owing to the special requirements required for dealing with this type of meat, much of their work had already been done.

The factory manager gave specific instructions to his two most trusted employees. These men had dealt with other late-night arrivals and would ask no embarrassing questions as long as they were paid well for their work — and their silence. The manager signalled to the visitors to follow him. Once inside the privacy of his office, he asked if everything had gone to plan. It was a courtesy question, nothing more.

'Not really,' the driver, the older of the two replied. 'Someone stuck their nose in where it wasn't wanted and I had to deal with him.'

The manager was curious but refrained from enquiring further. There are some details it is better not to know. Instead he removed the cash box from the safe and counted out the sum agreed beforehand. He thanked them, adding, 'I'll be in touch as soon as we need anything else.'

* * *

The phone at Clara's bedside rang. She rolled across the double bed, missing the warmth of her fiancé David's body alongside her. 'Mironova,' she croaked into the handset.

'Sorry to wake you, Clara, but it's bad news, I'm afraid. News of the very worst kind.'

'Why, what's happened, Jack?' As she was listening, she threw back the duvet and was reaching for her clothing as he answered.

'One our uniformed men has been killed. Gunned down in cold blood.'

Clara could hear the anger and distress in Binns' voice. 'Tell me the details.'

'It was Geoff Riley, based at Netherdale. He'd been out to Bishop's Cross on a routine matter. On the way back he called in to report a suspicious vehicle parked by Winfield Estate. Looks as if he was shot as he got out of his patrol car, we believe he might have disturbed a gang of poachers. I've briefed Superintendent Fleming. She's on her way.'

'Right, I'll set off as soon as I'm dressed. Lisa's on call; let her know, will you? I assume Professor Ramirez has been notified?'

'All being dealt with. He's organizing the forensic team.' Binns paused, but Clara waited, aware he wanted to say more. 'I know Jackie Fleming will have to be SIO on this one, but you'll be doing most of the detective work. Nail these bastards, Clara. Geoff Riley was as decent a bloke as ever put on a uniform. He didn't deserve this. What his wife will do, I've no idea. It was hard enough before, this will make things intolerable.'

'How do you mean?'

'Maureen Riley is the civilian clerical officer from Netherdale. You know her; she works alongside Tom.'

'Oh! I didn't know that. She's the one who transferred from Bishopton after the station there closed down, right?'

'That's correct.'

'What did you mean about her being unable to cope?'

'Geoff and Maureen have a son; the Riley lad is disabled.'

'Oh bloody hell, Jack, that's terrible.'

'I know. It makes you feel so helpless. That's one more reason for wanting to nail the swine that did this. I know it won't be easy, but you'll have all the backup you need. It's what Mike's trained you for. You're a damned good detective and, with what you've picked up from Mike, you can do it, if anyone can.'

As she dressed, Clara reflected on what Binns had said. The vote of confidence might have been good to hear, but it placed a weight of expectation on her shoulders.

CHAPTER THREE

Tony Hartley, head of the unit referred to by their rivals as the Soldiers, had a problem. He was on a fund-raising mission with a particular goal in mind, but things had gone wrong. In the midst of an earlier bank robbery he had lost three of his team. They had netted six-figure sums from the raid and a previous security van hijack, which was sufficient to fund the new drug-running operation. But that money paled into insignificance compared to what they were now earning. Such a highly profitable enterprise needed protection. He had got word to his boss, the major, and was awaiting a reply.

In a solicitor's office in Netherdale the morning post had been sorted and handed out. Prison Rule 39 is designed to allow correspondence between prisoners and their legal advisors without the contents being subject to scrutiny. When the solicitor received such a communication from Felling Prison with the letters OT discreetly written on the back of the envelope, instead of opening it, he placed it inside another envelope. After consulting a file, he addressed the outer envelope and placed it in his post tray. He made a note to add the appropriate charge to his client's legal fees. His abuse of the system could land him in trouble, but he knew he would be paid handsomely for the service.

Next morning at his house in Netherdale, Tony Hartley saw the solicitor's name on the franking mark on the envelope and breathed a sigh of relief. With luck, the major would have come up with an idea to solve his staffing problem. He opened it and began to read. The major didn't waste time on niceties.

'I appreciate the need to recruit. I hear the sergeant is back in the country now, and I'm sure he'll be looking for work — and money. And this time, make sure Nash doesn't get in the way.'

Tony Hartley finished reading, sat back, and thought about the message. Nash, his boss's nemesis and responsible for his imprisonment, led a charmed life where Hartley was concerned. This time however, there was no way Nash could even make a connection. He wondered briefly how, when currently serving a life sentence in a high security prison, the major had heard of the sergeant's return to England. They had all served together as sappers and when last heard of, the sergeant had been in jail in central Africa. Nevertheless, he'd be ideal for what Hartley required. Ruthless and professional, trained as one of the army's most efficient killers, the sergeant had become a 'security consultant', otherwise known as a mercenary.

Hartley scrolled down the contacts section in his laptop. All the entries were coded but he soon reached the one he was looking for. A cryptic note told him that the number belonged to the sergeant's sister, who was also his next of kin. He hoped that the woman hadn't moved house. He dialled the number, which rang out three times before going to voicemail. Fortunately, the woman had recorded a greeting which identified her. Hartley spoke slowly and clearly. 'This message is for the sergeant. Please ask him to contact Captain Hartley,' he recited his mobile number and rang off.

Five minutes later his mobile rang.

'You left a message.' Hartley could sense the tension in the sergeants' voice. Obviously, he was afraid the call might be a trap.

'The major suggested I call you. He thought you might be interested in some gainful employment. Extremely gainful. If so, we should meet.'

'Woolley Edge north, six plus twenty-four.' The phone went dead.

Hartley smiled. That was it then. He would meet him at Woolley Edge services on the northbound carriageway of the M1 at 6 p.m. the following day: problem solved.

* * *

Ron Mason, the sergeant, crossed to the table, coffee in hand, and sat down. 'Your security's crap,' he greeted Hartley. 'I followed you all the way from your car into this place. Now, what's the job?'

Hartley greeted the former sergeant then chose his words carefully, mindful that they were in a public place. 'We're having a lot of trouble with competitors in our supply department. A European company was already in the area. We need to eliminate them. Added to which, I lost three good men a while ago in an operation that went wrong, and I need to recruit.'

What might have been a smile crossed Mason's face. 'I read something about that so-called operation, in the papers — gave the impression of a complete cock-up. It sounded sloppy. Was that them, or you?'

'Them. They didn't follow orders. So, are you up for it? You know the team. All they need is a bit of smartening up. Like you said, security is one angle.'

'When do I start and where do I report?'

Hartley was about to reply when his mobile rang. He glanced at the screen before taking the call. 'Yes?' He listened for some time. 'Shit! OK, I'll deal with that myself,' he said. 'Who are they?'

He listened for a little while longer, grunted what could have been a farewell, and ended the call. He stared at the phone for a moment before looking up.

'Trouble?'

Hartley nodded. 'How soon can you start?'

'My kit's in the car.'

'I'll give you directions on the way out. Suddenly, your job has become urgent, we'll sort terms out later.' He lowered his voice. 'One of our couriers has been attacked. The dealer he was supposed to deliver to found him at the rendezvous an hour ago, bound and gagged. The package he was carrying, a very expensive package; gone. The hijackers made a couple of mistakes; they let our man see their faces. He recognized them, knows where they hang out; where we can find them. They're members of Euro-trash, our competitor's lot. Although the courier can't be certain, he thought he recognized something one of them said about where they were to take the package. That's why we need to move fast. We know who the enemy is and we know where they are. This means war. And, with you on board, we've the manpower to overcome them. It won't be easy. This man is a tough nut and he has some unpleasant characters around him, but that'll only make the job more enjoyable.'

* * *

Two days later at the meat factory, Ivan Kovac was reading an e-mail when his phone rang. He glanced at the display as he picked up the handset. 'Yes, Stanley?'

'We have a problem.'

'What?'

'The two men we used to hijack that shipment from the Soldiers two days ago. They've vanished. They haven't been seen since they dropped the package off.'

'I don't suppose they've been sampling the merchandise by any chance? Gone on a bender and not recovered? Alternatively, if they've decided to set up business on their own account I would be very, very angry.'

'No chance, certainly on the first count; all the stock is in place. And as for the second idea, I don't think they've the money to do that; or the balls.'

'If they have, they won't keep their balls much longer. If they're not out of it on the white stuff or flogging it round the streets, what do you think happened?'

'No idea. Worst case scenario is that they might have been seized as an act of retaliation by the Soldiers.'

'Worst case, why?'

'Because if that's what's happened it's more than likely that somebody inside our organization has been got at and talked. The alternative would be that our men were sloppy and got recognized. Either way, they know too much for comfort.' Stanley paused. 'Although from what little I know about our competitors I don't think they have anybody capable of extracting that sort of information. But,' he added, 'I could be wrong.'

'Thanks for cheering me up,' Kovac told him sarcastically. 'You'd better set everyone you can spare to looking for them. And another thing, the private detective e-mailed his report through with the Pollard woman's background. I'll phone you as soon as I've read it and decided where to start.'

'You still don't believe the press reports about the drowning?'

'Show me the body and I will.'

The report was long and detailed, but that was only part of the problem. Although Kovac's spoken English was good and he had mastered the difficulty of presenting his voice accent-free, reading the language was more difficult.

He made notes of anything significant, or that would provide some clue as to where the reporter might have chosen as a bolthole. The notes covered all members of Becky Pollard's family, her friends in both London and from her time in Yorkshire, together with her workmates at the *Netherdale Gazette* and the national paper she had joined.

He all but discounted her parents and the other close family members off his list. He felt sure Becky Pollard wouldn't risk endangering them by making them a target for possible collateral damage.

The more he thought about it, and the longer he studied the report, the more certain Kovac felt that the answer was in North Yorkshire and around the Netherdale area in particular. As he studied the list, two entries stood out. The chief constable, Becky Pollard's godmother, would be a natural choice given her personal attachment and her official position. However, it was the second name that interested Kovac even more; Detective Inspector Mike Nash. The private investigator had written at some length of their relationship prior to her departure for London. It seemed that the couple had been living together for some time.

Kovac felt sure that it would be to this man Nash that Becky Pollard would turn in such a crisis. The investigator had gone into great detail about Nash, outlining his career, which sounded remarkably successful following a stint in the Met; a dangerous opponent, then. If she had turned to him for help and shelter, Kovac felt certain she would have passed on all she knew. That in turn meant that Nash was an even bigger threat than Becky Pollard. Whereas she could only write about what she might have discovered, Nash could act on it. The whole of Kovac's empire was under threat.

He had to find out where Nash lived, and send someone to deal with him. But before that, it would be better to make absolutely certain. No point in wasting Nash if the danger from Pollard still remained. First things first, he would send someone on a scouting mission. Once they had confirmation, his men could move in.

He glanced at the photo that the private investigator had included as an attachment to the e-mail showing a smiling, very attractive woman. 'Sorry, my dear,' he murmured. 'If you're not already dead, then you soon will be. Your little game will be over. I'll introduce you to Uncle Stanley and you'll find out how he got his name.'

* * *

Clara Mironova drove from York to Netherdale for an early morning meeting with Chief Constable O'Donnell and Superintendent Fleming. The previous day had been her day off and she had driven to York to meet her fiancé Major David Sutton and stayed overnight. It had been their final chance to get together before he went on an overseas posting. Had he not been leaving, Clara knew that with the pressure she was under she would not have even taken a day off, but this was different. She was now burdened again with the anxiety all army wives and girlfriends feel when their loved ones are sent to a war zone. In her case the distress was heightened by the knowledge of the type of specialist work David was involved in.

He had been ready to quit the army but, with the prospect of unemployment, had decided to sign on for a further tour of duty which had sparked off an angry confrontation. However, all that was forgotten in the emotion of their farewell.

In an attempt to dismiss her fears and distress, Clara reflected on other things that had happened in the time since Nash had gone on leave. Principal among these was her realization of the amount of work he did, much of which she hadn't been aware. This was highlighted by the volume of paperwork that crossed her desk, papers she didn't usually get to see. She had often teased him about doing nothing. Now she appreciated the amount of work he did get through. Not that she would have admitted as much to him.

In the Riley murder inquiry, there had been no witnesses, so there were no statements to read. By contrast, given the location of the crime scene, they had called in a variety of scientific specialists whose evidence might prove crucial should they be able to bring a prosecution to court. On the passenger seat, Clara had the reports from each of these experts, copies of which were with the chief constable and Fleming. These reports would form the basis for discussion. But that wasn't all Mironova had. While waiting for David to arrive in York, Clara had read the reports and begun to develop a theory and a possible link. Whether this would lead to an arrest or conviction she was unsure.

They sat around the chief constable's crescent-shaped desk. O'Donnell opened the debate. 'What do you make of the expert opinions?' She looked first at Fleming for a response.

'The analysis of the blood seems to confirm the poaching theory. Identifying it as being from a deer means we're looking for someone prepared to kill to avoid arrest. That suggests that they might have form. Perhaps they knew that would lead to a longer term of imprisonment than standard for this offence. As far as physical evidence goes, we've a boot print and a couple of tyre tracks. These may or may not belong to the killers. Most important, Professor Ramirez recovered the bullet from PC Riley's body. It was a large calibre bullet that would have passed through the body had it not hit the breastbone, where it lodged. If we recover the weapon, that should give us a match. The calibre of the weapon is another indication that poachers killed our officer. That's as far as I've got, but I think Clara might have more.'

O'Donnell looked across at Mironova.

'I agree with Jackie up to a point,' Clara hesitated, 'but I think they were involved in more than poaching. I believe they were scared we could connect them to other unsolved crimes. Forensics found dog hairs in the deer's blood. Owning dogs isn't unusual for poachers, although I don't think many of them take them deerstalking. However, people who need to control sheep also need dogs.'

'Sheep?' The chief constable stared at her. 'Are you suggesting shepherds murdered PC Riley?'

'No, ma'am, not shepherds — rustlers. You remember the farmer who had his flock stolen? What if there's a gang stealing livestock to order? I asked Tom Pratt to do a bit of research.'

She turned the pages in her file. 'These figures are only approximate, and the data is from last year, but the NFU suggests that over sixty thousand sheep were stolen in the UK during the first ten months of last year. That's two and a half times the number for the previous year.' She read on a little further. 'There have also been large increases in the theft of cattle, pigs, and game birds.'

'That's a lot of livestock,' Fleming suggested.

'I agree, and reading this report, the NFU blames high meat prices. I'd go further and add the recession into that equation. These figures suggest there are large gangs of professional criminals stealing stock on a regular basis; gangs ruthless enough to kill in order to protect their source of income. I believe PC Riley was unlucky enough to get in their way.'

O'Donnell shook her head and sighed. 'All of which makes catching them even more difficult and dangerous. Accepting that you're right, and I'm not suggesting otherwise,' — O'Donnell smiled — 'what baffles me is how they dispose of such large quantities of animals.'

'I think there has to be an element of collusion,' Clara paused. 'Someone has to be doctoring the paperwork. Added to which there has to be an abattoir or meat factory involved. There's no other way such a large amount of meat could get into the food chain. Once the stock has been butchered, there's no chance of identifying the source. For all we know the next meal we eat, be it a bacon butty, lunch in the canteen, a pork pie from the butcher or dinner in a restaurant, could contain stolen meat.'

'I'm inclined to agree with your theory,' — O'Donnell glanced at Fleming who nodded — 'which makes it depressingly unlikely we'll be able to bring the killers to trial. Unless you've thought up an approach to identify the gang?'

'There is one thing that might be worth trying,' Clara said. 'Although it would be very difficult to identify the people involved, we might be able to find the vehicle they use. The van used to transport the deer would be near impossible to trace, but for a flock of sheep they would need an HGV; and a specialist one at that. There aren't many on the road, which shortens the odds no end. The other part of that equation is that they wouldn't want to travel too far with their load, or use a vehicle that would stand out, so the truck is likely to be a local one.'

'Good thinking.' The chief closed her file, signalling the end of the meeting. 'Keep me updated.'

O'Donnell watched them leave her office, reflecting on what Mironova had told them. The way Clara worked was uncannily similar to how Nash operated. He'd maintained all along that Mironova had the makings of an excellent detective. His absence looked set to give Clara a chance to prove him right.

CHAPTER FOUR

When Clara got home that evening, it was dark. She had been working late and had lost track of time. She walked in, switched the lights on, and looked round. The apartment felt cold, unused, as if she had been away far longer than forty-eight hours. She left her bag in the hall and wandered into the lounge. She had become so used to David being around the place that now, when she needed his help and support, a shoulder to cry on, she felt his absence even more keenly. Suddenly, despite the air of confidence she exuded at work, she felt very much alone and vulnerable.

Unsolved crimes were piling up around her and in her tired state she wasn't sure she could cope. At work she'd become accustomed to having someone to talk problems through with. As a member of the police team, she knew she made a valuable contribution. Now, plunged into the unfamiliar role of leader, she began to realize, for the first time, that the position was not without its disadvantages. It was lonely work being captain and suddenly, with something of a shock, Clara realized that she missed Mike Nash as much as she missed David. In a completely different way, she thought with a wry smile. Damn the pair of them, why had they both deserted her when she needed them so badly.

That was a little unfair, she acknowledged. David had taken the only option available to him and, if that meant time apart, it was no worse than thousands of other couples had to put up with.

If David's actions were easily explained, the same could not be said for Mike. Clara went into the kitchen, brewed herself a coffee, and sat at the kitchen table, nursing the mug. She knew she ought to eat something but she was long past hunger and couldn't be bothered to make the effort. Instead, she sat puzzling over the conundrum that was Mike Nash and in particular his recent untypical behaviour.

Why had Mike suddenly decided to take Daniel to France and for the whole of the summer holiday? It wasn't as if the little boy had any special fondness for his French home, other than his great aunt Mirabelle who he visited regularly.

She remembered the first time she met the boy, on the day Mirabelle had brought Daniel from France to Mike; the father that Daniel had never met, although he knew every detail of Mike from his now dead mother. Daniel, the son Mike was unaware of. That aside, how on earth would Mike amuse himself for the six weeks he would be away? What could he possibly find to entertain himself with when he wasn't even able to watch cricket live or on television?

Clara sat bolt upright, her mind racing. Cricket, there was something Mike had told her about cricket this summer. What was it? She cast her mind back to earlier in the year in the office at Helmsdale. It was a day when the county was being buffeted by gale force winds and lashing rain. The last item she thought would come up for discussion on a day like that was cricket. Then Mike had come in, a triumphant smile on his face. When asked why he was so happy, he'd announced with some pride that he had been lucky enough to obtain a couple of tickets for himself and Daniel to watch one of the test matches during the summer.

Clara got up and strode through to the lounge, fired up her laptop, and found the website she wanted. There it was, commencing during the first week of August. Under normal circumstances there was no way Mike would miss that, having paid good money for the tickets. Even if he was prepared to forego the pleasure, Daniel would certainly not be happy. Had her initial thought after he announced his leave been correct? Was Mike more affected by Becky's death than any of them believed? He was prey to deep emotions and Clara wondered if grief stronger than they imagined had taken hold of him. But surely, if that was the case, wouldn't a prolonged visit to France to stay in the home that Daniel had inherited from his mother, with all the painful memories it held, only make things far worse?

Clara shut down the laptop and wandered restlessly around the flat. She looked at the whisky decanter on the dresser but shook her head. 'Not on an empty stomach,' she told herself firmly.

She sat down on the sofa, still clutching her empty coffee mug. As she glanced down at it, she remembered that her coffee had been the source of many insults from Mike over the years they had worked together. For some inexplicable reason, this silly memory acted as the tipping point and she burst into tears.

* * *

Mironova's sleep was unsettled but she was still first to arrive in CID the following morning. Her dark mood of depression from the previous night had lifted, but there was work to be done, and the sun was shining. She set to work reviewing case files and had just finished making notes on the final one when her colleagues arrived.

She wandered out of Mike's office, which she was occupying for the duration, into the general office. 'Whose turn is it to make coffee?' she demanded.

Viv Pearce glanced across at Lisa Andrews, on secondment from HQ. 'I told you,' he remarked. 'She's getting more like Mike every day.'

'I'll make it,' Lisa said hurriedly.

As they were waiting for the drinks, Clara phoned Netherdale.

Tom Pratt divided his time between the two stations. Helmsdale only operated on a part-time basis and unless there was a major incident, closed overnight. Today Tom was at their headquarters. Clara explained what she needed. Pratt listened in silence.

'That's a task and a half,' he said. 'It could take weeks to get all that information and, even then, I couldn't guarantee that I'd got all of them.'

'Start with DVLA. I don't want every HGV; all I'm after are those that are in use for transporting livestock. I'm not sure, but isn't there some way of finding out if they've been converted for use as cattle wagons?'

'I don't honestly know,' Tom admitted. 'I can give it a shot, but I'm not promising anything. What's behind all this anyway?'

Clara explained her theory of the deer poachers' involvement in sheep thefts. 'It may turn out to be the only way we'll get some clue as to who killed PC Riley.'

'In that case, I'll get straight on with it,' Pratt promised.

Shortly before lunchtime, Clara took a call from the manager of Good Buys supermarket. 'How can I help?' she asked.

'I have a suspected shoplifting case, but I'm not sure whether it's one we can prosecute as we don't have the culprit in the store.' He explained the circumstances.

'I'll send DC Pearce over to talk to you,' Clara promised. She put the phone down and instructed Viv.

'Shouldn't uniform deal with that?'

'By the sound of it, this is quite unusual, so see what you can make of it.'

* * *

The store was busy. Pearce walked across to the enquiry desk and discreetly showed the assistant his warrant card. He was obviously expected, because only moments later he was shown into the manager's office, where they were joined by another man in the livery of the security company on duty in the store.

'Tell Detective Constable Pearce what happened,' the manager instructed him.

The guard began hesitantly. 'I thought there was something suspicious about two women, but I couldn't be sure. The company policy is not to be over-confrontational in situations like these. It was after we reviewed the CCTV footage that we knew we'd been done over.'

'It's a bit different from the national stores,' the manager explained. 'Being a local company, we're mindful not to upset customers because that way our trade can suffer badly. On the other hand, we can't simply turn a blind eye to people stealing from us. If nothing else comes of this, at the very least the women concerned will be watched next time they come into the store and if they try the same trick, they'll be gently escorted out — without their shopping,' he added with a wry smile.

'Tell me exactly what happened.' Pearce nodded to the security guard.

'They came into the store around mid-morning. Nothing unusual in that, a lot of mums drop their kids off at school or playgroup and then come in here. Like I said, I wasn't able to prove anything at the time but when we looked at the CCTV we were able to track them as they went round the aisles. They loaded their trolleys with identical items then one of them set off for the tills. She paid for her goods and left the store while the other one continued to wander around. She was over in the far corner, on the face of it looking at clothing. Incidentally, after the first woman left her, the second woman didn't put anything else in her trolley.'

The guard paused, collecting his thoughts, and continued, 'The woman still in the store then got a call on her mobile. As soon as she got that, she set off towards the tobacco and service counter. At that point, shopper number one came back in, minus trolley, and passed shopper number two her till receipt for the identical goods. Number two then strolled out without paying, and number one went over and bought a packet of cigarettes. In other word, they got a couple of hundred pounds worth of goods for half the price.'

'That's a new one on me,' Pearce admitted.

'Me too,' the manager agreed. 'But I spoke to someone from head office about it and they had a similar case reported a couple of days ago from one of our other branches, but the CCTV evidence on that occasion was inconclusive.'

'Makes you wonder if this is the same couple of women. In which case they're probably under the impression they're onto a really good thing. I'll need a statement from you' — he looked at the guard — 'and a copy of that CCTV footage. I take it you intend to press charges if we can identify the women.'

'Absolutely,' the manager confirmed. 'We have to let the criminal fraternity know that although we're a friendly, local company that doesn't mean we're a soft touch.'

Pearce headed back and told Clara about the duplicate trolley scam. She listened with growing interest.

When he'd finished she shook her head sadly. 'Sometimes I wonder how successful such people would be if they put their minds to something legal. But they seem to get more pleasure out of finding ways to circumvent all the security measures people put in place to defend their property. It's almost as if they regard it as a challenge. When you've finished your lunch get some stills taken off the CCTV footage. I want them distributing to uniform branch and putting on all the notice boards. Make sure copies go to all the supermarkets in our area together with a warning. Ask them to display the photos prominently. Even if it doesn't result in arrests, the photos might act as a deterrent.'

* * *

Tony Hartley looked up as Ron Mason entered the makeshift office in the rear of an industrial storage unit. 'What have you found out from our "guests"?' Hartley asked. 'Have they told you what they did with the drugs they stole from our courier?'

Mason smiled faintly at Hartley's description of the two men from Kovac's gang they had abducted. 'Yes, and more besides. What I did get out of them could prove useful. Certainly something I got right at the end, before the second one went beyond talking. I'd already confirmed the information we had about where their distribution centre is, but then I also found out how they get the stuff into the country. It's quite a neat arrangement really, all to do with lobsterpots.' He went on to explain and saw Hartley's eyebrows rise in appreciation.

'Interesting. I suppose they didn't tell you where the package they stole from us has gone, did they?'

'They did, but it's far too late for us to be able to retrieve it. They told me that piece of information early on, when they were still very cocky and arrogant. That was before I started applying pressure. Their attitude soon changed, believe me.'

Hartley did believe him. He'd seen Mason at work before, seen the results of his interrogation techniques too. 'Where did it go?'

'The cheeky bastards sent it out to their own dealers. By now it'll be up for sale or on the street.'

'I take it you've already disposed of them? Have you found a suitable hiding place for the bodies?'

Mason smiled, but it was a cold expression that contained little humour. 'No. In view of what they'd done and the need to establish our position and reputation, I thought it better to send a message to 'Euro-trash', I believe you call the opposition, that we mean business. So I made sure they were left in a place where they're certain to be found. I also asked our men to spread the word, whenever they get the opportunity, as to how they died — and why.'

Hartley nodded. 'Yes, I suppose that was a better way of doing it. Right, now we can move on. There's another shipment due soon. That means I'll need to brief our fishy friends. Have them come in, will you?'

The four men were dressed identically, neat collar and tie, smart white coat, as befitted their work as salesmen. 'Are the vans ready?' Hartley asked.

'Almost,' one of them replied. 'They're all fuelled up and the refrigeration units need to be brought up to temperature, we just need to know the timescale. Have you had word yet when that will be?'

'In a couple of days. Mason will let you know when. You'll need to be on the quayside, stocked up by the wholesalers and ready to move by first light. The special delivery items will be in the fish boxes. There will be two packages for each van. When you reach your sales territory, flog your fish around the villages exactly the same as normal. That in itself is starting to become quite lucrative, so don't neglect it. At some point in your rounds you'll be approached by someone whose enquiry will identify them as being one of our dealers. The wording they have been told to use is quite specific, so listen very carefully. They will ask if you have any green-lipped mussels, the freshwater variety. Your reply should be that you only have frozen ones. They will then say that the frozen ones will have to do, and they will ask for a kilo of them. At which point you handover the product in exchange for the cash. There should be twenty grand in each bundle, so when you return here, you should have one hundred and sixty thousand for me. Is that understood?'

CHAPTER FIVE

Ivan Kovac was growing more and more worried. Two of his men were still missing and the possible threat posed by the missing reporter and the information he believed she carried needed resolution. Despite Stanley and his other men reporting no untoward activity around any of their business premises, he waited impatiently. He was reluctant to authorize and continue major operations until he knew with absolute certainty that they were safe.

Thirty-six hours after he received the private investigator's e mail, Kovac heard from the man detailed to check on the chief constable's house for any sign of Becky Pollard. 'There's nobody here except the woman copper and her husband.'

'How can you be sure? They're hardly going to show themselves at the window, are they?'

'I'm sure because, like you, I didn't expect them to be visible. So this morning, after they both went to work, I got into the house and had a good look round.'

'You broke in? You idiot, that'll flag up that something's wrong.'

'I didn't say I broke in, I said I got in. They won't even know I've been inside. I'll tell you one thing, for a senior police officer, her security's crap.'

'So you reckon the Pollard woman isn't staying there? Any evidence she's been there and moved on?'

'No, I'd plenty of time to look round. I went into every room, checked all the spare bedrooms, toilets, bathrooms, wardrobes, the lot. Not even an extra toothbrush, no clothing, suitcases, nothing. If she has been there at any stage she's long gone and taken everything with her.'

To be fair, the O'Donnell house had always been Kovac's less favourite option. He was more convinced than ever that the woman would prove to be found hiding out with the detective, Nash. He's probably screwing her silly in lieu of rent, Kovac thought, remembering the comments on the private investigator's e-mail about Nash's reputation. He glanced down at the photo of Becky Pollard. Hardly surprising if he was, Kovac thought, she's a good-looking woman.

An hour later, a second phone call left him more mystified than ever. This time it was Stanley who reported to him. 'I decided that rather than entrust Nash's place to anyone else, I'd do the job myself,' Stanley told him. 'I thought that if the answer was positive it would save time if I was already on site. Then I could do two things at once, so to speak. Before I set off, I rang Helmsdale nick and asked to speak to Nash. They told me he was on leave and offered to put me through to some detective sergeant with a foreign sounding name. Needless to say I declined their kind offer, but I'd found out that Nash wasn't at work so I didn't have to waste time hanging around the nick watching for him. They're not my favourite places at the best of times. Can't think why.'

Stanley was being humorous. That wasn't a good sign. If he'd had anything positive to report he'd have been more excited, more businesslike. Not cracking jokes.

'So you went to his home,' Kovac encouraged him. 'What did you find?'

'He lives out in the wilds just outside a small village, really remote. The house must be worth a packet, but that's not all. I saw Nash's car on the drive. And guess what, he's got a bloody great Range Rover. I tell you what; it's a scandalous waste of public money giving gas-guzzlers like that to middle-ranking coppers. Either that or they're overpaying him something wicked.'

'Stanley, this isn't Top Gear. I couldn't give a toss what car Nash drives. Did you see a woman?'

The more impatient Kovac became the more it seemed to amuse Stanley. 'There was a woman, certainly,' Stanley conceded. 'She was helping Nash load his car with luggage, so I reckoned they might be off on holiday.'

'Becky Pollard? Please tell me it was Becky Pollard?'

'No, I don't think it was. Not unless she's changed her appearance radically.'

'So, she knows she's in danger. It makes sense she would dye her hair, perhaps put on some fake tan to disguise her fair complexion.'

'She could have done all that, I suppose,' Stanley admitted. 'However, I doubt if the best make-up artist in Hollywood could have changed Becky Pollard into the woman I saw with Nash.'

'Why not?'

'Because they would have had to change her skin colour completely and add four inches or so to her height.'

'High heels could . . .' Kovac began to say when the significance of Stanley's earlier remark hit him. 'What was that about her skin?'

'Not only is the woman taller than Pollard, she's also black. Incidentally, she's about the fittest-looking bird I've seen in a long time. The thing is, I thought if I asked around discreetly I might get a bit more info. So I went into the village shop and dropped a casual remark about the woman I'd seen. A lovely coloured girl, I described her as.'

'And, what did they tell you?'

'I think you can count Nash out as being Becky Pollard's protector,' Stanley told him, obviously enjoying drawing the story out. 'I found out the reason he's on leave. Apparently, it came as a surprise to the shopkeeper, but he's just got engaged. The girl I saw him with, Alice or Alicia, something like that she's called, is his fiancée. The grocer, who in addition to being a randy old bastard is also an unstoppable gossip, told me all about it. Apparently, they'd been in to buy supplies for their holiday yesterday. By what the shopkeeper was saying they couldn't keep their hands off one another. He said Nash introduced her and was really proud of her, told him they're off on an extended holiday.'

'That's all very well, but none of that stops him hiding Becky Pollard at his place, does it?'

'No it doesn't, not in itself, but you must remember, I've seen him with this woman of his, you haven't. I was watching and boy, talk about steamy. Nash won't have the time or energy for anything else except her, the lucky bastard. I bet he hates having to get out of bed in a morning. Mind you, I can't say I blame him for that. If I'd someone as fit as she is warming my bed, I wouldn't want to leave it, even to take a piss.'

'All right, all right, I get the picture. The problem is, if the Pollard woman is alive and she isn't with Nash, and we know she isn't with the chief constable, where the hell is she? We don't even know where to start looking.'

'One good thing,' Stanley pointed out, 'if she isn't with them, she isn't likely to be telling them anything they can act on.'

'Of course she can. She can e-mail them, talk to them on the phone.'

'Not that easy to e-mail them, seeing we nicked her computer in London, but even if she'd done that, surely we'd have had some activity from them by now? You don't think that news report was right and she could actually be dead?'

'Maybe, maybe not. It could be she's saving her info to get a big story, so she'll only release it to the police when she can make sense of what she's heard. Given the way that reporters behave these days I'm inclined to think that's what's happened. In that case, it makes finding her a bit less urgent and we can get on with our plans. Where are you now?'

'I'm at the Park.'

'Good, I'll drive over and meet you there.'

The distribution centre for Kovac's narcotics operation was known as the Park in an effort to maintain the secrecy of its location. It was late afternoon when Kovac arrived. He vanished into his office, a converted static caravan. He'd only been there a few minutes when his mobile rang. He glanced at the screen before answering. The display read INT'L. This, he assumed, would be the call he was expecting about the next consignment. Either that or someone from a call centre trying to refund the payment protection, which he had never paid, on a loan he had never taken out. He answered and once the caller identified himself, Kovac switched at once into French, a language he was far less fluent in than English. This wasn't too important, as his part of the conversation was limited to replies, mainly on the lines of 'yes, I understand,' or similar repetition of the caller's instructions. He ended by giving an assurance that the money requested would be transferred into the caller's bank immediately.

Using the guise of his meat production company, Kovac used the online banking facility to complete the promised transfer of funds before he summoned his assistant.

'I have news, some very interesting news. I've had word from France. Not only is our delivery ready for dispatch — but so is the opposition's. And I have their route and method.' He began relating what his informant had told him.

Stanley listened, his curiosity by now fully aroused. 'What do you plan to do?' he asked.

Kovac explained, watching his assistant's face register approval as he came to the final part. 'I think we should meet the Soldiers' supplier before they do. I have even got details of the vessel they will use. This way, we make sure they don't get their delivery. We can use the opportunity to dispose of more of their couriers; balance the odds a little. At the same time you need to make plans for our collection as expected. Notify our lobsterman, then we can have twice as much merchandise to sell, half of it free.'

Stanley discussed the details with him before heading off to inform their dealers to be ready.

Kovac had access to many sources of information. Unluckily, his sources didn't include army personnel records. If they did, and he was able to read Tony Hartley's file, he would probably have been interested in the annotation that revealed Hartley had been one of the finest surveillance officers in the service, second to none in planting and using sophisticated listening devices. Added to his skill with explosives, the report concluded, that made him a highly-valued asset.

* * *

Tony Hartley found the information culled during Ron Mason's interrogation of the two captured men from Kovac's team invaluable. Not least, the location of Kovac's distribution centre which Hartley had visited surreptitiously in the early hours of the previous morning and bugged the office. Several hours later, Tony Hartley listened to a recording of Kovac's and Stanley's conversation regarding their intentions of stealing his incoming delivery.

He called Ron Mason into his office, played him the tape, then made a couple of phone calls, the gist of which defied his companion until Hartley explained. 'Now we know they're planning to intercept our consignment, we let them have it. But before we do, we reduce the size of the order and get our contacts to make a slight adjustment to our merchandise — we make it unsaleable.'

Even Mason was shocked by the plan, and that didn't happen easily.

'And now from what we've heard, we also know when and where theirs is coming in,' Hartley continued. So, we play a game of tit-for-tat, payback for what they've already stolen and plan to steal from us. We empty their pots, even if it's only lobster in them.' Hartley smiled and added, 'I'm partial to a bit of lobster. Tell the van drivers there will be a slight delay with their fish collection at the docks but they might be able to offer their customers lobster for sale as a special treat.'

Ron Mason looked at Hartley. For years while serving in the army, he had thought of him as no more than an average commander. It was only since meeting up with him again that he had recognized the man's ruthless efficiency; two qualities Mason admired. 'OK, but the problem remains, how did they get their information?'

'Not from this end, that's for sure. In which case, it may prove necessary for you to take a short holiday in Brittany soon. I hope your passport's in order.'

Mason smiled. 'All of them are.'

CHAPTER SIX

Inside the neat terrace house in Helmsdale, the young woman was excited, nervous, at times elated, at others afraid. Tonight, things were going to change, or so she thought. Knowing that what she was about to do was wrong didn't stop her wanting to do it. So far it had all been innocent, fun, but not wicked. She grew even more tense as the time approached. Glancing at the clock every five minutes didn't help, any more than repeatedly checking her appearance in the mirror did. Trying to rationalize what was happening was no better.

She hadn't needed to go to the supermarket that day, the day she met him. The trip was more from boredom than a need for supplies. She'd been ambling from aisle to aisle collecting the few items on her mental list, staring at the stacked goods with lacklustre interest. She wasn't bored because her husband was away; she was bored with her life. Worse than that, she hated her life. It was much better when he was away working on the rigs, even though she had no family close by, no friends she could call on. It hadn't always been like that, but one by one her friends had dropped away, daunted by her husband.

Someone had asked once if she minded him being away for long periods. That would have been funny had it not been so poignant. She'd felt like screaming at them, 'Yes, because while he's on the rigs he's sober, and while he's on the rigs he can't come home drunk and beat me up for no other reason than that he wants to. I really do miss that!'

She hadn't done, of course. She'd done as always, bottled it up. Sometimes, she found it difficult to remember why she'd married him or what had attracted her to him. Now, she wasn't sure which she hated most, the sickening brutality she knew would follow once she smelled alcohol on his breath, or the nauseating grovel of his apology once he'd sobered up and seen the extent of the damage that he'd inflicted on her in his drunken rage. If she'd anywhere to go, or anyone to turn to, she knew she'd walk out without a backward glance — without a trace of regret.

Her daydream had been rudely interrupted as her trolley collided with a man standing in the middle of the aisle staring at a display of breakfast cereals. She began to apologize, but he would have none of it.

'My own fault,' he'd said with a cheerful smile. 'I wasn't even thinking of buying them, merely passing the time.' He looked at her closely. 'Gosh, you're pretty,' he said, then, 'sorry, I shouldn't have said that.'

It was a long time since anyone had told her that, or anything like it, nor did she feel pretty. She'd smiled back. 'You don't need to be sorry, but I do think you might need an eye test.'

'There's nothing wrong with my vision *and* I stand by what I said.'

'Why are you passing the time here? Are you unemployed?'

'No, I work from home and sometimes I get bored with my own company.'

She'd sighed. 'I know that feeling only too well.' Before she knew quite what was happening, he'd offered to buy her a coffee in the supermarket cafe and she'd agreed. Over the drink they chatted and the common bond of loneliness soon became apparent. He told her he was divorced, and that his wife had moved somewhere down in the West

Country together with their two children. 'I miss them, although I don't miss her,' he'd said, his face clouded with unhappiness.

'What went wrong? What caused the split?'

'I found out she was sleeping with my best friend; had been for a couple of years.'

'Did you confront them?'

'No, I'm not really the confrontational type. I just walked out and never went back. I don't miss her, not for herself, but I do miss the kids and the company.'

She'd seen the pain, the sadness in his eyes, and the loneliness that mirrored her own. When he'd asked, she agreed to meet him again, for a stronger drink this time.

At their next meeting he'd acted with perfect decorum throughout the evening. He'd taken her to a country pub, miles from Helmsdale. 'I thought it best, less chance of anyone who knows you being in here,' he'd told her.

That sort of consideration was something she was unused to, just as he'd dropped her at the end of her street to prevent any neighbours seeing her getting out of a stranger's car. Before she opened the door, she'd leaned across to kiss him goodnight; the flicker of response she got from him told her all she needed to know.

She returned to the present, realizing with a shock that the time had come. Once she walked through that door, once she walked to the end of the road, once she got into his car, she knew she would have committed herself beyond recall. She picked up her handbag, looked around the room as if for the last time, and walked out, closing the door firmly behind her.

It was late when they left the pub. There had been only a few regulars in the bar, villagers she guessed, who had no interest in the couple sitting quietly in the corner making two glasses of wine and two orange juices last the whole evening as they talked. When they walked across the car park, she took his hand, clasping it with fingers that trembled slightly.

As before, he drove her back towards Helmsdale but as they approached Kirk Bolton he swung the car off the road towards the car park by the river. 'Do you mind?' he asked.

'No,' her voice was slightly husky, fear and longing at war. Her heart was thumping violently. Could he hear it, she wondered?

His hand rested on her knee, the touch burning through the fabric of her jeans as if it was on fire. He unfastened his seat belt and switched the engine off. As he reached across to unbuckle hers his hand brushed her breast then returned to caress it gently.

'Stop,' she said. 'Stop for a minute. Put the headlights back on.'

'What is it?'

'I thought I saw someone. Over there by the picnic tables.'

'Oh Lord!' He turned the ignition key and switched the headlights to main beam. Passion died as they stared at the figure slumped over the picnic table. 'Stay there, I'm going to take a look. He may be ill. He could be a tramp.' He didn't think so; didn't know whether he'd convinced her.

As he got out of the car she felt the draught of air and shivered, not so much from the cold, but the certainty of what he would report on his return. She watched his shadow, elongated by the headlights, as he approached the motionless figure. Watched as he stood alongside the corpse for a long moment, then he moved and for a few seconds he disappeared behind a large bush. Was he being sick? She could hardly blame him if that was the case.

He reappeared and walked swiftly, almost ran back to the car. 'Let's get out of here.'

She looked across, saw the grim set of his features as he started the engine, and swung the wheel to his right; heard the tyres spurting on the gravel, echoes of his anxiety to leave this place.

'Is he . . . ?'

'He's dead. But that's not the worst bit.' Something in the way he said it should have prepared her, but there are some things you can't prepare for.

'What do you mean?'

'I think he's been beaten to death. His face . . . it's horrible. Close up it looks like . . . pulp. I'm so glad you didn't have to see it. I wish I hadn't. But that's not all.'

'Not all? But what else is there?' she asked her voice beginning to rise in panic.

'He isn't alone. Behind the big bush — there's another one.'

'Another body?'

'Yes, and by the look of it, he's had the same treatment.'

'Oh my God, what are we going to do? We have to report it.'

Gravel spurted from beneath his tyres as he accelerated out of the car park. As he turned on to the main road he said, 'I know that, but it would be awkward. Give me time to think.'

She was silent, her hands clasped tightly on her lap as she stared at the hedgerows flashing past the windscreen, praying he would find a solution. She wondered how they'd landed in this mess. Others seemed to get away with it, did this sort of thing time and again. They hadn't even . . . It had all seemed such an adventure, now it was threatening to become sordid. She could imagine people gossiping, pointing her out and sniggering.

He broke her train of thought. 'I can't report it to the police from my mobile or my home phone. If I did, they'd trace the call and want to know what I was doing out there, and with whom. That would mean involving you, and I can't allow that. No way can I risk that. You mean too much, I . . . er . . . I don't want to spoil things for you.'

She felt suddenly cheered by his considerate thought, his protective words. It was a watershed moment, although she didn't realize it at the time. 'We can't simply allow them to lie there until someone else finds them. It could be hours, days, maybe. And there are foxes and things. We have to tell someone.'

‘I’ve had an idea. When we get to Helmsdale, I’ll go in one of the pubs. There’s one just off the Market Place that has a public phone in the back entrance. I could slip in the back door without going through the bar, use the phone, and be out again within minutes. You can stay in the car. If I park well away from the building, no one will see you.’

Half an hour later he walked briskly back across the pub car park and got into the car. ‘That’s it, done. Now let’s get out of here, in case they send someone to check up.’ They pulled out into the Market Place and he turned the car in the direction of her house. ‘Are you OK?’

‘I think so. It’s just thinking of those poor men, it’s well, it’s really awful.’ She shuddered.

‘I’m sorry,’ he told her, ‘this isn’t how I wanted the evening to end.’

‘Me neither,’ she said before she could stop herself. ‘It wasn’t your fault. Anyway,’ — she swallowed, nerves threatening to overcome her — ‘does it have to end like this?’

He glanced sideways. ‘What do you mean?’

She abandoned her last reserves of caution. ‘I don’t really want to be alone, do you? We’ve both had a dreadful shock. And didn’t you say your flat was near here? I could do with a stiff drink and I’m sure you could too.’

‘We could go to my place, but I wouldn’t be able to drive you home if I have a drink.’

‘I know that. I wasn’t planning on going anywhere else.’ She turned as she spoke and her eyes met his as he glanced quickly at her.

‘Are you certain? I mean, absolutely certain.’

She was certain; and growing more so by the minute. She reached over and placed her hand on top of his as it rested on the gearstick. ‘Oh yes,’ she breathed. ‘I’m really, really sure.’ She giggled, which she guessed was in part relief from the stress of the trauma they had both endured. Much more though, from the decision she had made; a decision from which there could be no going back.

CHAPTER SEVEN

Mironova was nodding off in an armchair, trying to summon up energy to drag herself to bed, when the phone rang.

'Clara? Jack Binns here, I'm on my way to Kirk Bolton. We've a pair of bodies on our hands. Unidentified males, found sometime this evening. We got an anonymous call from a public phone in one of the Helmsdale pubs.'

Mironova was instantly awake. 'Where did you say?'

'Kirk Bolton. In the picnic area alongside the river where all the courting couples go. The one the locals refer to as "leg over lay-by".'

'OK, I know where you mean. Have you called Fleming?'

'Already done. And Mexican Pete; he'll meet us there. He asked where Mike was. Said Nash would be beside himself at being away and missing three bodies to drool over.'

Clara smiled at the reference to the pathologist. Although Spanish by birth, his nickname was derived from *The Ballad of Eskimo Nell*. 'Mexican Pete seems to have developed what he considers to be a sense of humour. I'm on my way. Can you raise Lisa Andrews for me? And, Jack, I really appreciate your help.'

* * *

The crime scene was already illuminated by a powerful generator-driven arc light, supplemented by the headlights of two patrol cars, the pathologist and CSI teams hadn't arrived. Clara walked over to a pair of traffic officers who were busy setting up a cordon of incident tape, their faces changing colour, tinted by the emergency lights of their vehicles. 'You lads are well organized.' She pointed to the generator.

'Jack Binns got us to call in at the station and collect it en route,' one of them told her.

'Where is he?'

'Playing at boy scouts.'

The traffic officer pointed towards a van where she could just make out Binns and another officer wrestling to erect the tent needed to protect the bodies. Would they need two? Did they have two? She couldn't remember. It would be galling to have to borrow one from another force. She heard the sound of approaching vehicles, before a trio of lights swooped into the car park. These contained the pathologist, the CSI team, and DC Pearce.

She was surprised to see Viv. 'I thought Lisa was on call tonight?'

'She was, but we swapped. It's some sort of anniversary, and you know what that means.' Pearce made a vulgar gesture with one hand across the other forearm.

'Lucky for some,' Clara muttered.

'What's the score?'

'Two — nil, I think.'

'What do you make of it? Are they walkers? Have they been mugged?'

'I don't think so.' Clara illuminated the body with her torch. 'Look at the way he was dressed. Suit, tie, leather shoes. Not exactly hiking gear, is it?'

'He might have driven here.'

'What in?' She gestured to the car park. 'Ours are the only vehicles.'

She turned to the pathologist, mentally bracing herself. Ramirez could be acerbic at the best of times. Being called out late at night was likely to cause his temper to be shorter than usual. 'Good evening, Professor.'

Ramirez turned. 'It was, until my phone rang. I was enjoying a film at the time.'

Clara couldn't resist it. 'What was it? *Invasion of the Body Snatchers*?'

The pathologist glared at her. 'No. Now, let's see what we've got, shall we?'

Ramirez conducted his preliminary inspection, allowing the photographer to conclude before signalling one of the forensic team to help him lift the body from the picnic table. Their struggles met with no success. They repositioned themselves and began to manhandle the body again, which proved no easy task.

'The feet have been jammed under the stretcher of the table,' Pearce pointed out.

'I can see that now,' Ramirez snapped. 'Presumably it was done to prevent the body falling over.'

After several more minutes and a succession of swear words, mostly in Spanish, they managed to wrestle the body clear of the furniture and laid it on a plastic sheet. At first sight, the body presented an absurd picture, with legs, back and arms frozen in a bent position, like a giant upturned crab, Clara thought. It was only when they saw the man's face that every vestige of humour vanished.

'Good God, what has happened to him?' Pearce exclaimed.

If any of them had harboured the slightest lingering doubt regarding how the man died, that too vanished. The face was a shapeless mass of bruises, a swollen, soggy and discoloured mess. They could just make out that several teeth were missing, whether knocked or pulled out they couldn't be sure. Any attempt at recognition would be futile, that was beyond certainty.

Ramirez looked up and beckoned the detectives closer. 'There's no sign of any ID on him. But what do you make of this?' He pointed towards the man's body. Ramirez parted the shirt, which Clara noticed was unbuttoned for the most part, they could see further bruising lower down the torso. The bruises covered all the area that was visible to them.

'Beaten the same way all over?' Mironova guessed.

'I think so.' He signalled the photographer over to continue. 'I'm beginning to get an idea what happened to him, but I'll wait until after I've examined the other body and conducted the post-mortem to confirm that, one way or another. Have you noticed his clothing? The shirt was like this when we found him, and the trousers were unzipped.'

'He was naked when he died, and the killer dressed him?'

'That's the way it looks to me. I'll be holding the post-mortems in the morning. I think you should be the one to attend.'

'I'll be there,' she told him grimly. 'Now, do you want to finish with this one first, or have a quick look at the other one?'

'I'll look at the other one, briefly. I see no reason for both of us to miss out on our beauty sleep. Not that you need it,' he told her gallantly.

Binns was standing close to the incident tape in conversation with Jackie Fleming. Clara hurried over to join them. She reported what she'd seen of the first victim. 'We're about to look at the other body, if you want to join us?'

'No, the fewer people trampling around the scene, the better. I'll see them when we go to the mortuary. When's he doing the PMs?'

'Tomorrow morning. With the university having broken up for the summer, he's no lectures to conflict with his work for us.'

'OK, get away from here as soon as you can. And let me know when you arrive in Netherdale in the morning. We need to start planning for a major murder inquiry.'

Clara voiced both their thoughts. 'I wish Mike was here, instead of swanning off.'

Jackie shrugged. 'Nothing we can do about that and I can't see there's much more we can do here until daylight. CSI will want a fingertip search of the area, which will mean getting uniforms organized.' Jackie turned to Binns. 'Can you sort out a team, Jack? We'll be at Netherdale General in the morning, so you can liaise with Viv and Lisa Andrews. Instruct one of the patrol cars to stay here. Make sure nobody disturbs the scene. We don't want any amorous couples loitering within tent.'

They all groaned at the pun.

* * *

The mortuary at Netherdale General had been modernized the previous year, with the creation of a separate viewing area behind glass. This enabled official viewers to be able to see the occupants of the tables without having to endure the sound or smell associated with the grisly process. It didn't protect them from the horrendous sight of victims as badly mistreated as the men Ramirez was examining.

Both men's torsos were almost covered in a rainbow of bruising, with black, blue and yellow replacing the natural skin tone in all but the smallest segments.

Fleming spoke into the two-way microphone installed in the glass screen. 'It looks like a punishment beating.'

'I don't think punishment was the objective, at least not the principal one,' Ramirez replied, his voice muffled by the mask he was wearing. 'But I'll be able to confirm that once I've finished.'

As they watched the pathologist and his team at work, Clara wondered about the identity of the dead men and why they had been killed in such a brutal fashion. And was the beating the cause of death, or were other factors involved? She was startled out of her daydream when Ramirez spoke again. 'I've almost finished. If you care to go through into my office, I'll join you. My assistant can tidy up here. There's nothing further you need to see.'

I didn't need to see any of it, Mironova thought, as they turned for the door and walked through into the drab chamber the pathologist called his office. It was as cold and cheerless as the rest of the mortuary. Clara wondered again how anyone could work in such uncomfortable and depressing surroundings. They were joined almost immediately by Ramirez, who was carrying a clipboard.

'Ok, let's start with cause of death, which was a massive heart attack in both cases. I guess they were triggered by the extreme pain inflicted.' Ramirez paused. 'There comes a point when the level of pain becomes intolerable, and the overreaction to that causes system shutdown.'

'That would still class as murder though, wouldn't it?'

'Undoubtedly,' the pathologist's voice was as grim as his expression, 'especially so, given what was done to them.'

'Have you any idea what was used to beat them with? Not fists, surely?'

'No, you should be looking for our old friend, the blunt instrument. Something with a smooth surface, like a baseball bat.'

'You seemed to indicate there was something different about this beating than the normal working over?'

'Indeed there is. It was far from normal, if there is such a thing. I had my suspicions last night, although it is something I've never encountered before. I have read accounts of such cases, but it's not the sort of thing one expects to see in this country.'

Ramirez saw the puzzled expression on both detectives' faces and hastened to explain. 'As I suspected, the men weren't killed at the picnic site. They were transported there. The lividity in the corpses confirms that. You should be looking for men who have been missing for at least a week, or thereabouts. During that time, they were imprisoned, bound and gagged, as the ligature marks and some of the minor bruising about the mouths indicate, and beaten, not once, but twice or three times, possibly even more. The gagging would be necessary, particularly for the repeat beatings, these took place over a period of approximately four days.'

The pathologist paused, obviously waiting to see if there was any reaction from his listeners. When he saw none, he continued, 'You don't know what I'm referring to. Do you?'

Clara and Fleming looked at one another. 'No, Professor,' Jackie replied.

'There is a system of torture used in certain countries where civil liberties are unknown and, for all I know, it might also have been used by Special Forces elsewhere to extract information from prisoners. Someone discovered that if you inflict heavy bruising on a prisoner, leave the bruises to set and then return several days later and attack him or her once more, the second beating on top of the effects of the first one, causes pain that is beyond human endurance. It is, I believe, extraordinarily effective. I venture to suggest you should look for someone with Special Forces experience. Although, to be fair, I suppose these days they could have got the information through the internet. There seems to be very little that isn't available online.'

'That is sick,' Clara muttered. She could feel the nausea, merely from the impact of what Ramirez had told them.

'That's no exaggeration,' the pathologist agreed. 'Do you have any missing persons who fit the description? Identifying them could point you to the reason someone wanted information from them, or even, with luck, the murderer's identity.'

'I'm afraid at this point, we've no idea who they are,' Fleming told him. 'I've checked all the MISPER cases reported nationally within the last month and there's nobody matching the descriptions.'

'Then all I can do is circulate their dental records and see if we can get a match.'

* * *

When Fleming and Mironova reached the Netherdale headquarters, Tom Pratt was waiting for them. 'One of the victims found at the picnic site has been identified via his fingerprints,' he told them. 'I don't understand why you didn't use a fingerprint reader last night.'

'That's all very well in theory, Tom, but you can't even get a mobile phone signal out there, so any device stands no chance.'

'I see, anyway, forensics tried to get you at the mortuary, but you'd already left.' He handed Fleming a folder. 'The man has three convictions for drug related crimes, plus one for possession with intent to supply. Maybe what you found last night was the aftermath of a transaction that went wrong.'

'I don't think so. I can't imagine even the keenest drugs dealer walking fourteen miles into the depths of the countryside to meet a punter. Nor can I imagine a punter being that desperate to score.'

Clara saw Pratt's puzzled expression and explained Jackie's statement. 'There were no vehicles at the picnic site. Both victims had obviously been transported there, by what Mexican Pete said, probably after they were killed.'

'So you think it was a dump site?'

'Yes. And given the way they died, we think they must have been held prisoner and tortured non-stop before they were killed.'

'It sounds almost as if you could have a turf war on your hands.'

Fleming sighed. 'I'm very much afraid you might be right, Tom. And that's the last thing we need at the moment.'

'Anyway, I won't keep you any longer. The chief wants to see you both. She wants to hear what you have to say on this case, and to bring her up to date on any other outstanding business.' Pratt smiled. 'By the sound of it, perhaps I should order your lunch now?'

'Never mind lunch; by the time we're finished it might be dinner.'

CHAPTER EIGHT

The meeting with the chief constable concentrated on the double murder. O'Donnell listened to the reports of both detectives, paying particularly close attention to the possibility of a drugs connection outlined by Jackie Fleming.

'Have you any leads?' she asked.

Fleming was about to shake her head when Clara said, 'There is one thing that might give us a clue; the phone call.'

'Sorry, I'm not with you.'

'Whoever found the bodies phoned the emergency services from the Cobblers Arms pub in Helmsdale. Now it may well be that the caller was a perfectly innocent citizen, or on the other hand it might have been the killer wanting to draw attention to his handiwork. That could be what happened if, as we believe, the men were killed as part of a turf war between rival drug runners. Either way, what they didn't take into account is that the Cobblers Arms has CCTV covering the car park. I've asked Lisa to check the footage. We might get lucky.'

'That sounds promising.' O'Donnell smiled. 'Good work, Clara. Off the cuff, I can't think of an innocent reason for someone to be stopping at a picnic site miles from anywhere at that time of night.'

'Oh, I can think of one, ma'am, but whether you'd class it as innocent or not is a different matter.'

O'Donnell laughed. 'Right: now onto other business.'

The next item on the agenda was the murder of PC Riley, but here, neither detective was able to report any progress. 'Clara's got Tom checking out all the cattle wagons in the area, as we discussed previously,' Jackie said, 'but given the nature of this district it's a mammoth task.'

The chief constable then asked about the other unsolved crimes and between them, Fleming and Mironova had to give account of the series of burglaries, muggings, shoplifting and other offences they had on their workload. Clara had just finished reporting on the duplicate trolley shoplifting scam when Jackie leaned forward and cleared her throat to speak.

O'Donnell stopped her with a raised finger. 'Before you go, I'd like you both to have a look at something you should be aware of. This report arrived by e-mail this morning.'

She passed them both a thin sheaf of papers, the heading to which, Clara saw, was National Drugs Intelligence Unit. Both women started to read.

There are two major sources of supply for class-A drugs, principally heroin and cocaine, operating in the north of England. We have no idea as to the identity of the suppliers. That includes both the end dealers and the wholesalers, for want of a better word. The availability of hard drugs in large quantities throughout the region has increased dramatically during the last twelve months.

Although intelligence is severely limited, to the best of our knowledge the increase is believed to be purely down to the activities of one existing and one new player. The newcomer is well funded, ruthless and has more or less swept all opposition aside in certain areas.

Attempts to penetrate this network have been completely unsuccessful. We have tried various methods, including an attempt to infiltrate them via an undercover officer, but failed. Normally, with organizations like this whose activities cover such a wide geographic area, it has proved possible to identify and suborn a weak link, but in this case, such attempts have proved fruitless. The difference appears to be in the way the networks are put together. Although this is only a theory with nothing in the way of hard evidence to back it up, we believe that they operate on a cellular basis, much the same as certain terrorist organizations.

Our second major problem has been identification of the supply route. The scale of their deliveries suggests they are able to smuggle drugs into this country undetected. Not only do we have no clue as to the method by which the drugs are brought in, but we have no evidence as to how they are brought from the point(s) of entry to the local distributors and dealers. In previous cases, this part of the operation has been a fruitful way of tracing both ends of the supply chain, but all our efforts in this respect have met with a completely negative feedback.

Given the extreme gravity of the problem, we are taking the unusual step of issuing this briefing bulletin to all senior detectives in the region.

After she had completed her perusal of the contents, Jackie looked across at the chief. 'This lends even more urgency to the request I was about to make. I believe we ought to ask Mike Nash to return from leave immediately. Don't get me wrong, I'm not decrying Clara, far from it, she's a first-class detective, as good as we could hope for. But the way things have deteriorated since Mike went away, she and the rest of the team are in danger of being snowed under. The deterioration and Mike's absence are unconnected, merely coincidental. But there is no doubt in my mind that an extra pair of hands, particularly those of an experienced detective, would help us no end in what I have to say is close to being a crisis.'

The chief constable looked at Clara, then at Fleming, and shook her head. 'No,' she told them, 'I'm sorry, but that is something I'm not prepared to do, or even consider. I insisted Mike take this leave, he needs the break. He has been through some harrowing times recently. Not only by the news about my goddaughter, but also earlier events that were equally distressing. I took the trouble to check the rotas for the past twelve months. Mike has hardly taken any time off, in spite of the fact that as a single parent he should have been spending at least a part of any school holidays with his son. May I mention in passing, and this is no criticism of either of you, that you both took leave during those holidays and you are not parents. So I will not even consider asking Mike to come back, even though I know he would say yes.'

Fleming's disappointment was obvious, but she soon recovered. 'Very well, ma'am, I accept that, but if you're not prepared to ask Mike, what about requesting assistance from one of our neighbouring forces?'

'I've already considered that approach, in the light of the latest murders I sent out requests this morning but I'm not too hopeful. I've already had one chief constable on the phone to tell me that he'd made a similar request which was turned down and was on the point of asking me to lend him someone. It's only at times like this when there's a sudden escalation in the crime rate, that the true effects of the cutbacks and the reduction in personnel become painfully obvious. I regret to have to say this, because the potential effect on morale concerns me deeply, but I believe it's a situation we will all have to learn to live with, like it or not.'

* * *

Local radio carried the first report of the finding of the bodies, but Kovac never listened to those stations. The severity of the crimes was such that it was considered important enough to make national radio. The news item carried a description of the rural location where the bodies had been found, a brief mention of the mysterious 999 call and stated that local police were puzzled as to how the victims got to the scene. It was only when the reporter mentioned the name of the village of Kirk Bolton that Kovac realized the dead men were his two missing couriers.

There could be no mistake. Two of his employees were missing; had been absent for almost a week. Now two men had been found dead in the same area in what police were describing as suspicious circumstances. Kovac was only too well aware what that phrase meant. Putting two and two together, he knew that this had to be an act of reprisal. It seemed as if the opposition had declared war, in which case it was time they were made to understand that he was prepared to go to any lengths to protect his empire. He had fought hard to get to the position he was in; he wasn't prepared to relinquish it without a struggle. And if that meant others getting hurt, so be it. He picked up the phone and called Stanley.

'Have you been listening to the news on the radio?'

'No, I've been busy.'

'Switch on a news bulletin. Our men have turned up — dead. When we intercept that shipment of the Soldiers, I think we will have to demonstrate what a serious mistake they've made and show them that every escalation will be matched by our retaliation.'

* * *

The trauma the couple had shared in the picnic area might have ended their relationship before it began, but instead it had driven them together. That night had been a turning point, in more ways than one. When she got into his car at the start of the evening, she couldn't have foreseen the dramatic events that would have followed, could never have guessed she would end the night at his flat, in his arms, in his bed.

The morning had brought some awkwardness, until he'd asked her, gently, if she'd any regrets. She'd stretched, luxuriously, and as she did, her toes brushed against his leg. It might have been accidental. 'No regrets,' she told him firmly, then whispered, 'no regrets at all.'

After a leisurely breakfast, which was so late it was almost lunch, he'd begun work on his laptop. He hadn't mentioned her leaving, indeed he chatted intermittently as he worked, promising to have it all finished by late afternoon. After watching him for a while, at his suggestion she wandered away on an inspection tour. The flat was large with four bedrooms and ample space for a family. For one man alone, it was huge. Except that he was no longer alone, was he? As she thought it, she realized that her mind was already made up. If he asked her, she would move in with him. The decision surprised her, but certainly didn't shock her.

She was leaning on the door of the kitchen, mug of coffee in hand, when she felt his arms slide around her waist and up inside her jumper. She leaned back as his hands cupped her breasts, feeling his renewed arousal.

'I can't concentrate on my work so I was going to suggest a late lunch,' he said. 'But I think I'd prefer to wait until dinner. It isn't food I need. I want you.'

She put the mug down and led him towards the bedroom. By the time he had closed the bedroom door, she was already under the duvet; her clothes lying discarded on the floor. He removed his shirt and was about to join her when there was a loud hammering on the front door.

'Who on earth is that?' she asked, half fearful that her vengeful husband had found her. Then she realized she didn't care if he had. Last night had signalled the end of her married life, and hopefully the start of a new chapter.

He hurried to the flat door. Two women, flanked by two uniformed police officers, were standing outside holding warrant cards. One woman spoke, asked him to confirm his identity, then introduced herself. 'I'm Detective Sergeant Mironova, Helmsdale CID. This is my colleague DC Andrews. May we come inside?'

He nodded and stepped aside ushering them and one officer into the lounge. The second uniformed man remained on the doorstep.

'You called the emergency services to report two bodies you'd found at the picnic site near Kirk Bolton. How did you know they were there?'

He gasped. 'How did you find out I made the call?'

'CCTV picked up your registration number. Now, why were you at the picnic site, and how did you know about the bodies?'

'I . . . I found them. I drove into the car park and saw them. Well, I saw one to begin with. I . . . I got out of my car to see if he was injured. He wasn't breathing. That was when I saw the second body.'

'Why did you go there?'

'I . . . er . . . I wanted to . . . that is, I needed to relieve myself.' He knew it sounded false.

'I'm sorry, I don't believe you. There are public toilets at the far side of the car park. You would have no cause to go anywhere near the picnic tables. So, I'll ask you once again, what were you doing at the picnic site?'

He stared at the women, unsure what to say.

The answer came from behind them. 'He went there with me. He wanted to go there so we could make love.'

The detectives turned at the sound of the woman's voice. The fact that she was wearing nothing but a man's shirt didn't escape either of them.

'He didn't want to tell you, for the same reason he didn't identify himself when he made that call. He wanted to protect me, because he knew if our names became public I'd be upset by the scandal and publicity — as would my husband. However, I no longer care what either the public or my husband think, so there's no reason to hide the truth.'

'Thank you.' Mironova smiled as she looked back at the man who now looked completely nonplussed.

Andrews began to take her details, noted her name and asked, 'And your address please?'

The woman looked across the room at the man who had become her lover, saw the questioning look on his face, the hope in his eyes and then the smile beginning to dawn. That exchange of glances was all it needed to confirm that she had made the right choice. 'My address is here,' she replied. 'As of now, this is my home.'

'I ought to give you a lecture about wasting police time,' Mironova told them severely. 'But somehow in circumstances such as these I don't have the heart. I will need you to make an official statement of what you've just told us, but we'll do our best to ensure it is confidential and try to keep your names out of the press.' As an afterthought, she smiled and added, 'And I hope you'll be very happy together.'

CHAPTER NINE

Viv Pearce was looking for Clara and found her in the kitchen. 'Clara, I've just been speaking to Jack Binns. One of his officers has come back from rest days and seen that notice on the board about the shoplifters at Good Buys. He's identified one of the women. He says she's a prolific thief, not just shoplifting, but receiving as well.'

'Some good news at last. Check her out, please, and let's see if we can get a warrant arranged. You and Lisa can have the pleasure. Arrange to take some uniforms with you. Superintendent Fleming's coming here for a meeting but I'm sure you'll manage without me.'

The exterior of the house was far from prepossessing. Although the paintwork at the windows and front door looked reasonably clean. Lisa guessed this owed more to the attentions of the council than their tenants. The curtains at the windows looked as if they hadn't been washed since they were new; and that had been a long time ago. The garden could best be described as unkempt, bordering on wilderness. Amidst this display of tawdry living was one sign of mild prosperity she found surprising. On the hardstanding alongside the house was a newish mobile home. By contrast, it was in impeccable condition.

Pearce instructed the two uniformed men supplied by Jack Binns to make their way round the side of the house towards the back, while he and Lisa remained at the front. He hammered on the door, waited a moment and tried again. Although no one answered, it had clearly provoked a response, for he and Lisa heard the sound of a door slamming at the back, followed by a shout.

The officers returned, accompanied with great reluctance, by a man whose presence was not of his own volition. The man the officers were grasping by the scruff of his neck was in his early twenties. He was making strenuous efforts to break free but his attempts to escape were hampered considerably by his newly acquired fashion accessory; a pair of handcuffs.

'This bloke scarpered out of the back,' the officer said, 'but we managed to collar him.'

At that point the front door opened a few inches to reveal a woman whose age could have been anywhere between forty and sixty. Lisa gestured to the handcuffed man. 'Is this yours?'

'That's my son,' the woman snapped. 'He's done nowt wrong.'

'Of course not. They never have. That's why they run away at the sight of police officers. Does it have a name?'

'Newsome,' the woman told her reluctantly. 'Dwayne Newsome.'

'Good,' Lisa smiled. 'See; we're making progress already. So you must be Eileen Newsome, right?'

The woman nodded, as if wary that it might have been a trick question.

'OK, Eileen, I want to know something and I think you might be the one to help me. It's all a bit puzzling to be honest. We came here today to talk to you and we have a search warrant for these premises. But given that you told me a minute ago that Dwayne hasn't done anything wrong, why do you think he tried to leg it out of the back as soon as we knocked on your door? Of course it could be that he's just naturally shy but somehow I don't think so. Or might the reason be that he's been up to something he doesn't want you to know about. What do you think he's been doing?'

Lisa walked over to Dwayne. She leaned forward and as she did so, caught a whiff of something familiar on his breath. 'What have you been smoking, Dwayne? That's not nicotine I can smell, is it?'

She spoke to the uniformed men. 'Caution and search him, will you?'

One of the officers pulled a small plastic bag from the youth's jeans pocket. He handed it to Lisa, who sniffed cautiously. 'Ah yes, I thought so.'

'It's only cannabis,' Eileen blurted out. 'Surely you're not going to do him for a bit of weed.'

'Shut the fuck up, Ma!' Dwayne shouted, the first time he had spoken.

'Tut, tut, that's not a very nice way to talk to your mother, Dwayne.' As Lisa was speaking, the group stepped forward to enter the property and Pearce handed the search warrant to Eileen Newsome.

'What's all this about,' Eileen demanded.

'Your visit to Good Buys supermarket, the one where you left without paying for over a hundred pounds worth of shopping. The image on the CCTV footage is unmistakeably you.' Lisa looked at Eileen Newsome, whose face registered shock.

'Oh dear, I don't think this is proving to be the Newsome family's luckiest day. Where's your husband, Mrs Newsome? Is he inside?'

'No, he's been out for nearly two years now.'

Lisa frowned sternly at the officers, who were struggling not to laugh. 'No, Mrs Newsome. I meant is he inside the house?'

'He's not here. He's taken the dog for a walk.'

'That's unfortunate. And, I do hope you don't have any other relatives here, because if you did we'd risk running short of handcuffs. I'm also sorry to have to tell you, but there's another problem. When you get to the police station, we'll have to separate you and your son. We haven't got the extension with the family rooms finished yet.'

She gestured to the uniformed man waiting with handcuffs. 'Now, caution Mrs Newsome too, charge her with theft and take them both inside, then we can get to work.'

Mother and son were settled uncomfortably in the lounge, where one of the officers was left watching them.

Lisa glanced round at the room before returning her gaze to Eileen. 'Look on the bright side, it'll probably be a whole lot tidier after we've finished.'

An exhaustive search yielded nothing more than a tobacco tin on the coffee table containing Dwayne's smoking requisites. When they entered the roof void however, they found a treasure trove of stolen items that had been stashed among the joists. Amongst these were several recognizable from the recent spate of burglaries outstanding on the crime sheets. Alongside the stolen property was a quantity of clothing and electrical goods all still packaged and labelled.

'I think we have enough,' Pearce commented. 'Let's ferry these two back to the station. Jack's men can continue bagging the property; and if the husband turns up tell him we'd like to speak to him.'

* * *

Clara and Jackie Fleming were delighted with the results and supervised the handing over of the prisoners to Jack Binns for him to make out the charge sheets.

'Eileen Newsome, shoplifting from Good Buys supermarket, and receiving stolen goods,' Lisa told him. 'That's nice and brief, but make the most of it, because when you get to Dwayne's turn, you could finish up with writer's cramp.'

After mother and son were led away to the cells, Binns asked the superintendent if he could have a quiet word. She led him to one end of the area. 'Is there a problem, Jack?'

'The Coroner has released Geoff Riley's body at last and it's the funeral in two days. I had a word with my superintendent, and he's given me the OK to attend, providing I can organize cover for the station here. I would like to go, if possible. Geoff and I go back a long way and I know Maureen, his wife, will expect me to be there. Uniform branch will be turning out in force, so it wouldn't be fair to ask one of them to forego the right to pay their last respects. I wonder if you could organize someone to stand in for me. I'll take the day out of my leave entitlement if necessary.'

'You'll do no such thing, Jack. Of course you have to attend the funeral. I'll make sure Clara and her team deputize for you. They'll cope. How is Maureen, do you know? I haven't had chance to go see her since it happened. She was put on compassionate leave immediately.'

'I haven't spoken to her either, but I saw her brother in town yesterday. From what I could gather, Maureen's distraught, which is understandable but she can't give way to it too much for fear of upsetting the boy.'

Binns saw Fleming's puzzled expression. 'Geoff and Maureen have a son, who is about the same age as Mike's boy Daniel, but the lad's both physically and mentally disabled. I'm not sure of the exact details, but I do know he attends a special needs school and Geoff told me the costs are a terrible burden, even with two salaries, so that must be a concern for Maureen.'

'Oh Lord, that makes things even worse, if that were possible. It's remarkable that you only get to find out what goes on behind other people's doors when something like this happens. Don't worry about tomorrow. Your shift will be covered, and you will be paid for it, all right?'

Binns nodded his thanks. 'Is there any sign of progress towards finding out who was responsible?'

Fleming shook her head 'Apart from the theory that he interrupted poachers at work; and recovery of the bullet that would give us a ballistics match, sadly, we're no further forward.'

* * *

It was mid-afternoon when Clara got a phone call from one of the officers involved in the search at the Newsome house.

'I'm still at the Newsome' house, although noisome would be a better description. How people can live like this, I don't know. I've seen cleaner, tidier pigsties. Anyway, I think someone from CID ought to come back out here.'

Fifteen minutes later Clara and Pearce arrived to find the officer waiting by the dilapidated fence that acted as a demarcation between the pavement and the garden. Clara got out of the car and walked carefully across the crumbling concrete towards the motorhome alongside the house. The officer opened the door of the vehicle and she and Pearce followed him inside. 'I found the keys to this hidden in a tobacco tin inside one of the drawers in the main bedroom. That made me suspicious. Why keep them hidden? So I thought I'd have a look. That's when I found this. I poked one of them and it feels like a block of something. That's when I called you.'

He pointed to one of the bench seats that folded out to make a bed base. The top was hinged to provide storage space inside and he had propped the lid open with a cushion. Clara peered inside and saw hidden among some blankets, four large parcels, neatly wrapped in black plastic. She put on a pair of latex gloves, removed one of the parcels and hefted the weight.

'What do you reckon?' Pearce asked.

'One thing for certain, I'm prepared to bet it isn't a bag of sugar. I think we're going to have to make a new charge sheet out for Mrs Newsome. The shoplifting allegation is the least of her worries now. I think there are grounds for refusing bail. I'll wait until I've interviewed her then she can go to the cells at Netherdale.'

'What about her husband?'

'That's a very good question. Didn't you say he was supposedly taking the dog for a walk, so where is he?'

Patrick Newsome's absence had now become highly significant.

* * *

Later, Lisa Andrews and Pearce were talking to Jack Binns, discussing what had happened at the Newsome house. 'The place is disgusting,' Pearce said. 'There are all sorts of smells, none of them pleasant. It's the sort of house where you walk across a carpet and feel it sticky underfoot. Makes you want to wipe your feet when you leave, then rush home and jump into a hot shower. I found myself itching, even after I'd done that. If I had to make a choice, I'd rather live in the motorhome than the house. It isn't a new one by any means, but at least it's reasonably clean; and smells a whole lot better. They can't have had it long, otherwise I feel sure it would be in a similar state,' he added.

'You said you'd arrested the mother and son. What about the father?' Jack asked.

'No sign of him. Clara thinks he's done a runner. We found a mobile phone belonging to Mrs Newsome. The last text she sent from it was timed just after we arrived at the house. It read "pigs at home" which we think was a warning. If so, it worked, because he seems to have vanished. Obviously, he'll have guessed by now that we've found the drugs, either that or heard on the grapevine. Unless we can find out where he's gone, and who might be harbouring him, we could be looking for a long time.'

'Has his wife said anything?'

Pearce grinned. 'Nothing repeatable. In between swearing at us, she claimed we'd planted the drugs. Obviously, she has no idea about police budgets. Getting hold of a few thousand pounds worth of heroin to frame her and her old man simply isn't possible, no matter how desirable the idea might seem.'

'Will you let Clara know Eileen Newsome's brief has arrived?'

Viv headed for CID and relayed the message, adding, 'He's here for Dwayne as well, so we'll be able to interview both of them.'

Clara noted that Viv didn't seem too excited by the prospect. 'Who's representing them?' she asked.

Pearce saw Clara's expression turn sour when he told her.

'You didn't expect anything else, did you, Clara? It stands to reason a scrote like Dwayne Newsome with a harridan of a mother like Eileen would have a devious bastard like that for a solicitor. What line do you think Eileen will take on the drugs?'

Clara considered the question. 'She'll say only what her brief instructs her to. I'd guess that between them they will try to shift all the blame onto her husband. With Patrick Newsome having gone AWOL, they've a perfect opportunity to fit him up for anything and everything from the Jack the Ripper murders onwards. If I know that slimeball who's representing her, I'd guess he'll instruct her to say that she lived in terror of Patrick. He'll get her to tell stories of physical and mental cruelty, throw in abuse of Dwayne from early childhood and claim that Eileen knew nothing of the drugs in the motorhome.'

'That's possibly true, but she won't be able to get away with the shoplifting charge, not with the video evidence. That's fairly conclusive, I'd say,' Viv pointed out. 'And I'm sure we can make the receiving charges stick.'

'I'll bet that doesn't stop him encouraging her to try spinning a yarn. If she's to stand a chance of making the abuse and domination charges to stick, she'll have to make it realistic by telling us and the court, if they'll listen, that the only reason she went into Good Buys was because Patrick bullied her into it and she was too afraid of what he would do to her if she refused.'

'Surely the fact that she had an accomplice weakens that defence considerably?'

'It might, except for the fact that unless we can find that accomplice, or Patrick, we can't disprove Eileen's story. Any joy in tracing either of them?'

'Not yet, although another of the uniformed lads said he recognized the woman's face vaguely. The problem is, the image lifted from the CCTV isn't too clear, even though

I did my best with it. The guy said he thought the woman lived on the Westlea, but he couldn't be sure. I checked the file and interestingly enough the Newsome woman has never had any associates before. It's too big an estate to go knocking on doors, so I've circulated the photo again and asked Jack to keep reminding his troops about it. As for Newsome, he seems to have vanished into thin air, and short of a chance sighting, I can't think how we can collar him.'

'Well we'd better get on with it,' Clara said as she got to her feet and grabbed a pen and folder.

When they emerged from the interview room, Pearce reflected that Clara's prediction about the line Eileen's defence would take had been uncannily accurate. In fact, she could hardly have got closer to the mark had she scripted the interview herself.

CHAPTER TEN

Patrick Newsome had been lucky. Lucky that he'd been out of the house when the police had come knocking on his door. The text had come as an unwelcome shock, to put it mildly. When he read the message 'pigs at home' his immediate reaction had been that the police had come for him. It was only later, when he'd been watching from a safe distance and seen his wife and son carted off in a police car, that he'd realized he wasn't their initial target.

Later, overhearing the neighbours in the pub discussing the matter, he'd discovered that his wife had been the one they were after as the woman who'd nicked a load of groceries from the local supermarket. Dwayne, the stupid bastard, had been identified and arrested in connection with a string of burglaries, purely by chance, it seemed. Patrick cursed his nearest, but not dearest. How could they be so thick? The temptation to steal had been too much for them and in doing so they had threatened his prime source of income. To say Patrick was furious would be the understatement of the year.

Now he had to consider his options and the more he thought about them, the bleaker they seemed. First things first, he had to find somewhere to go, where he and his dog, could hole up without fear of discovery. Thinking of his dog provided a possible answer. He knew Sharon would like her. Sharon loved dogs. Within hours of the raid, as his wife and son were staring at the bleak cell walls of Helmsdale police station, Patrick had left town and travelled to Bishopton.

He hoped Sharon would be alone. She hadn't taken up with anyone else that he knew about since her partner's death. Patrick had never liked the man Sharon had lived with, partly through jealousy perhaps. He'd always considered Sharon as his, even after he'd married Eileen. Which was a little churlish, but the news that the man had died in prison a couple of years back certainly hadn't upset Patrick.

From time to time since then, especially when his family infuriated him by their stupidity, Patrick had considered leaving, abandoning Eileen and Dwayne, and moving in with Sharon. He'd resisted, up to the present — apart from the occasional visit. Now the idea was far more appealing. He had little doubt that Sharon would accept him. He had something he thought she would want. But then he'd known Sharon a long time.

The council estate, or as they were now called, social housing clusters, was situated on the west of Bishopton, in the low-lying land close to the River Helm. The estate was far smaller than the Westlea and, for the most part, the houses were better kept. Patrick walked to the last house on the row where the estate ended and the pastures used for grazing sheep began. He smiled; his dog would be in her element here. He knocked on the door and stepped back. He knew that before opening it, Sharon would be looking to see who her visitor was from behind the net curtain at her lounge window.

He heard the chain rattle, then the door opened. 'Hello, stranger. I wondered if I might be seeing you, sooner or later.' She glanced down at the dog. 'This your partner in crime, then? You'd better come in before any of the nosey bastards round here see you.'

She opened the door wide, then, as soon as they were inside, slammed it shut, replaced the chain and slid the bolts for good measure. She turned and looked at her visitor. 'Well, go on then, tell me all about it? What's the slag and your dopey son been up to? And, come to that, what have you been up to?'

Patrick began to explain, marvelling at how she already knew about the arrests. There wasn't much got past Sharon. She ought to have been a spy. As he spoke, Patrick watched her carefully. She hadn't changed much in all the time he'd known her. A little bit broader in the beam perhaps, and maybe the breasts weren't quite as pert as they had been, but she was still a handsome-looking woman, even though she was well on the shady side of forty. Her hair had always been one of Sharon's specialities. Different styles, different shades. Over the years there had been too many changes to count. Now, she'd let it grow to shoulder length and the colour, Patrick, who was no expert, could only think of as damson. But then, fruit wasn't his speciality either.

She listened to his story, wondering how the man she'd known for so long had ended up in such a mess. Her mouth hardened with anger as she identified the reason; Eileen, the greedy, grasping, cold-hearted slut he'd been stupid enough to marry. He'd married her in a fit of temper after he and Sharon had fallen out; a stupid row. Before they'd had chance to make up, he'd taken off and married that bitch.

When he'd finished his tale of woe, Sharon sat looking at him for a moment. 'It strikes me the cops might be the least of your worries. If your sponsors get wind of what's been going on, they might get concerned about what you and the slag know about their operations. They sound like the sort of people who wouldn't take too kindly to publicity and might be prepared to take decisive action if they felt the threat of exposure. And I doubt the slag will sit there quietly and take the rap for everyone else. As for the thicko, what do you call him, Dwayne is it? I take it you haven't been daft enough to tell him anything about the drugs?'

'Neither of them knows anything. I may be daft but I'm not fucking stupid. All Eileen knows is that we drive to the coast, pick up a parcel, and then deliver it.'

'You know that, but do the people you're working for know it? If not, they might direct their attention towards you.' Sharon accompanied her words with a bloodthirsty gesture, drawing her index finger across her throat. 'If I was you, I'd find somewhere safe to stay, well out of the way until the heat dies down. I certainly wouldn't consider running to them for help.'

None of which cheered Patrick up in the slightest.

'I suppose you're right,' he agreed gloomily. 'The problem is I've nowhere to go, not with the dog. Nowhere safe, that is. Unless — I don't suppose you'd risk putting me up for a day or two, would you? Just until I figure out what's best to do.'

Sharon stood up and stretched, giving Patrick an excellent view of her figure. She walked round the kitchen table to face him and leaned over him. She took hold of one of his hands and tugged it gently round her waist. She placed both her hands on his shoulders and began to move, slowly, rhythmically, suggestively. When she spoke, her voice was husky. 'Stay as long as you want. Do you know how long I've had to go without you? Damn near twenty-three fucking years! Or twenty-three non-fucking years, to be precise. If you stay here you'll have to put that right. Do that for me and I'll shelter you and the dog, no matter what the risk. Now, I suppose I'd better nip to the shops and pick up some dog food. You stay out of sight while I'm gone.'

She picked up her purse from the kitchen worktop and walked over to the door. Before unfastening the chain, she looked back and grinned. 'Upstairs would be the safest place to hide.'

* * *

The day following PC Riley's funeral, Clara arrived at the station before 7 a.m., but despite that, Sergeant Binns was already on duty. 'I thought I'd better get an early start,' he told her, 'I know both Nuisances are due in court this morning, so there's a lot to do.'

'How did yesterday go?'

'About as bad as you'd expect. Maureen was almost hysterical, but that was only to be expected. Fortunately her family was out in force, so there was plenty of physical and moral support for her and the son. Poor lad was completely baffled by everything that went on. I don't suppose the significance will dawn on him until his father doesn't return.'

'She comes from a big family then?'

'Her father is chairman and one of her brothers is in charge of furniture and fine art auctions, over at the auctioneers at Broughton-On-Helm. Her cousin runs the farm sales and she has another brother who is head gamekeeper to Lord Slingsby-Darrow. His lordship was also in attendance yesterday, together with all his brood.'

'There was a big turnout then?'

'Oh yes, Broughton church was full to overflowing. A lot had to stay outside. I think that might be of some comfort to Maureen when she thinks about it later on, because it showed the respect people had for Geoff. As for me, well, it was good to see old Lord "slings and arrows" and Maureen's cousins without having to caution them or threaten them with a cell overnight. It shows how even the wildest bunch can settle down given time.'

'You had some bother with them when they were young then?' Clara was fascinated by this glimpse into the less reputable past of certain prominent locals.

'A fair bit, but most of it was relatively harmless. More youthful exuberance than vindictiveness and usually fuelled by large quantities of beer. The trick was to nip it in the bud before it got out of hand. The problem was, if you did happen to upset one of them you'd have the whole pack of them down on you like a ton of bricks. And before you knew it, you'd have a battle royal on your hands.'

'How did Lord Slingsby-Darrow fit into the picture?'

Binns gave her a sly grin. 'The oldest way in the book. He'd been giving one of Maureen's cousins a good seeing to from the time they were both sixteen, if not before.

Eventually, of course, the inevitable happened and he put her up the stick, but to give him his due, he did the honourable thing and married her. They've been married over twenty years now and, judging by the gathering of young slings and arrows on display yesterday, she must have been popping them out every two years or so. Mind you, I reckon they're still as keen on one another as they were when they were kids, judging by the way they were holding hands.'

'Jack, you are without doubt, the dale's biggest gossip.' Clara smiled. Then added a sober note, 'Did anyone mention the murder, or was that subject taboo for the day?'

'That's a rather odd thing. Nobody said a thing, apart from the vicar in his eulogy. I expected them to and I was dreading it to be honest, although I'd rehearsed my answers to some questions I thought might be asked, but nobody did.'

Clara saw him frown. 'What is it, Jack?'

'The more I think about it, the more it worries me. For them not to ask anything whatsoever about the investigation simply isn't natural. I know these people and I'm concerned they might believe they can deal with this their own way.'

'You think if it was poachers, then they might know who shot Geoff Riley?'

'No, not for certain. I mean, they might suspect someone, they might even have drawn up a short-list, but they can't know for definite. Any more than we can.'

'Why are you worried then?'

'Put it this way, three of them are landowners, another is a gamekeeper and a couple are farmers. They're far more likely to have a good idea who might be involved in poaching around this area than we are. What concerns me is if they did discover anything more definite or if they thought they knew who killed Geoff and, if they believed the culprit might get away with it for lack of solid evidence, the sort that would stand up in court; then they could be tempted to, well, take matters into their own hands and that would be really bad news.'

'I think it would be a good idea if you were to have a quiet word with one or two of them, don't you? A gentle sort of warning that if any of the poaching fraternity suddenly turn up riddled with twelve bore pellets, we'll know where to come looking.'

'I'll do that.'

Binns changed the subject. 'What happened about those packets found in that mobile home? Did they contain drugs? Forensics should have come back with results by now.'

Clara laughed. 'You haven't read your charge sheets yet this morning. Eileen Newsome's got far more to worry about than mere shoplifting, especially if her husband doesn't turn up to share the blame. The parcels contained over two hundred thousand pounds worth of heroin at today's prices. Which means, she's now facing charges of possession with intent to supply. Patrick Newsome appears to have done a runner. You don't happen to have an idea where we might find him, do you?'

'Sorry, no, Patrick isn't exactly one of my close social circle. Come to think of it, I don't think he's much in demand in any social scene. He has one or two boozing mates on the Westlea, but that's about all. I'll have a word with my lads and see if they can come up with some names. If there is anyone on his calling list, I feel sure they'll be known to us.'

Clara went into CID and began to go through the files stacked on the desk. She settled to her task, feeling more cheerful than she had for some time. This was partly the result of a phone call the previous evening from her fiancé, David. He'd reported that he was safe and well and that he was well clear of any danger zones. The operation he had been on had been completed and he and his men were resting up, awaiting further orders.

As she tackled the files, Clara's optimistic mood brightened further. The other reason for her cheerful frame of mind lay in the reports she had received from the various technical support officers tasked with examining evidence supplied following their raid on the Newsome house. Those results would be sufficient to prove their case against Dwayne Newsome. The hoodie he had been wearing had been tested and what might prove to be a vital piece of evidence taken from it. It was hair, and it definitely did not belong to Dwayne. If the hair could be matched to a recent mugging victim, there would be a further charge to add to the list.

The net result of their raid would be to clear up many of their unsolved cases, which only left the most serious ones, the murders of PC Riley and the two victims found at the picnic site. In another mood, Clara might have been disheartened by this, but she refused to allow herself to get depressed by it, or by the fact that they were still no further forward in tracing the source of the drugs found in the motorhome. That topic was fresh in her mind when Lisa Andrews walked in.

'I've been thinking,' Lisa announced. 'It's to do with the Newsome place. There was something illogical about what we found there.'

'Illogical? In what way?'

'Well the house was a real mess, scruffy, smelly, and dirty.'

'That's certainly no exaggeration from what little I saw of it. What's your point?'

'It just seemed to me illogical that they should have such a revolting house, and yet they've a rather smart motorhome on the drive.'

'Well, people like the Newsomes are more interested in their toys and gadgets than they are in new home furnishings.'

'I know that, but I checked up on the price of motorhomes and I was quite staggered at how much they cost. A vehicle similar to the one on their drive is worth thousands. I mean quite a lot of thousands. My thought was that they must have bought it on the drip, so I did an HPI check and it showed up clear. I couldn't believe that even the most lax of finance companies would have passed either of the Newsomes as creditworthy. My other thought was that it could be borrowed or hired, but the DVLA record shows

Patrick Newsome as the registered keeper. It's also properly insured, which I admit surprised me. The insurance premium alone could set them back over fifty pounds a month, plus all the other running costs. So if anyone can tell me how they manage all that with no income apart from benefit cheques, I'd love to hear it.' Lisa looked at Clara for an answer.

'Given that we know they were involved in drug trafficking, perhaps buying the motorhome would be a good way of laundering the money?'

'It would, except that the dealer would need proof of where such a large amount of cash originated. They have to check up by law. So I started wondering if there was more to it than that.' Lisa went on to outline the rest of her theory.

Clara thought about it for a while. 'You could be right,' she admitted. 'I'll tell you what; I'm due to meet with Jackie Fleming and the chief constable later. I'll see what they think. If they agree that it's worth following up, we'll start working on it. And don't worry; I'll make sure they know it was your idea.'

CHAPTER ELEVEN

The chief listened to Clara report the successful outcome of the search of the Newsome house, followed by Jackie Fleming who catalogued the crimes they could now add to their clear-up statistics.

'That's good,' O'Donnell told them. 'However, there are still three unsolved murders. Has there been any progress with those enquiries?'

They admitted there was nothing new. 'There is one concern, ma'am,' Mironova said. 'PC Riley's in-laws might try direct action if they think nothing else can be done.' She repeated what Binns had told her.

'It might be worth having a word with them,' O'Donnell instructed. 'Both to warn them off and to discover if they have any suspects we don't know about. If they can give us a name or two, point us in the right general direction, that might lead to the breakthrough we need.'

Clara agreed. 'I've already suggested to Jack Binns it might be wise to speak to them, I'll get him to ask. He knows them better than anyone. They might open up to him.'

'Is there anything else to discuss? I've a meeting to attend in Manchester, and I need to set off soon.'

'Just one more thing,' Clara said. 'It's to do with the Newsome family. It's an idea that Lisa came up with that might be worth following up.'

'What is it?'

'It's to do with where we found the stash of heroin.' Clara explained about Lisa's enquiries into the ownership of the motorhome. 'When she found out how much those vehicles cost, she wondered how they could afford it. That was when she remembered what I'd told her about the report from the Drugs Intelligence Unit. Her idea is that Newsome and others like him are being used to bring the drugs inland from the coast. That would give them the cash to fund vehicle purchases. And thinking about this area, what's more natural to see than a motorhome travelling between here and the coast, especially in summer?'

'That's true,' O'Donnell acknowledged. 'My husband complains when we get stuck behind one.'

'What use can we make of it, though?' Fleming asked. 'Even if Lisa's theory proves to be correct, I don't see how it helps?'

'Lisa thinks it's worth checking others in the area, to see if anyone else has been buying vehicles that are way beyond their apparent means.'

'If the people behind this racket have got to know about the drugs seizure they'll have gone to ground, surely,' Fleming suggested.

'I'm not so sure. Who will have told them? We haven't announced it. Patrick Newsome certainly won't have told them. He'd be far too frightened about reprisals. In any case, knowing how such gangs work, they'll have made sure they can't be traced.'

O'Donnell nodded. 'I agree with Clara. I think it's worth pursuing. For the effort involved, the rewards could be enormous. Breaking up just one of these gangs would be an immense bonus. I'll leave it you two to sort out the ways and means.'

Despite her earlier statement about the meeting she had to attend, after Fleming and Mironova left, O'Donnell picked up the phone. 'I have news that I think will interest you.'

* * *

Patrick Newsome was content — certainly as content as a man on the run from the police could be. He was lying on one side, watching Sharon. She was asleep, her face relaxed, smiling in her dream. Was that about him? Patrick wondered. Certainly their passionate encounter before they slept was enough to cause pleasant dreams.

He should have done this long ago. As he looked at Sharon, as he remembered their lovemaking, he wondered what on earth had caused him to stay with Eileen as long as he had. It certainly wasn't her looks, for she couldn't hold a candle to Sharon in the beauty stakes. Nor was it from love, for any affection between them had died long ago, probably stillborn at that.

No, Sharon was a far better choice. Would she let him stay? Would she consider making it a permanent arrangement? Patrick hoped so and couldn't see a reason why not. It wasn't simply for the sex, although that was terrific. Other things linked them together, things they didn't talk about, but were tacitly understood.

There would be problems, though, obstacles to be got out of the way. Eileen was the biggest of these. Presumably, the police had searched the motorhome and found the drugs by now and Eileen would waste no time, spare no effort in putting the blame fairly and squarely on him. He knew her far too well to harbour any illusions that she might stay silent and take the rap for him. That would involve a level of loyalty; loyalty that Eileen simply didn't possess.

Although he was relaxed, he felt isolated. Being out of touch with what was going on was a bit unnerving. When he thought about the type of people he worked for, Patrick knew they would be less than happy about his silence. Arguing that it was through no fault of his would not stand him in good stead. They weren't the kind to accept excuses, even if they listened to them.

Now he was just grateful that he was absent from the house when the police descended on it. Fortunate that he'd been able to turn to Sharon, come here for a bolthole and shelter until the heat died down. The only problem with that was the heat might not die down for a long time. He might be forced to lie low for months, years even. He grinned; the idea of spending such a long time imprisoned in Sharon's bedroom did have its redeeming features.

Where Patrick had been unlucky was that at the time Eileen had sent the text warning of the police at their house, his mobile battery was already running low. Before he had chance to do anything about this, the phone had died. Without the charger he was helpless to call anyone. All the people he needed to speak to were only available via the contacts list on his mobile. Above all else, he needed a replacement charger, the one Sharon owned didn't fit his older style mobile. But he wasn't exactly in a position to go shopping.

Patrick glanced sideways. There were a couple of phone shops in the town, Sharon would have to buy one for him. Once the mobile was fully charged he could phone the people he worked for. Telling them the bad news about the loss of the drugs consignment from the motorhome wasn't going to be pleasant, but it would be necessary. If he didn't give them the information and they found out by other means, they might suspect he still had the goods; that he had concocted the story of the police raid to hide the fact. If they thought he was holding onto the drugs, maybe even setting up for himself in competition, the consequences would be unpleasant, to say the least.

Patrick thought of the man he'd met only once, the man with the fearsome reputation. He thought of the weapon the man always carried, and something inside him cringed in terror. No, he certainly didn't want to meet Stanley again.

There was another reason he needed the phone charged up as soon as possible, also connected to the people he worked with. Patrick's gaze strayed to the chair near the bed, and the clothing he'd dumped on it in his haste to get into the sack with Sharon. He thought about the contents of one of the jeans pockets, and what those contents represented. Yes, getting that charger was vital. He would have to try and get Sharon to go shopping first thing in the morning. Patrick thought he knew how to persuade her.

* * *

Sharon entered the phone shop, clutching the piece of paper with Patrick's mobile details on. Patrick might not be every woman's idea of a perfect partner but Sharon didn't mind that. She didn't mind his lurid past or his slightly dodgy reputation either. She was convinced that much of what he'd done, or what he was rumoured to have done, was down to that woman's influence. Sharon never thought of Eileen Newsome by name, to her she was always 'that woman'. Not that Sharon spent much time thinking of her, not a moment longer than was strictly necessary. In fact, whenever she did, Sharon got wound up and angry by the knowledge that the woman had cheated her of so much of Patrick's life and done her best to ruin him into the bargain.

Sharon was by no means blind to Patrick's imperfections. If love is blind, in Sharon's case it was the blindness of ignorance. She didn't ignore his misdemeanours; it was simply because he omitted to tell her all of them, or their gravity.

She was unlucky in the first phone shop and fared no better with the second so-called specialist. However, her luck changed when she went into Good Buys supermarket. A short while later, she left the store, the blister pack containing a replacement charger nestling amongst the groceries in her carrier bag.

Patrick was pleased with the charger, appreciative when she explained the trouble she'd had in getting it. If he had any concerns, they surrounded the possible reaction from the people who paid him to bring drugs in his motorhome, or rather the one they had provided for him. The news of the potential loss of such a valuable consignment was not likely to be well received. While Sharon had been out shopping, he'd switched the TV on and watched the local news bulletins, and retuned the radio to Dales FM. Nowhere was there any mention of drugs, so he still harboured hope that the packets were still hidden under the seat where he'd stashed them, unlikely though it seemed.

He plugged the charger in and was shocked to see that the phone didn't register anything. 'This is going to take longer than I thought,' he told Sharon. 'I don't think I'm going to be able to use the phone until morning, by then it should have some charge.'

'Oh well, we'll just have to think of some way to pass the time until then.'

CHAPTER TWELVE

A week before the grim discovery of the bodies in the picnic area, far away, in a small town in France, a young North African girl, Shakila, stood behind the kitchen door of her home listening to her parents' conversation. She listened, hardly daring to breathe for fear of discovery. The conversation was about her. They were talking about the anger and distress she had caused, and the shame they felt she had brought upon them. Shakila could hear their fury reflected in their voices.

She heard her mother ask, 'What are you going to do about this? The situation is intolerable. It is your duty to act.'

Shakila listened to her father's angry reply. 'You know very well what I have to do. It is what is expected of me. More than that, it is demanded of me. If it isn't done, we will become pariahs and everything we have worked for will be lost. Not only that, we will never be able to obtain good marriages for our other children. Shakila has brought disgrace on all the family. She refuses to cover her face, refuses to wear discreet clothing. She causes a scandal every time she walks down the street. She is disobedient, hangs around with young men who are not of our people, not of our way of life. And now she has insulted one of the most prestigious families in the region by refusing to entertain their son in the marriage that was arranged for her years ago. A marriage that cost me a lot of money to fix. Money that could have gone into the dowry of her sister. By refusing to honour that marriage contract she leaves us with no choice. I have talked the matter over with our eldest son and my brother. We are agreed, so when they come here in two days time we will ask her one final time. If she persists in her obstinacy, we will have no choice. Then we will have to decide.'

'Decide what?'

Shakila heard the fear in her mother's voice. It reflected the pain in her own heart. Although she listened for her father's answer, in truth, she already knew it. The confirmation, when it came, was no less of a shock.

'Decide if we can allow Shakila to remain a dishonour to us, or if we rid ourselves of this stain forever. Only by doing that will we regain the respect we have lost.'

Although it was a warm evening, Shakila shivered uncontrollably. Her eyes widened in fear. She clasped her hand tightly across her mouth to stop the scream that threatened to burst forth. Silent tears coursed down her cheeks. Tears of terror mixed with tears from the pain as she bit her finger almost to the bone. She had just listened to her own father pass sentence of death on her. The house she once knew as her home had become her prison, the room she had slept in since infancy was now a condemned cell. Her own family, those she had held dearest, those she had loved the most, were now her enemies. They would soon be her executioners. She had little chance to escape the doom that awaited her. Her choices were stark; her prospects less than bleak. Either she had to choose marriage to a man she loathed; or escape. If she could not face the one or achieve the other, her own family would kill her. But if she succeeded in getting away, where would she go? How would she travel? She had neither money nor passport.

For the moment, all she could do was remain silent; pretend she didn't know what was planned and think of a way to escape. She had two days before her brother and uncle arrived. Two days to live. Shakila crept silently to her room and closed the door. She wedged a chair against it then cast herself down on the bed. It was only then that the flood gates truly opened, and she wept uncontrollably in solitary desolation.

* * *

Shakila had packed everything she dared take with her into a rucksack. It was as much as she could secrete without her mother noticing. Her room had been searched more than once recently. These searches were unannounced, often without Shakila being there and she knew if she took too much out of her wardrobe it would give the game away. What she dare not take would have to be abandoned, a small but inevitable price to pay for her life. The day before her brother and uncle were due to arrive dragged slowly by, each hour causing her mounting stress as she fretted that her plan might be uncovered.

The first phase had been easy, or relatively so. Knowing that her father only banked the shop takings on a Friday, Shakila had removed as much as she dare from the house safe, without making it obvious that the cash was missing. Two-thousand euros was not much on which to build a future, but the alternative was no future at all.

Eventually, as the house quietened down for the night, Shakila started to entertain the hope that her plan might stand a chance of succeeding. During the interminable day, neither of her parents had spoken to her, averting their gaze whenever she was near. Was that from anger, or shame at what they intended to do? With something of a shock, she realized that she no longer cared. By planning her death, they had severed the last fragile thread of family loyalty that had remained. If she succeeded, Shakila would leave without a trace of regret.

It was two a.m., when she guessed the family would be fast asleep, that Shakila made her move. She cautiously slid her bedroom window open. It moved easily, for she had greased it the previous day. Every detail she could think of had been taken into account and planned well. She reached below her bed, pulled out the rucksack, and lowered it out of the window, letting it fall onto the soft earth below. Although it made only a slight thudding sound as it landed, to the girl above, her nerves stretched to breaking point, the sound seemed as loud as a cannon's roar. She turned towards the inside of the house and listened, trying to catch the slightest whisper of sound that might indicate that someone's sleep had been broken. There was nothing, but she waited, distrustful even of her own senses.

Eventually, impatience overruled caution and she climbed out of the window, a manoeuvre she had practiced several times the previous night. She reached across and clung to the drainpipe, her ladder to freedom, her escape route to survival. The next part was the trickiest. Holding on to the pipe with one hand and with her feet braced on the support brackets bolting the drainpipe to the wall she reached across and pushed the window closed. If the house became cold someone might wake up and notice. If they noticed, they might come and investigate. Shakila had checked the weather forecast which promised a strong breeze from the north. A draught could have given her away as easily as a slamming door. It might be unlikely, but she wasn't prepared to let chance shorten her odds.

With the window in position, she managed to half-climb, half-slide down the pipe, reaching the ground without mishap. Once on solid ground she groped about to locate her rucksack, found it and turned to face her next obstacle. There was no point opting for the gate which squealed loudly in protest even if someone threatened to open it. Scaling the garden wall, topped by broken glass, was the only alternative.

Standing in front of the two-metre-high wall she carefully edged her foot along the base. She moved position twice, repeating the action each time. Eventually, her foot made contact with a brick lying hidden in the grass. She had placed it there to denote the point where there were hand and footholds in the otherwise smooth brickwork. She removed the bath towel from between the straps of the rucksack and spread it on top of the wall. With this protection in place she cautiously felt for the gaps and began to climb. When she was able to grip the wall top in safety through the towel, the rest was easy. She dropped the rucksack over the side and jumped down. Quickly she dragged the towel away and tossed it into the neighbouring garden.

She picked up the rucksack, slipped the straps over her shoulders, settled it comfortably and turned to head for the town. It was a twenty-minute walk, although at the time it seemed far longer. During the journey, she never once looked back.

In the town centre she made straight for the taxi rank. Many of the drivers were of North African descent like her. These, she avoided, opting for a white man who told her in halting French that he was from Poland. After a short discussion, Shakila climbed into the back of his taxi. Once she had settled, she took a hundred euros from her stolen hoard and gave him it, part payment for the journey. As she handed the money over, she told him sternly, 'No tricks, no funny business. Drive me straight to where I want to go. No questions. And no talking. Get it?'

He nodded understanding, any thoughts he might have had of not complying being negated by the look in her eyes; or possibly by the sharp carving knife in her hand. Four hours later, at about the time when her mother would be waking up and thinking about going to her daughters' rooms to rouse them, Shakila climbed out of the taxi and gave the driver the rest of the fare. She watched the car drive away, the last link with the past she had left behind; then turned to stare at the capital's famous landmark. She walked swiftly towards the Eiffel Tower, but after a few hundred metres she entered the nearest metro station.

By the time her mother entered her room, found it empty, and raised the alarm, Shakila was on a train heading for the coast. She was determined to try and reach England. She had never been there, but one of her teachers and some of the other girls said it was a good place, a land where freedom was valued, and that thought was like a breath of fresh air to Shakila. Quite how she would get there without a passport or papers, she hadn't worked out. Somehow, it seemed less important than what had gone before.

Shakila's first instinct had been to head for the ports giving the easiest access to Britain, those closest to the south coast of England. However, during the long taxi ride, she had chance to rethink her original idea. She had read stories of immigrants trying to get to Britain via those routes. Their efforts almost always ended in failure, to such an extent, that the French authorities had set up what was in effect an internment camp close to the coast.

She knew she could not afford such a risk. It would mean being returned to her family and almost certain death. Instead, she headed further south. As she had been pondering the difficulty, a stray memory came to her aid.

It had been a year earlier, when she was still at school. A classmate had told of her summer holiday, which had sounded idyllic. 'We stayed near Brest in a small town called Camaret-Sur-Mer. It is a beautiful little town. It has a marina and a campsite where we stayed.'

'You spent the holiday in a tent?' To Shakila it sounded wonderfully adventurous, if a little uncomfortable.

'Of course not, although I wouldn't have minded. My parents rented a small chalet, like a log cabin. Although of course it is a sleepy little place, not like Brest, where all the big ships come, the marina has lots of power boats and yachts from all over the world.' She lowered her voice and whispered, 'I met this beautiful Swedish boy who was on one of the boats. It belonged to his father. We used to meet on the beach every night. He has promised to write to me.'

Shakila had reflected on how different the girl's exciting life was to her own miserable, caged existence. Not for her the freedom of meeting a lover on a beach. No beautiful Swedish boys would be allowed near her. Now, however, the town of Camaret-Sur-Mer, with its marina filled with boats from all over the world, seemed like the ideal place to try the next phase of her freedom bid.

If she could rent a chalet for a few days, it would give her chance to inspect the marina, possibly find a boat that would take her clear of French territory. And if she was really lucky, Shakila thought, she might even find one with a beautiful Swedish boy on board, who would be prepared to aid her escape. The only reservation Shakila had was what a beautiful Swedish boy might want in return for taking such a risk but she put that thought firmly to the back of her mind. If there was no suitable boat or the price demanded was too high, she supposed she could always try Brest where the bigger ships might give her an opportunity. Wherever she set out from, if the worst came to the worst she could always stowaway.

Mindful of the need to preserve her dwindling hoard of euros, she opted to walk the sixteen or so kilometres from Brest train station to Camaret, hopeful of arriving before nightfall. The choice of a campsite was a good one in several ways. Not only was it far cheaper than staying in hotels, but the campsite didn't demand to see paperwork, or look askance at someone arriving with no more than a rucksack as luggage.

After parting with a further two hundred euros, Shakila secured a chalet. She had to eat, and sleep. This would deplete her cash a little more, but the hunger pangs of a healthy eighteen-year-old could not be denied any longer. Apart from a barely edible snack on the train, she hadn't eaten anything for twenty-four hours. Not having slept for far longer, she would have to go to bed. On the way to her chalet, she had noticed a restaurant with a takeaway section. Although her instinct was to go inside and sit down, order a meal and dine at her leisure, she realized with something of a shock that this option wasn't open to her.

As she was booking in, Shakila had seen the television in the reception area. The news bulletin had been about to start as she left the building. For all she knew, her parents might have already reported her absence to the police. A nationwide search might be on for her. Perhaps she would be featured in the newscast. Perhaps there would even be a photograph. Recognition would almost inevitably lead to exposure; exposure would lead to detention.

The danger of being seen would also limit her mobility severely. Choices of where to go and when must be governed by the need to avoid crowds and the heightened risk of detection. With this in mind, Shakila went to bed early. If she wanted to survey the marina it would have to be undertaken before the beach and sea front were thronged with holidaymakers. An early start was essential.

She did not sleep well, due in part to the stress she was under and to the romantic antics of the couple in the adjoining chalet. Despite this, Shakila was up, dressed and out of her room before first light. She set off in the direction of the marina and from a nearby headland was able to get a long-distance view of the boats moored within the breakwater.

From her vantage point she realized there was one major obstacle. At the end of the pontoons to which the boats were moored was a high wall with a big gate, obviously designed to keep out people who had no business to be inside. People like her. Even if she was able to identify a suitable boat, she would have to devise some means of getting inside. To be so close, and yet be unable to advance her escape plan, was frustrating.

She sat on a rocky outcrop, looking at the lie of the land, pondering her options, which were, she admitted, severely limited. As she stared at the curve of the bay with the strengthening sunlight reflecting brightly off the calm blue water, Shakila began to get the glimmer of an idea. She tried to estimate distances, wondering about currents. If all else failed, there was one desperate measure she could try.

In the reception area at the campsite there was a small shop, whose shelves were crammed with anything and everything a holidaymaker might need. Shakila set off back again; her funds were about to be further depleted, by a take-away breakfast and the cost of a swimsuit.

She returned to her chalet to eat and added the swimsuit to the few possessions in her rucksack. She didn't doubt her ability to swim round the headland to the marina, but she wondered how difficult the task would be with the added burden of the rucksack. The label on the bag proclaimed it to be waterproof but was that claim one that stretched as far as prolonged immersion in sea water, she wondered.

Identifying a British registered boat didn't present that much of a challenge in itself, she knew she'd be able to pick one out by the pennant it displayed. But even if she saw a British craft, there was no way she could find out when it would be sailing and, equally important, what the boat's ultimate destination would be. Shakila had a terrible vision of stowing away on board a vessel that didn't leave the marina for weeks. Hunger alone would force her to surrender.

The alternative was equally terrifying. What if the boat did set sail, but instead of heading north-east, set a southerly course entering the Mediterranean, perhaps to end up off some remote Greek island or the Turkish mainland? Shakila would be forced to go ashore without being able to speak a word of the language, or any knowledge of the laws and customs. At least she was reasonably fluent in English and her study of British history had given her some knowledge and insight into the people.

One thing was certain; her original idea of how she would arrive on British shores was a plan in ruins. She needed a radical rethink. Either that, or a miracle. Although she wasn't to know it, miracles come in all shapes and sizes, and sometimes, they are cleverly disguised.

CHAPTER THIRTEEN

Early that evening, Shakila though it was safe to leave her chalet. The foreshore was all but deserted. By then, many of the holidaymakers would be preparing for their evening meal. When she reached the headland, she sat on top of a sand dune, staring across the bay towards the marina. She tried to think. How could she by-pass the security at the gate? The alternative was a long, difficult swim in unknown waters. Even if she reached the marina, how could she board a vessel that was soon heading for Britain?

The prospect seemed hopeless and Shakila had to face the unpalatable fact that her attempt at freedom had almost certainly ended in failure here, so close to her ultimate goal. Her dream of escape, a new life in a land where she could be sure vengeance wouldn't follow her was in ruins. She would be captured, returned to the family she hated and who hated her. In the fullness of time, when the glare of publicity had faded, she would simply disappear. Butchered most probably, her remains fed into the local waterways by those closest to her. Despair overcame her, and Shakila began to weep, tears of loneliness and desolation. Only a month had passed since her eighteenth birthday. Now, she felt sure it would prove to be her last.

'Kes Kur say?' The question was in an attempt at French, but the speaker's accent was certainly not French.

Shakila looked up, startled by the interruption and the unfamiliar tone. She saw a woman in early middle age, with bleached blonde hair. As the questioner saw Shakila's face, her eyes narrowed and she stared at the girl.

'Je connais vous . . . Oh, bugger it. I can't get used to this ruddy frog speak. Do you speak English, love? Because I reckon I know you.'

Shakila nodded, unable to say a word. Was this the end? The woman spoke again, and Shakila listened carefully, frowning at the effort of concentration needed to decipher the unfamiliar language when delivered in a strange, broad accent unlike any used by her teachers at school.

'I know you. Your picture's in this morning's paper.' The way she said 'picture' made it sound like a baseball player.

Pitcher? Was that really how you pronounced it? Shakila wondered.

'You're that girl who's missing. The coppers are looking for you, aren't they? Isn't your name Shakira?'

'Shakila,' she replied wearily. She began to cry again. 'But now you will give me to the police, and everything is finished.'

The stranger sat down alongside her and put a comforting arm around her shoulder. 'Now hold on, love. Don't take on. It's not worth it, believe me. Nothing is. This will all be over with soon, and you've the rest of your life to look forward to.'

Shakila's tears increased. When she eventually calmed down a little, she said in slow, careful English, 'You do not know. You cannot know. You would not understand. I have no life ahead of me. When I am returned to my family I will vanish. Someday, a body may be discovered. Possibly.'

'What the hell are you on about? Is this some daft game you're playing? Like one of those virtual computer games where you pretend to be someone else?'

'No, madam, it is no game. In the ways of my people and the ways of my religion, in their eyes I have offended so deeply. I cannot be allowed to live. My existence is a blasphemy, almost. We have strict rules we must obey as a female. In dress, in conduct and with marriage arrangements that might have been made when we were children. I refused to comply with many of these and my rejection of a man I found repulsive was the final defiance.

'I have brought disgrace upon my family. My parents no longer regard me as their daughter. Neither my mother nor father spoke to me in the week before I escaped, they would not make eye contact with me. My meals, such as I was allowed, had to be taken in my room, brought to me by my younger sister, who was forbidden to speak with me. Then, I heard my mother and father talking, plotting my death. I had two days to get out before my brother and uncle returned home. If I had remained, I would have been executed and my body disposed of.'

'Hell's bells! Are you kidding?'

Shakila began to cry again; heartrending sobs.

'You're not kidding, are you? I've heard stories of stuff like this, but I thought it was only fiction. An honour killing, that's what you're talking about, isn't it?'

'Oui . . . I mean, yes, madam, that is it, precisement. And now you know it is not from the pages of the fiction writers' alone. And now it will come about.'

'No it bloody well won't, Honey. Not if I've owt to do with it. Just steady on a minute and let me have a little think.'

Shakila obeyed, half fearful, half wondering if she dared entertain some hope that all might not be as bad as it seemed.

Her comforter spoke again. 'How did you land up at this spot? I mean, it isn't exactly Gay Paree, is it? And what were you planning to do next? How were you hoping to get away?'

Shakila explained, as best she could. When it came to her plan to swim with her rucksack over to the marina and pick out a boat with a British flag, her companion shook her head. 'You wouldn't have stood a chance. First off, swimming at night with a rucksack and hoping to find one boat amongst all that lot that was going to England. You'd have had more chance of winning the lottery. No, you were bound to fail.' She paused and studied Shakila for a moment, then asked, 'How good a swimmer are you? Did you seriously think you could swim from here to the far side of the marina towing a rucksack?'

'I do not know. If I had not the rucksack I would have succeeded. I was in my school the best swimmer.'

'Then today might just have been your lucky day, Honey. See that boat at the far end of the marina?' She pointed to a large cabin cruiser that Shakila had noticed earlier, one of the most expensive-looking craft in the bay.

Shakila nodded. 'Is that your boat?'

'It is, love. Mine and my husband's. What's more, we're leaving later tonight. And, we're on our way back to England. My husband has gone to Brest to do a bit of business, but once he gets back, we're away. If you can get on board without being spotted, then we'll take you with us, how does that sound?'

Shakila couldn't speak, choked as she was with emotion, but her face said it all for her.

Her new accomplice laughed and continued, 'The boat is called the Blooming Rose. Here's what I suggest. You nip back and gather your stuff in your rucksack and put your swimsuit on. Bring everything back here and then start swimming. I'll take the rucksack and get it through the gate. They won't stop me. All you have to do is swim to the end of the marina. There's a ladder on the seaward side of the boat. If you climb up that, you'll not be seen. Besides, I'll be looking out for you. Get on board the boat and you've cracked it.'

'Cracked it?' The idiom defeated Shakila.

'Achieved what you set out to do, love.' The woman smiled at her. 'I know it's not the ideal solution, but it's the best I can come up with at short notice. Is there anywhere in England you were aiming for. Anywhere in particular, I mean?'

Shakila spread her hands in a gesture of helplessness. 'I do not know anyone in your country, so I could not say.'

'We're headed home, to the north. A place called Yorkshire. Have you heard of it?'

'I know of puddings.'

Shakila's saviour laughed again. 'Fame for my county at last. Anyway, best get on with it. Off you trot, sharpish. And don't get seen. Remember, if I recognized you, others can.' She saw Shakila's hesitation. 'Go on, get your skates on . . . I mean hurry up.'

Shakila turned to go, then, on impulse, turned back and put her arms around her new friend. 'Merci, madam, merci, merci.'

As she walked swiftly back to her chalet avoiding the more popular paths, Shakila repeated the name of the boat. The Blooming Rose sounded quite romantic, she thought. She wasn't to know that the owner had named the vessel after his mother-in-law, and that blooming, in that sense, was a mild expletive.

Shakila's elation was tempered by caution. Could she trust her new friend? Dare she place her future in the hands of a stranger, a foreigner at that? And what would the reaction of her husband be to the news that they were carrying an illegal migrant?

In reality, Shakila knew she had no choice. She must risk the voyage, must risk the kindness of strangers. Her decision was made, but had it been made out of wisdom or naiveté? In the long run, she could hardly be worse off than she already was.

Wearing jeans and a T-shirt over her swimsuit she left her key in the chalet door rather than risk returning to the campsite reception and headed back to the headland. Sure enough, the Englishwoman was waiting, sitting on a rock staring out to sea. A lazy plume of smoke drifted into the night air from the cigarette in her left hand. Curiously, the sight of the woman smoking comforted Shakila slightly. Perhaps it was the air of normality that eased her mind.

It was now almost dark, the lights from the town and the marina glowing brighter by the minute. The older woman watched in silence as Shakila took off her shoes, and then helped pack the discarded clothing before gesturing towards the sea. 'Luckily, it's quite calm tonight, but be careful, the water will be cold. Cramp is always a danger. As I remember, there isn't much of a current and, if you're as good a swimmer as you say, you should be OK. One more thing, swimming in the sea is a lot different from a heated indoor pool. Apart from the cold, there's the salt content of the water. Try and avoid swallowing any. Apart from it tasting unpleasant, with what gets dumped in the ocean, you could get sickness, or the trots.'

'The trots?'

'Dysentery.' The word was accompanied by a graphic gesture. 'Go on. Get off with you while there's no one around. Just remember, keep going at a steady pace, don't try to rush, and don't thrash around in the water too much, nothing that might draw attention to you. I'll be waiting on the boat.'

On impulse, Shakila hugged her, then turned and walked into the water, giving an involuntary gasp at the cold. She plunged into the sea, striking out with bold, confident strokes. The Englishwoman watched her for several minutes, until the girl was all but lost to sight. 'Aye,' she murmured, 'you can swim, right enough.'

She picked up Shakila's bag and slipped one of the straps over her shoulder. As she made her way towards the marina, she mused on what Shakila had told her. She and her husband hadn't been blessed with children. If blessed was the right word. From what she'd heard that evening, she wasn't too sure she regretted the lack of family. If Shakila's story was anything to go by, family wasn't all it was cracked up to be. She would have liked a daughter, but although she had no regrets when that hadn't happened, the thought of what Shakila's parents had been prepared to do made her blood boil. She increased her pace, partly through anger, partly in order to be back at the boat before either her husband or the girl got there. She wondered what the business he had gone to Brest for was about. He was being very secretive but she'd learned to put up with that sort of behaviour from him over the years. Was it anything to do with money? They'd suffered a lot because of the recession. Just how much, she wasn't sure, but from his attitude she knew things were far from rosy on the financial front. Their savings wouldn't be giving them much of a return; that much she did know. The boat had been a luxury they could afford, but buying it just before the banking crisis hit hadn't turned out to be the wisest investment of all time. With their income stream reduced to a trickle, the upkeep of the boat was rapidly becoming a millstone. If times were better, they would have sold it, but then, if times had been better, they wouldn't need to. Even if they could find a buyer, the price offered would be a fraction of its worth. So they were stuck, unable to afford to keep it, unable to afford to sell it. Catch 22.

She had only been back on board the Blooming Rose a few minutes when her husband arrived. She saw the taxi draw up outside the marina gates, knew it was him by the stride as he hurried along the quay towards the pontoon where the boat was moored. She wondered how near the girl was. He climbed aboard and greeted her with a kiss on the cheek.

His first words came as a surprise. 'We're not leaving tonight, love. There's been a delay. We'll go in the morning.'

She eyed him suspiciously. 'Why's that? I thought you were dead keen to be off. At least that's what you said before you vanished on your mysterious mission this morning.'

'Ah, well, there's a little job I arranged for us. Nothing too arduous, we just have to collect something and deliver it on the way. And we get a nice little fee for doing it. The problem is the stuff we're going to be carrying won't be ready until tomorrow.'

'Stuff? What sort of stuff? What's this about? Nothing illegal, I hope?'

He tapped the side of his nose. 'Nothing for you to worry about.'

'I don't like the sound of it.' She would have said more, pressed him harder, but she had her own secret and realized this was the ideal time to tell him. He could hardly object, not in the circumstances. She explained about Shakila and the trouble the girl was in. When she finished telling her story, she waited for his reaction. She didn't have to wait long.

'You've done what? You stupid cow. Do you realize what will happen if we're caught trying to smuggle an illegal immigrant into the UK? The fine alone would bankrupt us and there'd be the prison sentence to go along with it.'

'And that "little job" you've arranged for us to do? I'm no legal expert, but I'm damned sure the penalty for smuggling one terrified girl whose life is being threatened would be a hell of a sight lighter than that for running parcels of cocaine or heroin or whatever it is you've organized.'

The argument continued for several minutes and was only curtailed when a splashing sound from the starboard side of the boat announced Shakila's safe arrival. As she climbed the ladder onto the half-deck, he took in the girl's olive-skinned good looks, her attractive figure, and her long, shapely legs. 'Oh, all right then, in the circumstances I suppose we have no choice,' he muttered. Exactly as his wife had known he would.

Once Shakila was safely inside the forward cabin away from any prying eyes, his wife ordered him to make hot drinks for them. That would allow Shakila a chance to dry off and change without him drooling over the girl, and also give her chance to explain the slight change of plan.

Once she'd told her, she saw the dawning apprehension on Shakila's face and hastened to reassure her. 'I know you'd have preferred to leave under cover of darkness, but when we're ready to go you can stay in here. All we have to do is draw the curtains over the portholes and nobody will see you. Nobody will think it strange if they haven't been pulled back.'

The knowledge of what was before her, the ever-present fear of discovery and uncertainty about whether to trust her new friends led to Shakila passing a sleepless night.

When she'd reached the boat, she'd paused to recover her breath before climbing the ladder, had heard them arguing and knew that the man did not want her on board. Besides which, it sounded as if they were about to do something illegal; something to do with drugs. Had she gone from danger into worse peril? By committing her future to this couple, had she placed herself at far greater risk than if she had stayed hidden in France?

CHAPTER FOURTEEN

Tormented by doubts, Shakila was wide-awake when she heard the faint sound of a mobile phone, alerting the owner to an incoming message. This was followed by a mutter of conversation from the wheelhouse where the boat's owners were sleeping, then, the soft padding of footsteps across the deck. Shakila cautiously lifted the curtain away from one of the portholes and peered out. She was in time to see the figure of a man hurrying along the quay leading from the pontoons towards the security gate. Was he going to inform someone about her? Or was it something to do with their other mission? She waited, half hoping, half fearful. It seemed an age, but eventually she saw him return, carrying a cardboard box. That had nothing to do with her. Shakila began to relax. She waited until he had climbed aboard and then looked out again. The quay was deserted. No security men, no port officials, no gendarmes. He hadn't given her away; her fears had been groundless. But, there was still the voyage, and what would follow it.

Shortly after first light, Shakila, now alone in the cabin, heard the engines fire up. She felt the gradual motion as the boat slipped its mooring and edged out of the marina before heading for the open sea. The engines' roar deepened to a growl as the speed increased. Shakila lifted the curtain over one of the ports and saw they were already well clear of the coast, the town and the shoreline receding into the distance.

Quite unexpectedly, she realized the enormity of what she'd done, recognized how completely alone she was. She faced the daunting prospect of Britain, a country she did not know and where she knew only two people out of the scores of millions of inhabitants. These two, her companions on the voyage, had only promised to take her to Britain. Beyond that, she was on her own; alone in an alien country with no papers, no form of identification. What hope did she have of surviving undetected? And if, as she now believed would happen, she fell into the clutches of the authorities, would they listen to her plea to remain? Or would they simply turn her round and send her back to France to face the wrath of her family?

'Do you fancy coming up into the wheelhouse?'

Shakila looked up; she hadn't heard anyone enter the cabin.

The woman could see the girl was upset and could guess the reason. Fear of the future, uncertainly as to what Britain would hold for her would be enough to daunt anyone. 'It's a grand morning, and things will seem much brighter out in the fresh air. I'm going to make breakfast and then I'll take the wheel.'

She saw the girl's look of surprise. 'It's going to take us a couple of days or thereabouts to get where we're going. So we take it in turns to avoid one of us getting over-tired. Later, I'll show you on the map where we're heading. Come on, love. You can't stay moping in here all the time.' She lowered her voice, 'Later, when his lordship's having a kip, I'll let you have a turn at the wheel. You'll enjoy that, I bet.'

The first part of the journey passed without incident. The man had the helm, on the port side, with his wife alongside him in the navigator's seat. Shakila perched on one of the bench seats behind watching them steer the boat.

As they travelled, the Englishwoman explained the voyage. 'We have about five hundred nautical miles to go before we reach Whitby, which is our home port.' She pointed to the chart, tracing the route for Shakila. 'As we pass Guernsey you'll be able to see the island off to starboard, then we steer north-easterly until we're off Dover. The white cliffs.'

'Please, what is starboard?'

She listened carefully as the older woman explained the nautical equivalents of right and left. 'After that we run north-by-east up the east coast of England. Normally we would complete the trip in a day and a half, but we're taking it easy this time. We can't sail into Whitby with you onboard. If you disembark there you'd be arrested immediately and sent back to France. All vessels, big or small are watched by the coastguard, the UK Border Agency, or the police. They are always on the lookout for illegal immigrants.'

'How will I avoid them?'

'I think you were lucky to come with us. Before we reach Whitby we'll be going inshore at a remote bay, where you can easily swim ashore. The distance will be no more than a few hundred yards . . . er . . . metres. Then, after we've reached Whitby we'll drive back down the coast for you. We'll bring your rucksack with your clothes and things. You can stay at our house for a few days until you decide what you want to do. How does that sound?'

'Merci. Thank you both. You are so kind.' Shakila was again close to tears.

When her companion announced she was going to make lunch, Shakila remained, watching the husband steer the Blooming Rose. After a few minutes he glanced across at her. 'Is it true, what my missus told me, that your family was going to have you killed?'

'Yes, I heard my parents talk of it. They did not know I was listening.'

'And you're sure they meant what they said?' He shook his head in disbelief. 'Simply because you refused to marry some bloke they'd chosen for you? Is that right?'

‘There is more, much more. I am afraid in their eyes I was a very bad daughter. I did not conform in dress, or behaviour, or in worship. They said they believed I was possessed by devils. That may sound odd to you, but this is a very powerful belief where my family come from.’

‘I have heard of things like that, but to have you done in because you wear jeans and don’t do as they command . . . I didn’t think people still behaved that way, I thought all that was in the past.’

* * *

During the afternoon, the husband went into the cabin to sleep. ‘He’ll take over from me tonight,’ his wife explained. ‘I’ll make our dinner then have a few hours’ kip up here. Before that, how do you fancy taking the wheel?’

As she slid into the helmsman’s seat, Shakila asked, ‘Kip, is that another word for sleep?’

Her mentor laughed. ‘Yes it is. It means a short rest, like taking a nap.’

‘I think English is going to be more of a challenge than I knew. How do I drive the boat?’

‘Steer, not drive,’ she was corrected.

Shakila spent the next hour learning how to control the Blooming Rose. When it was over, she relinquished the wheel with real regret.

Despite her unfamiliar surroundings and the motion of the boat, Shakila slept long and well that night. She had been living on adrenalin for so long, that exhaustion had at last caught up with her. She awoke only once, when the boat slowed then ceased moving; she dozed back off. It was daylight by the time she was fully awake, the Blooming Rose had picked up speed again. She realized this would be her last day on the boat. She had come to regard the Blooming Rose as a haven, her sanctuary. Now she knew how fleeting that sanctuary was.

As the day wore on, Shakila’s nervousness increased. Eventually, soon after dusk, she heard her saviour give her husband the instruction to set a new course, one she told Shakila that would bring them close inshore. 'We're getting near to the point where we drop you off. The sea might look a bit choppy, but once we get beyond the headland into the bay where it's more sheltered, it'll be much calmer. The swim shouldn't be a problem; the only thing you've to be wary of is, again, the cold. This is the North Sea and the water temperature is very cold, even at this time of the year. When you get to shore you'll be OK, as long as you keep moving. Do you like running?'

The question was such an odd one, Shakila paused before replying. 'Yes, I was good at it in my school.'

'The best way to keep warm will be to run along the beach and back a few times. It will help dry you and the swimsuit off. It will be an hour or so before we get back to you. No point in escaping from being murdered only to catch pneumonia or die of hypothermia.'

Shakila went into the cabin to change into her swimsuit and pack her clothes. She left the door open, and even above the sound of the engines, she heard the couple's conversation.

'How does this drop-off work?' The woman asked. 'How will they know where to look for the packages?'

'They'll have someone watching from the shore,' he explained. I have to tie the packages to the buoy and when we've cleared the bay, I send a text message. I suppose someone comes along to collect — simple as that. When we round the headland after the drop, I'll take us into the next bay and we can get the girl away.'

They had almost reached the cove when they heard the sound. The three looked at each other, all gripped with fear, the same fear, but stemming from different causes. The sound was the unmistakeable roar of diesel engines. Loud, and getting louder by the second. 'Patrol boat!' the husband muttered.

'Stay in the cabin,' the woman shouted to Shakila. 'And for God's sake keep quiet.'

Seconds later, as Shakila crouched, trembling with fear the Blooming Rose was lit up by a powerful searchlight. At the same time she heard a voice, amplified and echoing from a loud hailer. 'Motor vessel Blooming Rose, heave-to! UK Border Agency. We are about to board you.'

In the wheelhouse, there was a moment's pause, as if the couple were weighing their chances of making a run for it before the boat began to slow down. The Blooming Rose lost way and wallowed to a standstill as the dark shape of the other vessel came alongside. Such was the skill of the other helmsman that there was only a slight bump as the two boats touched. Seconds later, two men stepped on board.

The boat owner looked at them as they entered the wheelhouse. 'Hey!' he exclaimed. 'Who are you? You're not Border Agency—' His speech was curtailed abruptly.

Shakila jumped at the sound of the shots. The cabin door was slightly ajar. Through the crack she could see into the wheelhouse where the man's body lay. His head was turned towards her, and the glare from the searchlight was strong enough for her to make out the bullet wounds, to see the trickle of blood that ran from the empty, eyeless socket. Shakila bit back a scream, but the Englishwoman more than made up for the girl's silence.

Shakila heard the sound of several sharp slaps. 'Shut the fuck up,' a voice hissed. 'Shut up or you'll get the same as he did. Now, where are they?'

The woman was silent now, staring in horrified disbelief at her husband's body.

'Where are they?' the killer repeated his question. 'Don't make me ask again. Where are the drugs? If you don't tell me, I'll have to let Stanley here persuade you. He'll enjoy that, but I promise you, you won't. Show her how you'll persuade her, Stanley.'

Shakila risked another look and saw the man she had heard called Stanley. She recoiled in horror at what he had in his hand. It was a tool used for DIY; a wickedly sharp knife with a short, retractable blade. He was waving this in front of the woman's eyes. Almost like a caress, he passed the Stanley knife along her forearm, and Shakila saw blood immediately begin to spill from the wound.

His victim pointed towards the storage space below the bench seats in the wheelhouse.

The gunman nodded to Stanley, who walked over and lifted the lid. 'There's only three parcels,' he reported. 'Is that right?'

'I expected six.' The gunman turned towards the woman. 'Where's the rest?'

'There isn't any more,' she stammered. 'I swear that's all he got.' She was shaking violently, staring at the gun, the knife, and her husband in turn.

'That has saved me some time and you a lot of pain. Now, I feel sure you're anxious to join your husband.'

He might have been inviting her to a cocktail party for all the expression in his voice, but as he finished speaking, Shakila heard two more shots and then saw the woman fall to the deck alongside her husband. At the same time, a wave caught both vessels and swung them round. Shakila saw the gunman's face clearly for the first time, illuminated by the stark beam of the searchlight.

The man with the knife climbed back on the second boat. 'What are you going to do about the boat — and them?'

'We can't leave it here, the water's too shallow. We'll have to take her out to sea and scuttle her. With luck they'll have been eaten away beyond recognition by the time they're found. If they're found,' he added. 'Help me stow the packages onboard and then you'd better check out the cabin, just to be on the safe side, make sure she was telling the truth.'

Shakila saw they had their backs to her as they loaded the cargo. Before Stanley climbed back onboard and headed for the cabin, his progress impeded by the bodies, Shakila had already slipped from the cabin and climbed into the empty storage locker where the drugs had been hidden. She lay trembling, her eyes screwed tight shut, her fists clenched, holding her breath. After what seemed an age, she heard him shout. 'It's all clear, I can't find anymore and there's no one else on board.'

He returned to the wheelhouse and attempted to start the motor. 'You'd better come here. We've got a problem. One or more of the bullets has smashed the console. I can't get the engines to fire. We'll have to tow her out to sea before we scuttle her. I'll have to stay on board and steer her.'

Shakila listened keenly. She had to get away, get off the boat before they towed the Blooming Rose out of range of land. But she knew there was no chance of her escaping detection with one of the killers at the wheel. She had to move now while they were in the bows securing the rope.

She crept across the wheelhouse, trying to keep low enough to avoid the glare of exposure from the searchlight. As she moved, the beam was swung towards the bow where the killers were still attempting to secure the line. This was her chance. She stepped over the bodies and reached the afterdeck. Without pausing to think, she slipped over the low stern into the water, gasping as the cold hit her, unawares. She was only just in time, for as she trod water, acclimatizing herself and getting her bearings, she heard the engine sound of the killers' boat change, and seconds later, the Blooming Rose, like some seaborne hearse, began to move slowly out towards deeper water.

She began to swim, slowly at first, then more powerfully as the urge to survive pumped adrenalin through her system. As she swam, tears coursed down her cheeks to be lost in the saltwater of the ocean. Tears for the couple who had rescued her and tears for herself. Even if she survived and made it to the shore, her future beyond there had suddenly become more desperate than ever. On top of the existing threats, there was now an even more potent one. She was the sole witness to a double murder. If that was discovered, the ruthless men who had killed two people without any more thought than if they were swatting flies, would not hesitate to put an end to her too.

If she managed to make it to the distant beach, Shakila knew there could be danger. She had overheard the couple talking, in the course of which it was said that there would be people there watching for the boat, waiting for the drugs. If they had heard the shots, and seen the searchlight, which she knew they must have done, what would they do to her if they found her?

In spite of her despair, she continued to swim. Better to survive. Survive as long as she could. Even if it was survival without hope.

CHAPTER FIFTEEN

The watchers on the cliff top were beginning to feel the cold. They had been waiting for what seemed an eternity, obscured from view by a bank of bushes. Their eyes and ears strained for what was happening out to sea. The first sound they heard was that of diesel engines. 'This sounds like the boat,' one of them said. Even as he was speaking, the sound was augmented by more engine noise. They looked at one another, aware that this wasn't what they expected. They saw the powerful beam of the searchlight capture the cabin cruiser. 'A patrol boat? That could ruin our plans.'

He had his night vision binoculars trained on the scene out to sea. 'Check this out.' He passed the glasses to his companion. 'I'm not sure that is a patrol boat. See what you think.' In the distance they heard the echo of distant shots. 'That sounds bad. What's going on out there?'

They waited. Moments later they heard more shots, the sound carrying clearly over the water. 'This is very bad. I think they're taking our boat in tow. Yes, they're moving, going out to sea. Hang on, I thought I saw something. It might have been someone going off the stern of the cruiser. I can't be sure, and don't know if they went overboard or were tipped over.'

'Might it be the packages? Can you still see the boats?'

'No, they're too far out now. Moonlight would have helped. Listen!' Much fainter, but still distinguishable, they heard the distant rattle of more gunfire. It continued for some time. 'Now what's going on?'

'Scuttling the boat, I guess. Those cabin cruisers are pretty sturdy. Puncturing the hull with a load of bullet holes is the quickest way to sink them. That's what I'd do to hide the boat and what happened on board.'

'So what do we do now?'

'Your guess is as good as mine. We don't know what's going on and we don't even know for sure if they've put the drugs over the side, or if that was a dead body. I'd guess whoever was in the second boat has snatched the delivery so I don't see that there's much we can do. We better make ourselves scarce. Someone else might have heard those shots.'

'What if the other boat comes back and they decide to land the drugs on this beach? Maybe we ought to hang around in case they send an inflatable inshore. See if we recognize anyone.'

'You really fancy meeting up with them, after what we've just seen and heard?'

'Not really, but let's wait quarter of an hour. If nothing happens by then, we scarper.'

'OK, have it your way. I think we should be doubly careful though.'

'I wasn't thinking of walking up to them and confronting them, demanding the drugs, or else. I just thought it would be useful to find out who they are before we report back.'

'I doubt they'll come ashore here.'

'You mean you hope they don't.'

'That as well.' He pointed to the binoculars. 'As you're so keen to identify them, those might help — if they do come within range.'

Scanning the ocean, sweeping the bay with slow, rhythmical searching movements yielded nothing. They were on the point of conceding the futility of their wait, when he was nudged in the ribs and the binoculars thrust at him.

'Have a look over there, towards the headland. Concentrate on the water, close to the tideline near those jagged rocks. I thought I saw something moving, but I couldn't be certain, not with the shadow of the headland behind it.'

He searched the area indicated. As minute followed minute, he expected to dismiss what could have been a trick of the light — or the dark. A moment later he said, 'You could be right, there might be something there. It could be driftwood, or wreckage from the boat. I'll try the zoom and see if I can make out what it is.'

'Wreckage from the boat would hardly have drifted this close to land yet, would it?'

'True.' He was still scanning the shallows close to the rocks. 'I think it could be a body.

'A body?'

He lowered the binoculars. 'Whatever it is, I think we should take a dekko. Come on. There's nobody else around. They would have been here by now if they'd heard the shots.'

There was only one path down the cliff, little more than a series of shallow steps cut out of the clay, with loose chippings, which skittered down the slope as they scrambled down. They reached the bottom and began to cross the beach, casting furtive looks round as they ran. Once they were on the level, they found the going much easier, despite the dry sand that slowed their progress. The ebbing tide had left the sand close to the waterline firmer underfoot and once they reached this their progress was swifter. After several minutes they reached the point closest to where they had seen the object and as they paused for breath.

'Look there!'

The shapeless bundle they'd seen from the cliff top was indeed a body. Together, they waded into the sea, gasping slightly with the cold and soon reached their objective. They lifted the inanimate form between them and, stumbling every now and then on several small rocks hidden under the water, dragged it back to the beach and laid it on the sand.

The leader took a torch from his pocket and shone it on the face. 'It's a young woman,' he exclaimed as he began feeling for a pulse. After a few moments he looked up. 'She's alive! Let's get her onto her side; she could have swallowed half the ocean.'

It seemed as if an age passed before the girl finally stirred in response to their ministrations. She gave a choking, coughing sound, and next moment retched violently, spewing a large quantity of sea water onto the sand. They hauled her into a sitting position. This prompted a further vomiting session, which returned another sizeable quantity of the North Sea to its rightful place.

'What shall we do with her?'

'We'll have to take her with us. We don't know who she is or what she was doing out there. She's going to be the only one who can tell us what went on. And we don't want her falling into the wrong hands.'

'What do you mean by "wrong hands"? You mean if the people from the other boat come back?'

'It isn't only them I'm worried about. Any of the locals round here could be involved.' He gestured in the vague direction of Norway, but his companion got the point.

'You mean even the police, or the coastguard?'

'Yes, even them. Remember what we were told; trust nobody.'

'OK, we take her with us, but if we do that it could make things very awkward in more ways than one.'

'We'll have to deal with that when it happens, but we ought to get moving. Apart from anything else if she starts blabbing, better for her to blab to us than anyone else.'

'It's to be hoped she's recovered enough to walk. I don't fancy having to haul her up that cliff.'

Shakila had regained consciousness but was afraid to show it. As she listened to their conversation, she knew her worst fears had been realized. These people had been watching and waiting for the Blooming Rose, expecting the delivery. That meant they had to be involved in the drugs trade; had to be part of the trafficking gang. They might even be linked to the men who had murdered the couple on the boat. Shakila had read horrific stories about these gangs, how they were constantly feuding, with different factions struggling for control.

Even if the two who had found her had not taken part in the murders, or were even involved with the killers, their response to someone who had discovered what they were doing was likely to provoke as violent a reaction. In terrible fear for her life, Shakila decided her only option was absolute silence and a pretence to ignorance of the English language. Her teacher had taught her many idioms when she learned English. One of these was the phrase 'from the frying pan into the fire'. Suddenly, Shakila was painfully aware of the aptness of this saying.

'Who do you think she is?'

'No idea, and there's no way of telling. She's hardly recovered enough to talk yet. She must have come off the boat, but she seems a bit young for a boat owner.'

'She could be the owner's daughter or something.'

'Until we get her talking we won't know. I can't see where else she could have come from. This is hardly the place for a midnight swim.'

'Get her onto her feet and see if she can stand up, or better still, walk.'

They lifted Shakila and held her, supporting her between them. She opened her eyes, reluctantly. Not that she could make out much more than the outline of her rescuers in the dark. Then a torch beam shone in her face, blinding her completely.

'Ah, you're conscious. Good. Can you stand up on your own?'

Shakila stared back into the torch light, willing her expression to register neither emotion nor comprehension.

'Do you understand what I'm saying? Do you speak English?'

'I don't think she does. If she was on the boat, she could come from France or Spain.'

'Damn, I hadn't thought of that. Then how do we find out what language she does speak? We need to find out what went on.'

'I think we should just get her out of here and into somewhere warm, otherwise she'll die of cold and won't be able to tell us anything in any language.'

* * *

Kovac steered the fishing boat into Whitby harbour and moored at the dock. Both he and Stanley picked up their deep-sea fishing gear and made a show of stowing the equipment for anyone who may have been watching. They grabbed their holdalls containing the packages, a bucket of fish, and headed along the quay.

'I'm going straight back to the Park with this gear,' Kovac told Stanley. 'With this bonus cargo, we can hold our regular supply in reserve when it arrives. Remember what happened earlier this spring, when the sea was too rough to bring anything in? I don't want that to happen again. After I've seen to the distribution, I'm going across to Leeds to the meat factory and check on things there. Here's the key to the cottage, you can stay on for the next couple of days and wait for our delivery. Once you've got it let me know, and I'll see you at the Park when I get back from Leeds.'

Kovac paused for a moment. 'I think I'll tell the dealers to give our best customers a small discount on this shipment. Seeing we got it for nothing, I think we should share the benefit. A goodwill gesture is always appreciated, and much easier to give when I'm not paying for it. Besides, it will ensure their loyalty to us.'

* * *

The night following the sinking of the Blooming Rose, the fishing boat again left Whitby. Its sole occupant, the owner, was cheerful, looking forward to the night's catch — and the profit he knew would result from it. Fishing from the ports along the east coast of England had been in decline for many years. Dwindling fish stocks in the North Sea, over-fishing and the resultant imposition of increasingly stringent quotas limiting the amount of fish that could be caught had caused many trawler owners and inshore fisherman to sell up. They had forsaken the sea and sought a more lucrative way to earn a living. It was a source of great stress, for in doing so they had to forego the life they enjoyed, one that had in many cases been bred into them for several generations.

The fisherman hired out his boat for visitors to take angling trips and gained only a small seasonal income but for some, like him, there were other ways to keep the wolf from the door. Ways that involved a product that was always in demand and on which there were no quotas, no catch limitations, bar the law of supply and demand. Ways that involved working for a bloke called Stanley.

Given the parlous state of his finances it was easy, when offered the opportunity, to close his eyes to what the product was and what damage it could cause; the wrecked lives, the dependency, the means people had to resort to in order to find the money to feed their habit.

The fisherman knew all this; knew it and ignored it. Taking drugs, as he saw it, was a matter of choice. Their choice, not one that was imposed on them as catch limits had been imposed on him and others like him. Fishermen's lives — and the lives of their families — had been wrecked by the actions of others, not by their own frailties.

The money was good and easily earned. All he had to do was choose a time when the tide was right and when he knew the coastguard wasn't going to be around, then take his boat out and empty his crab and lobsterpots. Sometimes they would contain crabs, occasionally lobsters too. But often there would be parcels, each parcel worth over a year's supply of lobsters, even at today's prices.

Tonight was no exception, or so he had been informed. It helped that his wife and the coastguard's girlfriend were pals. Through their friendship he knew that the coastguard would be miles away that evening, helping to intercept a suspect vessel that might be carrying illegal immigrants. The tip-off about the vessel had come via an anonymous phone call. The fisherman knew this because he had placed the call. He didn't know whether the container ship had illegal immigrants on board or not, but he needed the coastguard out of the way and this was the best way to achieve it.

It was half an hour after leaving the harbour that he neared the area where he had placed his pots. As he closed in on the first of his marker buoys, he became aware that something was wrong. His night vision was good, even though the night was dark, moonless. He could just about discern the silhouette of a boat alongside the buoy. For a heart-stopping second he thought his trick hadn't worked and that the coastguard was lying in wait to trap him. But the boat was too small and the wrong shape. Someone was stealing his catch. Not only his catch, but the far more valuable packages the pots contained.

He cut the motor and, bereft of power, the boat slipped silently through the water. He was within yards of the other boat when a freak wave hit the bow. The sharp slapping sound of the wave against the side, made the trio of men in the other boat look round. As they did, the fisherman caught sight of one of them, a man he knew well. 'Hey!' he shouted angrily. 'What do you think you're doing?'

The question was rhetorical, for he knew perfectly well. He was about to protest further, but one of the men picked up a boat hook and hit him. The ferocious blow struck the side of his head, knocking him senseless. He fell forward, to land headfirst in the bottom of the boat.

'He recognized me!'

The man who had delivered the blow answered. 'That's extremely unlucky. Unlucky for him, I mean.' The speaker's voice was calm, without the slightest trace of panic. 'Wrap the rope from one of the lobsterpots around his ankles and tip him over the side. When they find him, they'll think he tripped, hit his head, and drowned.'

Half an hour later, with the drugs and several lobsters retrieved, they set off towards Whitby. Two of them were silent, dismayed by the enormity of what they had done to the fisherman. The third was unconcerned, whistling cheerfully as he examined their haul. But then, Ron Mason was no stranger to violent deaths, many of which he had been responsible for.

By the time they had offloaded the drugs and lobsters into the waiting fish vans and the drivers had set off inland, out at sea the fisherman's cooling corpse was already attracting attention from a minor local celebrity. The huge lobster had evaded capture for many years, becoming so well known he was talked about in the pubs where fishermen foregather. He was even given a nickname, one hardly in keeping with his reputation as a voracious predator. 'Lobby' the lobster would dine well that night. A fisherman would often eat lobster. It is far rarer for a lobster to dine on a fresh fisherman.

* * *

Stanley slept late the second morning. The sun was streaming in through the bedroom window of the holiday cottage when he woke up. It was one of a row of properties owned by Kovac. The first intimation of trouble came from the sound. As Stanley got up and blinked, bleary-eyed, he saw the bright yellow flash of something big pass the window. He peered out, the heavy throbbing sound of the Sea King's engine and the accompanying whirr of the rotor blades reverberating in his ears as the air-sea rescue helicopter passed close by. He watched it head out towards the open sea, wondering what their mission was. Did it concern the boat he and Kovac had sunk two nights ago?

'You're wasting your time,' he called cheerfully to the departing Sea King. 'They're already dead.'

It was only later, as he was shaving, that Stanley thought that the Sea King might have been summoned to search for someone else. Even then, he didn't think to associate it with their courier. That came much later.

During the afternoon, he took a walk down to the harbour. He looked at the line of boats moored alongside the quay. These ranged from privately owned vessels to inshore fishing boats and tiny dinghies. His search was in vain, for there was no sign of the boat he and Kovac had used. Even that failed to ring any alarm bells. The fisherman was often absent for twenty-four hours or more at a time and, given the nature of the catch, was far more likely to return during darkness than in daytime.

It wasn't until he went into the pub that evening that Stanley heard the news. He listened to the locals talking about the fisherman's death, and their speculation as to how such an accident could have happened to such an experienced sailor. None of them was able to offer a reasonable explanation, other than carelessness, which they all agreed was totally out of character.

Stanley could have enlightened them, even though he had been nowhere near the man when he drowned. As he listened to the discussion, which had taken on a macabre twist with the recounting of the giant lobster which had been seen feeding off the corpse, Stanley knew the death was no accident, no moment of carelessness.

He finished his drink and strolled out of the pub. Once outside, he hurried back to the cottage. As soon as he was inside, safe from the chance of being overheard, Stanley phoned his boss. As he reported the event, he wondered what Kovac's reaction would be; although he had a shrewd idea he would be less than happy.

The response was as angry as he'd expected and even Stanley's comment that at least they had the shipment from the Blooming Rose as compensation failed to placate Kovac. 'It had to be the Soldiers. How did they know? How did they find out where we were bringing the stuff in? Some bastard has grassed to the opposition. When I find out who they are, I'll turn them over to you. And you can make them suffer as you've never made anyone scream before.'

Stanley waited until Kovac's stream of invective died away and ended the call. Unlike Kovac, he felt really cheerful as he prepared to drive back to the Park. But then Kovac had promised him a treat. He fingered the tool he carried in a small leather wallet on his belt, the tool that had given him his nickname. Soon, he felt sure it would be time for the Stanley knife to get another outing.

CHAPTER SIXTEEN

The house on the outskirts of Helmsdale stood some distance from neighbouring properties. It had been derelict for many years. Most of the windows were empty, mere gaping shells. Those panes that hadn't been totally wrecked were more hole than glass. It had been the target for vandals from time to time, but even they had given up on the place in the end, probably because they thought there was little more they could do to it, other than razing it to the ground. Scorch marks on the exterior brickwork and what remained of the plasterwork in two of the downstairs rooms showed that even that had been attempted. The failure was probably due to damp. Mould and fungus flourished, giving some rooms the impression they had been decorated by some mad surrealist painter.

Despite its unwholesome appearance and unhealthy atmosphere, the house was the nearest thing to a permanent home for a small group of people who lived there peripatetically.

Mains services had long been disconnected. Lack of a gas supply was almost certainly the principal reason the house hadn't burned down. Disconnection from the water main, while it created severe sanitary problems, had prevented them from being flooded out.

Electricity was another luxury the house didn't boast. For the residents, this wasn't deemed a great disadvantage, as much of what went on inside the property was far better conducted under cover of darkness. All four of them were addicts, which was what had drawn them together and drawn them to this place as well. To pay for their addiction they used the only asset they had, which was why one of the bedrooms in the house contained the nearest thing to an item of furniture in the whole building: a mattress.

With only their bodies as a means of earning money, they traded sexual favours for cash in that room. The disgust and self-loathing others might feel at being involved in this trade passed them by. The substances they ingested had long shattered any remaining respect they had for their bodies and if someone was prepared to rent them by the hour, what did it matter, so long as their money was good?

'I got extra gear.'

'Extra? How come? You win the lottery then?'

'Course I have. How else do you reckon I could afford a mansion like this?' He gestured at their surroundings.

She laughed. 'So tell me, if you haven't won the lottery, how come you can afford the extra? One of your regulars? Mr "I own a car showroom and I've got money"?'

'Nah! He came round pleading the poor tale, so would I let him have a freebie. I told him unless he paid up, no cash, no bash.'

'So come on, tell me, where did you get the loot?'

'Your friend "Mr Little Dick" gave me it. You remember, last week, the one who kept complaining how cold it was?'

'Oh, "you're tiny and it's frozen", that one?'

'Yeah, well, remember those photos and the video I took with my phone? Those of the pair of you hard at it? The thing is, I saw him yesterday when I was visiting my mam. He was going into the bank. Turns out "Mr Little Dick" is only manager of the Helmsdale branch of Dales Bank. He went quite faint when I mentioned your name, fainter still when I showed him the photos. Then he took a kind of fit and started throwing money at me. Lots of money. The more photos I deleted, the more he chucked twenties in my direction.'

'What about the video? That would be worth all the photos put together, and more.'

He grinned. 'Thing is, with all that money around I clean forgot about the video. I thought it might come in handy another time.'

'No wonder you bought extra gear. How much did you get?'

'Wait, it gets better. When I went to buy it, Greasy Palms gave me a whacking great discount.'

She shuddered at the mention of Greasy Palms, their dealer. Part of the bargain when they were really skint, which was often the case, was payment in kind in return for the gear. 'There's never such a thing as a freebie,' the dealer told them. His oily complexion gave rise to the nickname.

'A discount? What's up with him? Been converted to Christianity or something?'

'Hardly. It wasn't his doing. He told me his boss had insisted on it. Some sort of loyalty bonus.'

'What's up with them? They'll be giving Air Miles next.'

'I got you a chicken korma and a six pack of Stella out of the change.'

'Great. Let's dine, and then we can sample the gear.'

'Where are the others?'

'Out and about somewhere. Their loss. Come on, take me to my korma.'

* * *

The first thing he noticed as he approached the squat was there was no light showing. He frowned, that wasn't right. It was early, at least by their standards. And it was Friday night. But from what he'd been told, he expected at least one of them to be in. He'd left the Cock & Bottle earlier than intended, simply because he'd bumped into Greasy Palms and the dealer had told him what was waiting at the house. They had few rules, but one they stuck to was share and share alike. If they'd buggered off out and taken the gear with them he wouldn't be a happy bunny.

He went inside, reaching with practiced ease for the candle and matches he knew would be on the shelf alongside the hole where the front door had once been.

As soon as he had light, he went inside the front room. It was empty. He tried the other rooms on the ground floor. Equally empty. They must be upstairs. He grinned, that probably meant they'd taken some stuff and been celebrating. He tiptoed as quietly as he could, hoping to catch them at it. Always good for a laugh, that was. He found them in the front bedroom, as expected, but realized he was a little too late. They were lying on the sagging double mattress, stark naked.

The mattress had seen a lot of action in its time, and by the look of it, tonight was no exception. His housemates were totally out of it.

His eyes caught the glint of metal, and he saw the cans of Stella. Two of them were unopened. They would make up for his early departure from the pub. Then he saw the makings.

He wandered over and sat down, his back against the wall, opened a can and toasted the post-coital couple. As he reached for a needle, he murmured, 'My turn next. Share and share alike, remember. Just got to stiffen up the sinews first.'

* * *

Three days later, the smell hit the girl as soon as she entered the house. It filled her nostrils as she moved through the rooms on the ground floor. She called out their names, one by one, but got no response. She heard a faint rustling sound she thought came from upstairs. That must be where they were, and probably out of it. She wondered briefly where they'd got the money. If there was gear to be had, she was keen to share in it, but what was that awful smell? It wasn't the drains, this stench was far worse. As she climbed the stairs, the foul odour got worse. She clamped her fingers over her nostrils and pinched them tightly, breathing through her mouth in a vain attempt to keep the stink at bay. She paused at the head of the stairs as nausea threatened to overcome her. Something was definitely wrong. Very wrong.

Resisting the urge to turn and bolt down the stairs, she edged cautiously towards the bedroom. Her conviction growing that something really terrible had happened, she pushed the door back and entered the room, coming to an abrupt halt one pace inside. As her eyes got accustomed to the gloom, she saw movement. Two small, loathsome furry creatures, disturbed by this sudden invasion of their dining room, scurried away, to disappear in a remote corner. The other creatures remained, continued dining, totally oblivious of the room's only other living occupant.

She recoiled in disgust as she realized the three corpses on the floor were the remains of her friends. Their faces unrecognizable, their bodies bloated and distended beyond belief, the colour of their skin a sickly green, turning black. She was only able to identify them by the clothing one of them was wearing, and those that the other two had tossed on to the floor alongside the mattress. Maggots writhed and squirmed in and around every orifice, their number seeming to multiply even as she watched.

Later, she was never sure how long she had stood there, absorbing the horror of the scene. She forced back the vomit that threatened to overwhelm her and turned, walking slowly but unsteadily across the landing, down the stairs, and outside into the clean, fresh air. She took a large, gulping breath. Mistake! All she could smell, all she could taste, was the foul reek of death. She bent over and was violently sick. After several minutes, when she had recovered slightly, she risked a series of smaller inhalations in an attempt to calm herself. It failed.

The operator on duty in the police control room had difficulty in making sense of what the caller was trying to tell him. Apart from the fact that the signal from her mobile phone was poor, the girl was hysterical. After some minutes and several unsuccessful attempts, he managed to calm her down sufficiently for him to grasp the gist of what she was attempting to report. It was only when the full horror of what she said struck home, that he began hitting panic buttons.

It was fifteen minutes later, following the dispatch of a pair of ambulances and two police patrol cars, when one of the uniformed police officers called in his report. 'I think you'd better get CID out here,' he warned the duty officer. 'You'll probably want the pathologist and a CSI team as well.'

'What do I tell them?'

'You could start by telling them we've three dead ones here. All drug addicts. Been dead a few days by the look of them — and by the stink. The paramedics reckon they can't see any signs of violence, so they may have overdosed. Tell them there's all sorts of infestation, and it's getting worse. That should get their arses into gear.'

As the control room officer was relaying the details to DS Mironova, the bitter irony of the address he read out didn't strike him. But then, he didn't know that the derelict property was an abandoned police section house.

Experience had taught Clara to come prepared. Before putting on her paper suit and overshoes, she smeared her nose and mouth with a powerfully scented decongestant gel that she hoped would counteract the smell she knew would otherwise overpower her. No precautions she made however, could prepare her for the horrific appearance of the corpses.

She talked to the pathologist who was supervising the scene as the photographer recorded the sickening images. She kept the conversation as brief as possible, so great was her desire to get out of that room.

'What do you reckon, Professor?'

Ramirez shrugged. 'There are no apparent marks of violence on any of the bodies, if you discount those made by prolonged substance abuse, so take your pick. We'll have to wait until we get them back to the mortuary and conduct the post-mortems before we know more, and even those might not be too informative. To me, it looks like either an overdose, which seems less likely, given that it has happened to three victims at the same time, or some adulteration of what they were using. There again, we'll not know for certain until we get samples tested at the laboratory, however I have bagged several samples of what looks like heroin.'

'Is there anything else I should know?'

Ramirez gave her a thin smile. 'Not keen to hang about in here? No, I don't think there's much more to add. At a guess, I'd say they've been dead around four days or so, judging by the maturity of the maggots. Moving the bodies is going to be a tricky operation, given the gas, the fluids, and the slippage.'

'Slippage?'

'The skin becomes loose from the tissue and is liable to slough off the corpse at this stage. It's very moist and damp in here, which has accelerated the decomposition.'

Clara grimaced. 'Right, if that's everything, I'll leave you to get on with your work.'

'I don't blame you. I don't think even Nash would stay inside this room longer than necessary.'

Once she was outside, she removed her protective clothing and attempted to rid herself of the noxious stench of death that seemed to cling to her hair, even the pores of her skin. She talked to one of the officers who had been the first responders.

'We came here as soon as we got the triple nine. It would have only been a few minutes, because we were fairly close by when the call came through. Once we'd assessed the scene inside,' the officer shuddered, 'my partner and I taped the area off. Another car had also arrived by then, so rather than have them go into the house — for which I reckon they owe us a pint, we asked them to scour the area and try to find the kid who called the emergency operator.'

He gestured to the brightly coloured police vehicle at the roadside. ‘I told them I didn’t think she’d have driven off in an Aston Martin, and sure enough they picked her up only a few streets away. They knew it had to be her because of the state she was in; near to hysterical she was. She’s calmed down a bit now, so I reckon you’ll be able to question her soon.’

CHAPTER SEVENTEEN

Clara took the girl back to the station and placed a cup of tea in front of her, assessing her value as a witness. In other circumstances, Clara thought, she might be really pretty. However, shock, horror, and grief, combined with the effects of her addiction, had robbed her of any pretension to beauty. The girl, who looked to be little older than eighteen, was painfully thin, malnourishment adding a gaunt appearance, her cheeks sunken. She had already given what little details she knew of her friends' identities and Clara was trying to establish the facts.

'I've been away. I didn't go into the house until this morning. And then I wished I hadn't.'

'Away where?

'I went to visit a friend.'

'Where was that?'

'Netherdale, but I never got there.'

'Why not?'

The girl shrugged. 'I got into a fight.'

'A fight, how did that happen?'

'I needed a fix, but I couldn't get one without money. So I thought, if I could get one punter, maybe two, that would pay for the stuff. Anyway, I was on the lookout for one when out of nowhere this old bitch comes at me, shouting and screaming because I'm on her patch. She starts whingeing on about how bad trade is, even without the competition. I told the ugly old cow a paper bag over her head might help. Then she starts pulling my hair, kicking and scratching me.'

'What happened?'

'Well, I stood back and kicked her where it hurts. She went down, but then her pimp rushes at me. Came out of nowhere he did. Starts waving this big knife around saying he's going to carve me up into little pieces if I don't clear off.'

'What did you do?'

'We were outside that new residential development. You know the one, all maisonettes and superior one-bedroom apartment. Boxes, more like. Anyway, I ran off, and this guy chased me — so I hit him with a gnome.'

'You did what?'

'I'd run into the yard of one of the maisonettes. The owner had tarted-up the back yard with all sorts of ornaments, so when this pimp comes at me I crowned him with a garden gnome. If it hadn't smashed I'd have probably got away with it, but the owner rang the police, and I was arrested. I spent all weekend in a cell.'

If her alibi checked out, it was as cast iron as could be.

'So you came back here this morning and went to the house? That was when you found the bodies. Did you touch anything in the room?'

'No way! I took one step inside. That was enough. The sight, the smell and those bloody rats and maggots . . . After I was sick — I ran.'

'I'll want you to sign a statement confirming what you just told me and I'm going to get someone to check your story.'

After a long period of silence, the girl asked, 'What killed them?'

'We don't know for sure yet. They could have just overdosed, but we believe the heroin they took might have been contaminated in some way. We're waiting for forensic reports to be certain. If we're right, our biggest concern now is that there might be a load more from the same batch out on the street. It would help if we were able to trace the bad stuff. The only way to do that and be sure we get the whole batch is if we knew where they got the stuff from, or who their dealer is? I need you to tell me who that is.'

The girl looked horror-struck. 'The people we buy from would kill me if they found out I'd told you who they are.'

'They could only do that if they were able to get to you. And that wouldn't happen if they were in prison. Let's be fair, if we were able to catch them and prove they supplied what killed your friends, they'd be going to prison for a long, long time. Think about it and think about your friends. I saw the bodies too and I can tell you, one look at their faces was enough to tell me they died in extreme agony. Do you want to end up that way? Could you live with yourself if other people take the same stuff and end up like that, without you having done anything to help prevent it? Because the next few grams you buy could have that same lethal cocktail inside it. Right now, even as we're sitting here, someone could be handing over a large amount of cash for something that will kill them as surely as a bullet between the eyes. Don't you want to get your own back on the people who were responsible?'

There was a long silence.

Clara tried again. 'Tell me something. Why did you start taking the stuff in the first place? What was it that got you hooked?'

After a few moments, the girl replied, 'I was at Netherdale College. I'd got a place there on a nursing course. To help pay my rent, I took a job behind a bar. The landlord tried to . . . well, you know. Then, because I wouldn't let him touch me, he sacked me. My boyfriend found out, and thought I'd been shagging the landlord. That was what he was told. So he walked out on me. The worst of it was, he was living with me and contributing half the rent. I got depressed; then one night someone offered me a joint. I felt better after it, much better, so I went on a binge: a drink and drugs bender. The result was I got kicked out of college, kicked out of my flat, and finished up at the squat. The thing is, I only take the stuff now and again. I'm not a big user like them, but I've nowhere else to live and I can't go back home.'

She began to cry, and, after a few minutes, when she had recovered slightly, between her tears, she began to talk, to tell all she could about the drugs she and her friends had used, and where they got them. Clara made note after note, surprised by the girl's observational skills and her recall of names, places and her ability to describe faces.

When she had told Clara all she could, Mironova summoned Tom Pratt. She handed him the notes. 'I'm afraid there's quite a bit to that statement. Before you get someone typing it up, would you ask Superintendent Fleming to come down? She's up in Mike's office.'

When Jackie Fleming entered the interview room, Clara explained, 'This young lady has very bravely given us some highly-valuable information that I feel sure will help us track down and arrest those responsible for distributing the drugs that killed her friends. She's prepared to give evidence against them, providing we can give her the necessary protection. In view of that, together with the fact that with luck we should be able to wind up a big part of at least one of the gangs bringing drugs into the area, I think we should give her that protection. Added to that, she wants to enter a rehab programme, which I believe is something we should also assist in.'

* * *

Maureen, PC Riley's widow, had decided to return to work. Her relatives had been shocked by her announcement. 'It's too soon. You should take more time to grieve,' several of them told her.

That was the last thing she needed as she explained to her brother. 'After I've done the school run, I'd be sitting around at home on my own, moping. Everything there would be a reminder of Geoff. It'll be bad enough having to go home at night and face all that, without having it twenty-four, seven. Apart from that, it's what Geoff would have wanted me to do and, above all, I need the money.'

'Surely there are funds to cope with times like this? Compensation, insurance and all that.'

'There are, but they won't pay up instantly, and if I'm at work I can access the HR people to get the ball rolling quicker. In the meantime, I need money now.'

'I can help out. How much do you want?'

She put her hand on his arm. 'No, it's kind of you to offer, but I'm not begging. That wasn't why I mentioned it. I know I've only to ask, but I won't. Thanks, anyway.'

'I only wish there was something I could do. I feel so helpless.'

'Just let me go back to work and, if I get down, bear with me when I moan. That's all you can do. Honestly, being at work is the best thing for me right now.'

Although there was no way she could have known it, Maureen's decision to return to work was crucial, both in the timing of it and what followed. Had she not chosen that course, at that time, her husband's killer might well have escaped justice.

Her first morning was a difficult one, made more so by the nature of the clumsy but well-meaning kindness of her colleagues. It was after eleven o'clock before the tide of questions about her health, her plans for her and her son's future died down. The questioners touched on almost anything and everything that avoided mention of Geoff's name.

It was as the last of her inquisitors moved away from her desk that Tom Pratt approached her. Whereas Maureen's work was for the most part confined to reports generated by uniform and traffic division, Tom dealt almost exclusively with those from CID. Their work patterns were flexible though, allowing them to help each other out if one of them had too much to cope with. As she saw him walk towards her, Maureen braced herself for yet another painful quizzing.

'Relax,' Tom told her. 'I'm not going to ask any daft questions.' He gestured in the direction of the departing officer. 'They mean well, that's about the best you can say.'

Maureen smiled faintly. 'Thanks, Tom.'

'What I am going to do is ask if you've time to help me out preparing some reports. I'm a bit snowed under at the minute.'

'I haven't much to do,' Maureen conceded. 'That might be down to the fact that someone seems to have taken care of my work while I've been off. That wouldn't be you by any chance, would it?'

Pratt held his hands up in mock surrender. 'Guilty as charged. It seemed the least I could do. The problem is I've had a sudden avalanche of stuff from CID. I think they must have promised Clara a productivity bonus and as it's all come at once I've too much typing and too few hours. Would you mind typing a couple of reports to CPS for me?'

'Of course I'll help. Pass them over and I'll get started right away.'

He returned a few minutes later with the files and waited until Maureen had skim-read them. 'I don't think there's anything in these to frighten the horses,' she told him. 'Leave them with me; I'll have them ready before the end of today.'

'Thanks, Maureen, you're a star.' Tom patted her shoulder, a gesture of gratitude and affection. Strangely, that, and his comment, affected her more than all the insensitive questions.

After some time, Maureen had all but tied down the first of the files. The second promised to involve far more work, as there were a considerable number of offences and the associated witness statements to report on. She decided to take her lunch break first.

Having brewed a cup of tea, Maureen took it back to her desk where she opened her foil-wrapped sandwiches. She could have used the staff rest room, which was her normal practice, but in there she knew there would be a chance of encountering yet more questions.

As she ate, Maureen read the report she had typed up on her screen, checking it for both factual errors and spelling mistakes. Although she had recorded the details verbatim, she had not absorbed the sense of them. Now, as she went through the text, the meaning became clear. She reached one paragraph and paused, her half-eaten sandwich poised in mid-air, as the significance of the words struck home. Maureen had worked for the force for a number of years and had been married to a police officer for even longer. She knew there was something within this report that should have been followed up, but there was no mention of this having taken place.

She put her sandwich down and wiped her hands on a tissue, before thumbing through the work papers Pratt had given her. She could see no mention of the fact, so it wasn't something she had missed. She pressed the print icon on her computer and collected the sheaf of papers from her printer, before walking over to her colleague's desk.

'Tom,' she began hesitantly. 'I have a question for you. I know that strictly speaking it's none of my business, but I've looked everywhere in the file you gave me and I believe there could be an important item that is either missing, or which has been overlooked.'

She pointed to the relevant section of the report and explained what she had been puzzled by. Pratt read the report a couple of times, checked the paperwork he had given her, and then glanced up. 'I reckon you're dead right. It isn't surprising given the amount of stuff they've had to deal with. I'd better phone Helmsdale and have a word with them. I'll ask Viv Pearce, he'd be the one to handle it, if anybody. Apart from anything else, he's the only one with the technical know-how. I'll be sure to let him know it was your idea, too. Well spotted, Maureen.'

Clara and Viv were crossing the reception area en route to CID when the constable on desk duty stopped them. 'Tom Pratt wants you to phone him, Viv. He told me it was something to do with one of your cases. Said to tell you he's got an idea that might help you.'

As soon as they reached his desk, Pearce rang Netherdale. 'Tom, you wanted a word. What's this idea you've got?'

'It isn't my idea. I passed the papers to Maureen to type up the report for CPS. She came up with it.'

Pearce listened to Pratt's explanation. 'That's brilliant, absolutely brilliant,' he said when Tom finished. 'Say thanks to Maureen for me, will you?'

He rang off and turned to Clara. 'Listen to this,' he said, his voice reflecting his excitement.

CHAPTER EIGHTEEN

The pace of developments left Mironova breathless. Given the constantly stretched manpower, she was used to being busy but, as the week progressed, she had little time to concentrate on anything but work. In particular, the three deaths at the derelict police house plus the consequences.

Following their interview with the girl from the squat, Jackie Fleming had briefed the chief constable immediately. The matter of informing the public of the potential threat of contaminated drugs was left in abeyance until the results of the post-mortems, at O'Donnell's insistence.

'We can't afford to panic the public with a premature announcement,' O'Donnell had said, resisting pressure from her superintendent. 'We have to be sure of the cause of death first; more certain than we are at present. For all we know at this stage, they might have all eaten something containing poison, in which case the presence of the heroin would be a red herring. Added to which, if we let everyone know in advance that we're searching for the source of the drugs, it will mean when you do find out where the suppliers live they'll probably be sitting with their feet up in Mexico or Guadalajara. I appreciate the danger — that we're risking other people being exposed to potentially lethal drugs — but, without evidence, that's a risk we'll have to take. However, it does emphasize the need to resolve the testing quickly, so I'll have a word with the laboratory to add my weight to that of Professor Ramirez.'

With that, Fleming had to be content and phoned Clara to update her.

The only solace Clara could take was the thought of the hapless head of the laboratory who faced the prospect of being harangued by both O'Donnell and Mexican Pete. Clara only hoped the chief's intervention would have the desired effect, in time to prevent further deaths.

Next morning, Clara and Jackie Fleming attended the post-mortems of the drug addicts. The outcome was much as they expected.

Briefing them in his office following the extremely long session, which in itself was an ordeal they would have given a fortune to avoid, Ramirez told them, 'I'll need toxicology results to confirm the cause of death, but the heroin remains the prime suspect. Certainly, there is nothing to indicate otherwise. The two victims who were naked on the mattress died first, at around the same time, which would have been sometime late on Friday or early Saturday. The third one, the male who was fully clothed, died at least eight to twelve hours later. It may have been that he was more resistant to whatever killed them, or perhaps he didn't take as much of it, we won't know for a while.'

He turned the page of his report form. 'The man and woman on the mattress had both had sexual intercourse shortly prior to their death. Presumably that was with each other, judging by the fact that they were both naked, but I'll need DNA results to confirm that as well.'

Ramirez paused and thought for a few moments. 'Actually, now that I come to think of it, the difference in the times of death might have something to do with that.'

'Sorry, Professor, you've lost me.' Clara looked confused.

'If the couple on the mattress took the heroin then had intercourse, the physical activity would raise their metabolic rate, thus speeding their death.' He smiled, a little sadly. 'As the saying goes, at least they died happy.'

'When will you know about the heroin we found at the scene?' Jackie was anxious to know.

'I rushed the samples over to the lab late yesterday and I spoke to the boffins before you arrived. Apparently the chief constable has already had a word with their executive officer. The results should be back with me late today and, given the potential gravity of the situation, they will be with you about five minutes later.'

'The chief constable doesn't want us to go public on this until we're certain, but I think we should warn the hospitals in the area to be on the lookout for anyone exhibiting symptoms that might be down to whatever killed these people.' Fleming waved towards the examination room.

'I think that would be wise,' Ramirez agreed. 'If this is a contaminated batch of heroin we don't know how extensive that contamination might be. It could simply have been this one lot, which would make these people extremely unlucky. On the other hand, there could just as easily be several kilos more of it waiting for distribution. A ticking time bomb,' he added.

He saw Fleming's indecision and threw her a lifeline. 'Look, if the chief constable has banned you from telling the media, that's one thing. But warning Accident and Emergency departments in hospitals throughout this region to be on the lookout for a certain set of symptoms is quite another. Secondly, they're not as likely to panic, or rush to the media. If it simplifies matters, I'll warn them, shall I? In any case, it'll probably carry more weight coming from me.'

They both thanked him, their relief obvious. Before they left, however, the pathologist uttered one final, chilling message. 'Take my advice. I'd concentrate on nailing the source of these drugs. I don't think you can view this case in isolation. If it is contaminated and you don't track down the consignment in full, you could find yourselves dealing with more cases such as this — many more.'

* * *

Now they were in possession of the full facts from the post-mortems a further meeting was held in the early evening. O'Donnell listened as Fleming updated her. 'The heroin was the cause. I won't tell you what the substance used was as, for one thing, I can't pronounce it and I certainly can't spell it, but I've copied you both in on the e-mail. Mexican Pete has warned all local A and E departments of the likelihood of more cases, he's described the symptoms to look out for and told them what antidote to use. Fortunately, it's fairly easy to treat — if it's caught in time. The victims we found were unlucky that they were unable to get treatment. We've already heard of two more cases, but the patients have been detained as a result of the warning and, hopefully, should recover. I've sent Viv Pearce to interview them and try to discover if they use the same dealers. In the meantime, we've set up a raid for tonight on a man known as Greasy Palms who, on information from the girl who found the bodies, we believe supplied the victims at the derelict house.'

'In that case, once you've got him under arrest I'll get straight on to the media. I'll make sure a warning goes out in all the bulletins on TV and radio and appears in tomorrow morning's papers. It's at times like this I wish we had a dedicated press officer to deal with such matters, but not to worry. You'd better get to work and hope you find that dealer and seize the rest of that filthy stuff.'

Clara had been examining the laboratory report. 'By the way I read this,' she told them, 'it seems as if the substance was introduced deliberately. Does that make it murder?'

'It's a tricky point,' O'Donnell responded, 'and I think the problem would be proving intent. Whoever was responsible might claim, via their legal representative, that there was no intent to kill anyone. If they added the foreign substance merely to make extra profit, they could claim that they were unaware of any potentially harmful side effects. I think the very best we could hope for would be a charge of manslaughter, but the other problem we would face is identifying who actually cut the poison with the heroin.'

‘We might get lucky,’ Clara said.

As they were leaving the chief constable’s office, O’Donnell’s secretary stopped them. ‘DC Pearce would like you to ring him at Helmsdale as soon as you have a minute,’ she told Clara.

‘Use the phone in my office. I’ll round up the arrest team while you’re talking to Viv.’ Jackie suggested.

‘Hello, Viv, how did you get on at the hospital?’ Clara asked.

‘Both patients were very weak and had bad vomiting and diarrhoea,’ Pearce reported, ‘but they both confirmed that they bought the gear from the man you’re going to see, the one called Greasy Palms. But that was only part of the reason I wanted to speak to you urgently. ‘I’ve had some success, or rather the IT people have. You know that idea Maureen Riley had?’

‘She raised a query about Patrick Newsome’s phone didn’t she?’

‘That’s right. Well, they’ve been working on it for a couple of days now, but they’ve only just had a positive result. I have the details here. What do you want me to do?’

‘Nothing, for the time being. Head for the address of the drug dealer and meet us there. When we’ve raided that place, we’ll talk about this further. I think you may have to set your alarm for very early tomorrow morning. Alternatively,’ she added, ‘the way things are happening around here, you may not see your bed tonight. Better buy your Lianne a hot water bottle.’

* * *

The team that gathered outside the target premises consisted of Fleming, Mironova and Pearce, plus four armed officers along with a couple of uniformed men and a sniffer dog.

Much to the surprise of the detectives, the front door was unlocked. They rushed into the house, and had some difficulty locating anyone inside, until one of the armed men opened the door of the toilet situated on the half-landing between the ground and first floors. Sitting there, his face a picture of abject misery was the dealer. 'Found him,' the officer shouted. 'He's on the throne. No problem with resisting arrest, not with his trolleys round his ankles.'

Fleming gave the go-ahead for the search once the suspect had been moved to a more comfortable seat in his living room. Clara stared at him, remembering the girl's description. It was certainly accurate, she thought, noting the oily complexion that gave rise to the man's nickname. As Fleming administered the caution, Mironova's phone rang. 'Yes, Professor?' She listened for a few minutes, thanked the pathologist, and ended the call. She looked at Fleming. 'I think I might buy a lottery ticket tonight, because I reckon my luck's in. Which I reckon is more than I can say for this guy.'

She turned her gaze to the suspect. 'That was the pathologist who conducted the post-mortems on three people who we believe you supplied with drugs last weekend. Drugs we now know killed them. Guess what? He's just heard that the forensic team have lifted a partial fingerprint and possible DNA from the drug packets. And that fingerprint could be a match for you. What's more, they believe that when processed, the DNA will be identifiable, if we get a matching subject.'

If finding the dealer had been easy, discovering drugs on the premises was difficult. The team believed their luck had run out. In the bedroom the sniffer dog ran round the room, across the bed tucking its nose under the pillows as it moved. It searched the corners and round all the furniture before stopping, stock still, beside a fitted wardrobe, barked once and sat down. One of the officers opened the door and allowed the dog access. The dog stood, its tail wagging furiously. The officer shone his torch inside and noticed some light-coloured particles reflecting in the beam. He bent closer and was able to make out a join in the base. It looked as if the panel had been sawn in two. There seemed to be no reason for this bit of DIY, so he pressed one side of the panel. It shot up, almost catching him in the face.

He shouted for the detectives to come. They clustered around the wardrobe.

'Bingo!' Fleming said, as she looked at the neat array of three parcels all obviously ready for distribution with only one package open. Alongside them, lay a set of digital weighing scales and small plastic bags. 'If the analysis of this little lot matches the stuff found at the derelict house, I think we might have enough to charge him with manslaughter.'

'Particularly if his DNA eventually proves a match to the heroin wrapper,' Clara suggested. 'In fact, I think we ought to push for a murder charge.'

'A murder charge? I have to say I agree with the chief constable on that. I don't think we could make it stick.'

'No, but he won't know that. And even if his solicitor argues the point, if Greasy Palms thinks there's a chance he'll get life, he might be prepared to do a deal and give us the next link in the supply chain.'

'I like the idea. It's certainly worth trying. Now, let's get him to Netherdale and inside a nice warm cell.'

* * *

It seemed as if Clara's head had barely touched the pillow before her alarm was summoning her from a deep sleep. It was still dark outside. Hardly surprising, she thought, glancing at the clock. Half past four in the morning is not exactly the best time to be up and about. She dragged herself out of bed and sleepwalked into the shower room. Her only hope was that the effort and sleep deprivation would be worthwhile. Yesterday had been highly successful, was it too much to hope that their run of luck would continue today?

The team was in position shortly before dawn. Fleming gave the instructions. Clara stared at her, mildly envious that Jackie never looked tired, never appeared less than immaculately groomed. 'We go in through the front door. Two armed officers first, then the two uniforms, and finally DS Mironova and me. DC Pearce will go round to the back of the house with the other two armed officers.'

'Are we going to knock first?'

'I don't think so. We'll use the big red key.' Fleming gestured to the door enforcer, a mobile battering ram held by one of the uniformed men.

Patrick Newsome was dreaming. He and Sharon had been walking when the thunderstorm struck. Now it was raging all around them. He could hear the thunder. Loud, and getting louder. It must be quite close now, because he could feel the house shake with every reverberation.

He wasn't sure if it was the sound of the thunder that finally woke him, or the noise of Sharon's screams. He sat bolt upright in bed, blinking in the sudden brightness. For a moment, he thought it was due to a flash of lightning, until alongside him, the duvet clutched to her chest, Sharon screamed again. As the sleep cleared his befuddled brain and his eyes became accustomed to the light, Patrick saw the cause of Sharon's terror. He couldn't say he blamed her for being afraid. The sight of a stranger in your bedroom is unnerving: more so, when the stranger is pointing an automatic machine pistol at you. It would be enough to make any woman scream, even though the man's flak jacket was clearly labelled 'Police'.

As he was digesting this unwelcome development and what looked to be the end of his romantic idyll with Sharon, Patrick noticed that the bedroom they shared seemed to be suddenly rather crowded. Another gun-toting police officer plus two further ones in uniform had also arrived. Behind them, two people in plain clothes. Now Patrick was by no means averse to the presence of attractive women in his bedroom, in fact given the opportunity, he positively encouraged it, but he was far less enthusiastic when they were waving warrant cards that identified them as police officers.

'Will you do the honours this time,' Fleming invited Mironova.

Clara smiled. 'Patrick Newsome, you are under arrest . . .' she reeled off the caution. 'Now I'd like you to get dressed so that we can transport you to your new accommodation.' She glanced at Sharon. 'You'll be near your wife, Patrick. I'm sure she misses you — far more than you've been missing her by the look of things.'

Fleming and Mironova supervised the collection of Newsome's belongings, and after they watched Sharon get dressed, removed her from the house and placed her in the back of a police car. Sharon was protesting loudly enough to attract the attention of any of her neighbours who had managed to sleep through the previous disturbance. 'What are you taking me in for?' she complained. 'I haven't done anything wrong.'

'No?' Clara smiled. 'Sharon Meehan, I am arresting you for harbouring a fugitive.' When she had added the caution, Clara continued, 'That will be the first charge, we'll have to see how it develops from there. Playing it by ear, I think they call it.'

If Sharon was aggrieved, Patrick was far more resigned. As Pearce was supervising Patrick's installation in a police van, Newsome was unable to restrain his curiosity any longer. 'How did you find me?' he asked. 'I didn't tell anyone where I was going and nobody knew about Sharon and me.'

Pearce smiled. 'Blame it on technology,' he said. 'You have a GPS tracker installed on your mobile. We knew your number from the text your wife sent you, so once your phone was switched on, all we had to do was locate it from the signal.'

As he watched the uniformed officer secure the van, one of the others approached him. 'What shall I do with the mutt?' the man asked.

'Sorry?' Pearce frowned at the strange question.

'There's a dog in the kitchen. It's a Border Collie and seems quite a friendly animal. I'm not sure if it belongs to him or her, but we can't leave it here alone, obviously. We don't know how long they'll be away.'

'Oh, I see, better put it in your van and take it to the local shelter. There's a PDSA branch in Netherdale. I think that's the closest. Ask them to look after it for the time being. Explain the circumstances and tell them it should only be short-term. I feel sure at least one of these two will be out on bail soon.' Pearce made a mental note to record the dog's presence on his report.

After they reached Helmsdale, Patrick Newsome was made to empty his pockets and the contents, together with his other possessions, were listed by the custody sergeant. Viv, who had a considerable amount of jobs to do, wrote a quick note on a post-it and placed it on Lisa Andrews' desk. He knew she would action it when she arrived for work that morning. Anyway, it wasn't the most urgent thing they had to deal with, by any means.

Clara had been trying to deal with Sharon Meehan, listening to her constant denial of wrongdoing and her insistence therefore that she didn't need a solicitor.

'Sharon, if you calm down a little we can soon get to the bottom of this. So why don't you explain to me exactly why we found Patrick Newsome in your home?' Clara's frustration was beginning to show.

'He's a friend.'

'A friend? I would have thought he's more than that, considering where we found him — wouldn't you say? Or perhaps you've gone back on the game? Short of money are you?'

'I'm not on the game anymore!' Sharon looked shocked at the suggestion. 'He's a friend, I told you. He was just staying a while.'

'I see. And how long have you known him?'

'Years, we go back a long way.'

'Former client?'

'No, nothing like that.' Sharon was becoming annoyed. Her relationship with Patrick was genuine and this police officer was trying to humiliate her. But there was no way she would drop Patrick in it, she knew nothing as far as they were concerned. 'He wanted somewhere to stay away from that wife of his. Visits me sometimes when she gets too much for him to put up with.'

Further questioning didn't reveal anything that Mironova thought would be of use so she decided to release her. There wasn't anything she could prove and the CPS was unlikely to find sufficient to bring to court.

* * *

Viv joined Fleming and Mironova who were discussing Newsome's arrest and how to proceed against him.

'Given where we found him and the company he was in, I think it might be a good idea to interview Eileen Newsome again before we speak to her husband,' Clara suggested.

'What do you have in mind?'

'If one of us should happen to let it slip, quite accidentally of course, during the interview with Eileen, where her husband was when we arrested him and how much he appeared to have been enjoying himself before we so rudely interrupted, I don't think Eileen would be best pleased and might give us far more ammunition for when we interview Patrick than we have at present.'

'Clara, you have a really devious mind.'

Viv pointed to Nash's office. 'They say if you live with them, you get like them, and Clara's worked with Mike for a long time.'

CHAPTER NINETEEN

Lisa Andrews eyed the mound of paperwork that had been placed on her desk. It seemed as if she was going to have to pay for the rest day she had just taken. Before she could tackle any of it, she spent half an hour listening to Clara, who brought her up to speed with the events.

'I seem to have missed all the excitement,' Lisa remarked ruefully. 'I don't suppose there's much left for me to do, is there?'

'I wouldn't be so sure.' Clara pointed to Lisa's desk.

'I was trying to ignore it, in the hope that it might disappear. But I guess it won't go of its own accord, so I'd better get started.'

Lisa began examining the paperwork and discovered that the vast majority of it referred to a single subject, and that she had been the one responsible for generating it. The large sheaf of papers held together with a bulldog clip had been sent through by Tom Pratt. His covering note explained that these were the details of all motor caravans registered in the area. Tom pointed out that the list might not be one hundred per cent complete, because if someone had done their own conversion on a van, and neglected to inform DVLA, the vehicle wouldn't appear on the list.

She began scanning the first page, more than a little surprised by the number of vehicles there were. Halfway down the fourth page she saw a name that seemed familiar, although Lisa couldn't immediately remember why. She highlighted the entry, before continuing to scan the remaining pages. Without finding anything else of note she returned to that one entry and made a mental note to check the name with the others.

Lisa picked up the message left by Viv. 'Lazy bugger,' she muttered while conceding that he probably had enough to keep him busy. She headed for the custody suite and asked for Newsome's mobile phone explaining she wanted to see if there were any names in the contacts list that might be of interest.

The phone was fully charged but when she tried to access it, the home screen flashed up a message requesting a password. She switched it off. If Newsome kept quiet it would have to go to the tech boys. She glanced at the rest of the property. There were two credit cards, and Newsome's driving licence. Lisa's approach was thorough. She noted it was an HGV licence and the date of Newsome's one endorsement, which was for speeding. The only other items were his wallet and a key ring with several keys.

She picked up the key ring and examined it. It took a few moments before she realized the significance of what she was looking at. She frowned, in an effort to remember what she had heard and read regarding the arrest of Eileen and Dwayne Newsome and the search of their house. She thought for several minutes, before ringing Tom. 'It's Lisa; I need you to check something for me, if you would.' She explained what she was after.

'Let me bring the file up on my screen and I'll have the answer for you straightaway.' Tom came back on the line. 'No, Lisa, there's nothing wrong with your memory,' he told her. 'Why did you want to know?'

She explained, adding, 'I'd better have a word with Clara before she interviews Newsome. She may want to ask him about this.'

Clara's upbeat frame of mind was in no way diminished by what Lisa had to tell her. 'What gave you the idea Newsome might have kept something back from us?'

Lisa held up the keyring.

'Couldn't they be from his house?' Clara objected.

'No, I think I know what these two are for, but I can't be sure,' — she indicated two large bronze keys — 'but this other one is a mystery, so I checked with Tom and when he looked at the inventory of Mrs Newsome's property. She only had house keys, front and back; nothing that matched these.'

'I'll ask him about the keys when we get to interview him. I'm beginning to suspect there's far more to Patrick Newsome than we thought.'

Lisa grinned. 'I reckon Mrs Newsome might be about to discover that as well.'

'I'm not sure if Newsome will give us the information, but I think I know of a way to get his wife to tell us,' Clara said.

'By the way,' Lisa asked, 'does the name Machin mean anything to you? I thought when I saw it that it should mean something, but I wasn't sure.'

'Machin? Do you mean Lee Machin?'

'That's the one.'

'Is he out again? That shows how time flies, I thought he was still inside. Lee Machin is an unpleasant character who lives in a flat on the Westlea when he isn't being put up at the taxpayers' expense. His hobbies are porn, blackmail and flashing his todger in front of young girls. He lives with a scrawny female who puts up with his evil little ways because he keeps the pair of them in class-A substances. Mind you,' Clara added, 'if she didn't live with Machin, she might not need the fantasy world that cocaine gives her. In answer to your question, yes, I know Machin only too well. Why, what's he done now?'

'Nothing. At least nothing criminal.'

'There are those who would hold the view that his very existence is a crime.'

'Do you know, you're getting to sound like Mike?' Lisa grinned at the face Clara pulled. 'His name is on a list Tom Pratt sent me. You remember asking me to check out the owners of motorhomes in the area? Well, it seems Mr Machin has one.'

'You're joking? No way. That has to be wrong. Lee Machin hasn't enough money to be able to afford to buy a set of hub caps, let alone a motorhome.'

'In that case, do you think he might be another courier like Newsome?'

'I think it's a fair bet. How he got the money to buy something like that, I've no idea, but I can guarantee it won't be legal. Straight as a corkscrew, is our Lee. If I needed anything to convince me your theory about the drugs is right, the fact that Lee Machin is involved does it for me. I'm interviewing most of the day, but Viv should be back around lunchtime, I sent him home to get a couple of hours sleep because he's been up all night. Take him with you to the Westlea and have a word with our Mr Machin. He'll act like he's as thick as two short planks, but don't let that fool you; he isn't the halfwit he pretends to be. Oh, and watch out for his partner, a nasty little madam with a foul mouth on her. She's more than capable of sounding off; big style. Especially if she's under the influence, which she usually is. One more thing, be sure and wipe your feet on the way out. Neither of them knows one end of a vacuum cleaner from the other, and anything as basic as cleaning they regard as a waste of time and effort.'

Lisa rolled her eyes. 'Now I'm really looking forward to visiting them.'

* * *

With Clara's warning in mind, Lisa drove into Westlea estate with Viv in the passenger seat. As they passed through the first few roads where many of the residents had bought their property from the local authority, the houses were for the most part neat, brightly painted and well maintained, with tidy gardens, manicured lawns and closely trimmed hedges.

'It looks as if there's been a leylandii salesman round offering huge discounts,' Viv suggested. 'What's the great attraction about them above other hedges?'

'I reckon people go for them because they want quick results. They're fast-growing and evergreen, which gives greater privacy, and they only need trimming a couple of times every summer.'

There was no such evidence of pride in the appearance of Lee Machin's property. 'If an Englishman's home is his castle, then this is a ruin,' Viv said. 'I feel sure it isn't a coincidence that this place reminds me of Newsome's house and garden.'

'Hardly a leading contender for the Britain in Bloom competition, I agree. Not unless they've a category that awards prizes for cultivating weeds.'

'If what we suspect is true there might be even more weed inside the house than in the garden,' Viv suggested.

Lisa groaned. 'If you're going to make any more bad jokes I'll drive off and leave you to make your own way back.'

He ignored the threat. 'I don't suppose I ought to mention that the grass is overgrown then.'

'Any more?'

'No, I think that's it. I was going to mention snow, but I might have made a hash of it.'

'I sometimes wonder what Lianne sees in you. It isn't your sense of humour, that's for sure. Come on, let's get it over with. Which flat is it?'

Viv pointed to a dirty window on the ground floor. They walked up the broken concrete slabs that had once been a path and entered the block where Pearce hammered on the flat door. There was no response, so he subjected the peeling paintwork to a further assault. The only result from this was to dislodge a large piece of flaking paint that floated, feather-like to the ground.

As they waited, undecided, they heard a slight cough behind them. 'Shitheads are out.'

They swung round to find an old man watching them from the adjacent doorway. 'Sorry, what did you say?' Lisa asked.

'I told you, the shitheads are out. All three of them, Mummy Tart, Baby Tart, and Daddy Wanker. Buggered off about an hour or so back. Probably be out of it by now. Got their benefit money this morning, didn't they? They'll be well-juiced by the time they get back. By the weekend, Mummy Tart will be climbing the walls for more. Probably send Baby Tart out on the streets plying her trade.'

'You're obviously close friends as well as neighbours,' Pearce suggested.

'Bah! If I'd to pay council tax I'd claim a rebate for living next door to that scum.'

'Any idea when they'll be back?'

'If I had my way: never. It wouldn't break my heart if I didn't see any of them again.'

The old man nodded to them, a farewell gesture they realized, as he shuffled back inside and slammed his door. In the silence that followed, Lisa heard Pearce humming a tune. It was some seconds before she recognized the theme from *Neighbours*.

That did make her laugh, but then she asked, 'What do we do now? I hardly think they'll respond if we leave them a note, do you?'

'From what we've heard, they'll probably scarper. Mind you,' — Pearce gestured to next door — 'that'll make the old man's day. As we're here, I suppose it won't do any harm to have a look around.'

Outside the block he walked along in front of the window and peered in through the only gap between the curtains. 'Ugh! What a tip. How people can live like this, I'll never understand.'

Lisa joined him and shielded her eyes with her hands as she looked through the grimy film that covered the glass. Even the curtains at the window were soiled and she could clearly see cobwebs along the tops. 'Clara warned me about the state this place would be in. She certainly wasn't exaggerating.'

They retraced their steps and went round to the rear. Here, the wilderness was even worse than the front, if that was possible. 'It's like the Serengeti,' Viv muttered. 'Any minute now I expect to see a bull elephant walking towards us.'

One area had been cleared, however, the only indication of anything approaching maintenance they had seen. In the midst of the jungle, gleaming incongruously by comparison with its surroundings was a motorhome, its registration number indicating that it was no more than four years old. 'Is that the vehicle from your list? Or could it belong to someone in the other flats?'

Lisa checked the note she had made. 'Yes, that's the one.'

'No way Machin bought this with his own money,' Viv said. 'Apart from the state of the rest of this dump, they don't sound the types to be traipsing across to Scarborough with their buckets and spades.'

'Clara said much the same. Unless the dealer was offering a ninety-nine per cent discount and hire purchase terms on the balance.'

'I'm not at all sure that caravan dealers are either that generous or desperate enough for business—' Viv was in the middle of saying, when he stopped suddenly.

Lisa glanced at her colleague. Viv was staring at the motorhome, his expression stunned, almost as if the vehicle had suddenly turned into a UFO. 'What is it?' she asked.

'I'm trying to remember something I saw earlier. On the way back, can we drive round via Newsome's house? I want to check the motorhome that's on his drive.'

'We can, it's only round the corner from here. Why do you want to go there? It's not that much more luxurious than this palace?'

Pearce explained. 'In that case, let's go now,' Lisa responded. 'Although it will be hard to tear myself away from this delightful scenery.'

Newsome's house looked even more desolate, if that was possible, Viv thought. After they had checked the information they needed, which confirmed the accuracy of his memory, Lisa phoned the station and asked to be put through to Clara, only to be told that both she and Jackie Fleming were at Netherdale.

'They're conducting an interview with that drug dealer who was arrested last night,' Jack Binns explained, 'and straight after that they're going to talk to Eileen Newsome again, so it could be some time before either of them are available. Is it urgent? I could phone through and get a note in if absolutely necessary.'

'Would you do that please, Jack? We'll wait here for her to ring in case she wants us to take action over what we've found out.'

'Care to tell me what that is? It might help persuade her, because she's under a fair amount of pressure. I hear Mrs Newsome's brief has been jumping up and down. He also represents Greasy Palms, which doesn't surprise me. Like calling to like, I guess. Anyway, he's been demanding everything from his clients' immediate release to a full internal enquiry. Neither of which he'll get, he's just being bloody awkward. Nonsense, of course, but it isn't helping.'

Lisa explained why they needed to speak to Clara. Binns responded instantly, 'I can see why you think it's urgent. Leave it with me.'

CHAPTER TWENTY

The solicitor wasn't having a good day. Not that this was by any means unusual. It was the nature of his practice that he attracted a fair percentage of lost causes, clients others in his profession wouldn't go near. As such, there were many he had to consider as almost charity work, but those he knew had the wherewithal to pay him, more than compensated for these. He told his junior, it was a question of risk assessment and getting the balance right. On this particular occasion the balance was about perfect. One of his clients was a potential no-hoper; the other would pay handsomely for his services. The other plus point was that with both clients being held at the same police station, the travelling expenses would be minimal.

It hadn't helped that the first of his clients, Greasy Palms, when interviewed by two female detectives had completely ignored his professional advice to say nothing that would incriminate him. To be fair, with what the police had found at the man's house, he'd already done more than enough to incriminate himself. The client had asked him, more in hope than expectation, if there was a chance they could get a judge and jury to believe that the police had planted the drugs found in his bedroom wardrobe.

It isn't exactly deemed to be professionally sound to treat your client's statements to a dose of heavy sarcasm, but in this case the solicitor felt it was more than justified. 'The stuff was found in a secret compartment within your wardrobe, a compartment that had been constructed specially for the purpose. Are you suggesting that a jury will believe that the police turned up at your house with thousands of pounds worth of drugs and a Black and Decker? That they sawed through the base of your wardrobe and planted the drugs simply to incriminate you? I think even Perry Mason or Rumpole would have difficulty putting that across successfully.'

His client wasn't too sure who either Perry Mason or Rumpole were, but he got the message. That didn't mean he had to tell the police everything, but on later reflection, the solicitor had to admit that there might have been some point in what his client had done. He'd listened with dismay at the line the detectives had taken. Despite his reassurances, the client hadn't been convinced.

'Listen,' he told the accused man during the recess he'd requested, 'they're bluffing. All that business about charging you with murder if your DNA is found on the drugs wrapper is pure bullshit. Is it your DNA, incidentally?'

'Of course it is. Why do you think I'm shitting myself? Murder means life. Supplying that amount of heroin probably means close to life as well. There are lots of people gunning for me, and inside they've got a perfect opportunity. The longer I get, the worse my chances of coming out alive are. Added to which, if I get done for murder they'll put me in a high security wing with all the hard cases I'm trying to steer clear of. It'd be like issuing invites to my funeral.'

'You're going to have to face that risk wherever you get sent.'

'Yeah, but if I keep my head down and stay clear of trouble, in a couple of years or so they'll send me to an open prison, which will be a bloody sight safer.'

Eventually, unable to persuade his client to any other course of action, when the interview resumed the solicitor had to settle for confirmation from the senior detective that the worst his client would face in respect of the deaths at the derelict house would be a charge of manslaughter. That, in exchange for all the dealer knew about the organization supplying the drugs was the arrangement they settled on, one that was slightly less than satisfying all round.

Even when he listened to his client's revelation, the solicitor didn't appreciate the importance of what he'd heard. Nor, to be fair, did Fleming and Mironova at the time.

'I have to pay for the gear up front. It sometimes comes the same day; sometimes I've to wait a week. I get no warning it's on the way, until I got a note stuck through my door.'

'Is it a handwritten note?'

'No, it's always typed, like on a computer. It comes in a plain white envelope, no name or address on. Just a blank envelope, but I always know what is inside. All the note says is, "shipment arriving Thursday" or whatever day it's due. That meant I need to have the cash ready by then. Always cash. I'd wait in on the day. The guy turns up, takes the money and goes. It could be any time from first thing in the morning until late at night, but within an hour, the Royal Mail would arrive.'

'The Royal Mail?'

'That's what I called them, the blokes who delivered the gear. I'd get a neat parcel, wrapped in brown paper, which I'd have to sign for, just like the Royal Mail.'

'Did you know in advance how much you've to pay for the drugs?'

'Yes, that's in the note as well.'

'And the man who took your money wasn't the same one as delivered the drugs? That sounds an odd arrangement.'

The dealer shrugged. 'Maybe, but that was the way they insisted it had to be.'

'Did you ever get to meet or speak to anyone else?'

'No, they only rang me once, right at the start. I couldn't swear to it, but I had this idea that the man on the phone had a bit of a foreign accent. Well, not an accent maybe, not as strong as that, something in the way he spoke, it didn't sound natural like.'

'Can you remember what he said?'

'I remember one bit of it, too well. I'd been getting the gear from another bloke, see, and when they rang me, they said he'd gone out of business. That made a bit of sense, because I hadn't seen him for a few weeks. Gone out of business, that was how the bloke said it. I read later this guy had been found in that big reservoir near the M62, where they do the boating.'

'Had he drowned?'

'Yeah, but only after he'd been shot five times. I'd no choice but to get the gear from the new lot. On the one hand I'd people hammering on my door, shouting and complaining that I couldn't supply them, and then there was this offer, take it or leave it — but if you value your skin, don't leave it. The only good point was the new people gave me a bigger cut of the profits. Not much, but a bit more.'

Fleming sat back and nodded to Clara, who took over the questioning. 'Can you give us some names or descriptions of the men you did get to meet? What about the delivery men?'

'I didn't know their names. There were two of them, they used to alternate. I was never sure which of them would turn up. I can tell you something about one of them though. I saw him once, when he wasn't delivering to me, I mean. He was driving one of those caravanette things. You know, not pulled by a car.'

'A motorhome, you mean?'

'Yeah, I reckon they must have been paying him a bundle, because no way he could have coughed up for one of them.'

'Can you describe him? And the other delivery man?'

The dealer launched into detailed descriptions, and when he had finished, Clara asked, 'What about the man who took the money?'

She waited, seeing the troubled expression on the dealer's face. He clearly had reservations about this man, although he'd been quite open about the others. 'What is it? What's wrong?'

'I don't . . . that is . . . I'm not sure.' He looked at his solicitor for help. None was forthcoming.

'Everything you can tell us,' Clara reminded him.

He'd already said too much as well as too little. It was obvious to the detectives that he knew more; obvious to him they wouldn't settle for less. Giving the rest away was no longer an option, but the thought of the man he was about to describe chilled him.

'It isn't his real name,' he began, his reluctance obvious. 'Only a nickname, I think. And I only heard it once, and that was accidental. They call him Stanley, Stanley Slicer. Rumour is they call him that because of what he carries; a Stanley knife. He uses it on people who cross him. Or so they say. I don't know for sure.'

After they had managed to drag a description of the man called Stanley from the dealer, the detectives signalled an end to the interview and left the solicitor to confer with his client. When they emerged from the interview room Fleming said, 'The description of one of the delivery men fits Newsome, don't you think?'

'I do, and the description of the other one is just as accurate.'

Clara saw Jackie's look of surprise and explained, 'His name is Lee Machin. Viv and Lisa have gone to interview him. If we're in time we should be able to get them to arrest him. Then, if we go round there, we can search his place too. Now I need to try and catch Viv and Lisa before they head back to Helmsdale, and besides, word was passed during the recess that they want to speak to me.' As she took out her mobile, she added, 'I don't like the sound of this Stanley character. He sounds a very nasty piece of work. I don't fancy meeting up with him, but I would like to stick him where he belongs; inside.'

Fleming shrugged. 'The aggravating part of all this is, that we may not have to worry about it. Once they get wind of what's going on, the men in charge of these gangs usually vanish before we can get close enough to them, certainly before we can gather sufficient evidence to prosecute. Then they pop up again somewhere else under another name once the heat's died down.'

Sadly, Clara thought, Fleming's assessment was only too accurate. Perhaps this time though, it might be different. It would be nice if they were to get lucky for a change. She brightened. 'At least Lisa's theory about Machin was spot on,' she commented as her phone was answered. 'Lisa, where are you?'

'Still on the Westlea. Sorry to break you off, but there's something I think you should know.'

'Don't worry about that, in fact I'm glad you're still there. Have you spoken to Machin?'

'No, he wasn't home. There was nobody in. We spoke to a neighbour, who isn't their greatest fan. He said they went out over an hour or so ago.'

'OK, I want you to wait near his flat, close enough to spot him when he returns, but not in a position where he might twig that you're there. When he turns up, wait until he goes inside and then arrest him. We need him to be inside when you collar him. Charge him with supplying class-A drugs. Hold him there and get word to me immediately. I'll leave instructions to interrupt us, even if we're in an interview. Jackie and I will head straight out and then she can authorize a search.' Clara paused and added, 'He's been identified by the dealer we arrested as being one of the couriers. Is the motorhome there?'

'It is. It's about the only thing on the site worth more than scrap value.'

'Good. Now, what was it you wanted me for?'

Lisa explained what she and Pearce had discovered. 'The number plates on both Machin and Newsome's motorhomes carry the same supplier's name. It may just be coincidence, but we thought it might be worth checking.'

'I'm sure you're right. Let's see how things develop on that front. Now I must go. We're re-interviewing Eileen Newsome, and that's going to be fun.'

* * *

Eileen Newsome looked far from happy at the prospect of a further interview, obviously her idea of fun differed widely from DS Mironova's. She looked less and less delighted with life once the questioning began. This time Jackie had instructed Clara to take the lead.

'You'll no doubt be keen to know how your beloved husband is,' Clara said by way of opening the interview. 'In which case, I'm pleased to be able to tell you that he's fit and well.'

Eileen glared at her but said nothing, so Clara continued, 'I bet you're wondering how I know that. The answer is, because we have him tucked up warm and cosy in a cell at Helmsdale. Of course I don't think he's as warm and cosy as he was when we arrested him.' She glanced across at Fleming. 'He looked very content with life then, didn't he?'

Jackie was waiting for a prompt such as this. 'Oh yes, very content, I'd say. Although that might have been because he'd just . . . er . . . finished what he was doing before we burst in on them. I am glad we didn't interrupt them when they were still . . . er . . . busy.'

'Oh dear me no, that would have been most unfortunate.' Clara agreed.

'What do you think it was they were playing before we got there? I feel sure it wasn't snakes and ladders.'

'No, it was certainly more energetic than snakes and ladders, because Patrick was exhausted, fast asleep. In fact both of them were, so it must have been something really strenuous.'

'You may know what the hell you're talking about, but I've no idea.' Eileen spat the words out.

Clara's tone changed from frivolous to direct. 'We're talking about your husband Patrick. You do only have the one husband, don't you? Yes, I thought so. Well, when we interrupted him, Patrick was in bed with a very attractive young lady and neither of them had any clothes on. He looked quite sad when we arrested him and not at all pleased when we told him he could be moved here to be near you. In fact he seemed quite put out at being separated from, what was her name? Shelley? Tracy?'

'Sharon,' Fleming reminded her.

'Oh yes, Sharon, that's right. I knew it was one of those names that are popular with younger women. Did you know about her?' Clara paused and watched as Eileen Newsome's expression changed from nonchalance to thunder. 'No? Oh dear, how careless of me. That makes me wonder what else Patrick might have been up to that you're unaware of.'

'If that dirty ungrateful bastard has been dipping his wick with some tart or other, he can fuck off and never come back. I'm fed up to the back teeth with him. He got me into this mess. I told you that. If it hadn't been for him I wouldn't be here now. He made me do it. The shoplifting, I mean. I didn't know about the drugs. That's something else he didn't tell me about.'

'Oh yes, I remember you did tell me about Patrick putting you up to the shoplifting. He must have a real way with women, your Patrick. Apart from Sharon, I mean, we knew he was having his way with her. I have to admit I didn't have him down for so much natural charm, but I don't know him as well as you. To be able to persuade not one, but two women to go shoplifting for him, he must be like a sort of Fagin for the over forties. And all the time you're doing that, together with your pal, risking imprisonment on his behalf, he's busy, what was the expression you used? Dipping his wick into the lovely Sharon and setting up a really cosy love nest with her.'

'I've told you all I know. He never lets me know where he is one minute to the next. For all I know he could have been shagging half the women in the county. He goes out at night and comes home next morning knackered and smelling of cow shit. If he's been with a mucky tart he hides it well. Unless she's a farmer's daughter.'

'What do you mean?'

Clearly, Eileen realized she had said too much. Although they continued to press her for more information about

Newsome's nocturnal activities, Eileen remained silent. She had, however provided them with one valuable piece of information, that Newsome was absent from home for much of the time, even before his misalliance with Sharon. It was a long time before Clara realized what Eileen's oblique reference to cow shit signified.

The solicitor decided that he had by now spent long enough there. It had been what he deemed to be a long day. The general opinion was that half his clientele were now resident in the custody suite. Before leaving, the solicitor insisted that Patrick Newsome was charged with possession with intent to supply and stated that he would be back the following day to see his client. At that, he swept his notes and pen into his briefcase and marched out of the building.

* * *

Lee Machin had returned home and been arrested. A search of his house and the motorhome had been accompanied by a running commentary of invective from Machin's partner, almost all of which was unrepeatable. As Lisa was attempting to calm the woman, Pearce stared at her, and as recognition dawned, suggested that Lisa ought to handcuff her as well. Lisa looked puzzled but did as he suggested. Once they were out of earshot of their prisoners, Viv explained. 'Unless I'm very much mistaken I think we've just found Eileen Newsome's shoplifting partner. That woman looks very much like the one on the Good Buys CCTV footage. I'll go and caution her.'

The search of the motorhome had turned up another package of what looked like heroin, the hiding place similar to the one used by Patrick Newsome.

Faced with this evidence, Machin had elected for the strong silent defence. He hadn't said a word from the time Viv Pearce had placed the handcuffs on him. Throughout the search of his house, the subsequent interview at Helmsdale station and his incarceration in the last of their holding cells, he stayed silent.

Given the population of prisoners, the station had to remain open overnight, instead of the normal office hours. It didn't help that the remand wing at Felling Prison was full. As Binns handed over to his counterpart, drafted in from Netherdale specifically to cover the night shift, he remarked, 'You may get a visit from an architect. We're going to need a two-storey extension to the cell block if things continue like this.'

The night sergeant grinned and joined in the fun. 'What are we doing about breakfast for the prisoners? Have you booked a catering firm that specializes in large events?'

* * *

Despite the success they had enjoyed that day, any elation Clara might have felt evaporated when she reached home that evening. She was exhausted from the extremely long day, drained and empty and had no difficulty in identifying the source of her disquiet. She hadn't heard from David in over a week. She knew there were bound to be times when he would be unable to make contact when he was involved in an operation of some kind. That in itself was cause for concern. The sort of missions someone with his background and specialist training and skills was sent on were all extremely hazardous. The very same reason that he was unable to call her was the one that prevented her picking the phone up and ringing him.

She rooted through the freezer and picked out an individual quiche which she placed in the oven. She didn't feel particularly hungry but knew she ought to eat. Besides which, it would serve as a distraction. In the lounge she poured herself a whisky, savouring the smooth fire and enjoying the peaty aftertaste. She wandered around the flat, checking the oven timer more than once, wondering if it had developed a fault. Surely there had been fifteen minutes left on the display last time she had looked, which had been two laps ago?

She raised her glass and was surprised to see that it was empty. After a moment's hesitation she poured a second drink. Normally, she would have restricted herself to one, but tonight, she felt the need. 'It is a double malt after all,' she muttered.

CHAPTER TWENTY-ONE

On her way to Helmsdale the following morning, Clara called in for a brief meeting with the chief constable and Jackie Fleming. It was far more upbeat than their previous discussions had been. The arrest of the drug dealer, both his couriers and the seizure of a considerable quantity of illicit drugs were all contributory factors. A sobering note was introduced, in that there was still no progress towards resolution of the unsolved murders of PC Riley; the two men in the picnic area; and the deaths of the three addicts in the squat. However, towards the end of the meeting, Mironova was able to announce another possible breakthrough. She was encouraged by Jackie Fleming, who saw no good reason to take the credit for the work of the junior members of her team.

'We already know that Lisa's theory of the use of motorhomes to get the drugs into our area is correct,' Clara began. 'However, we now believe the significance of the vehicles used might be even greater than we thought previously. When Lisa and Viv were having a look round Machin's place, Viv spotted that both the motorhomes we've searched were from the same dealership.'

'How did he know that?'

'By the name they put on the number plate. Both vehicles were supplied by a company called Morag Caravan Park. Of course, it may be pure coincidence, or it could be that whoever is running the drugs has bought from the same place to get a better price. But what if the motorhome dealers themselves are the importers? If they are supplying large quantities of drugs they would need a business with a big turnover to launder the money. And given the very high cost of these motorhomes, I can't think of many better. All they would have to do is sell three or four of the flashier vehicles in a short space of time to make a six-figure deposit in their bank account very easily explainable. Nobody we've arrested so far seems at all willing to say much about the people they're working for, even Greasy Palms the dealer we threatened with a triple murder charge was less than forthcoming. If the man he referred to as Stanley is as evil as the reputation he was given, that isn't altogether surprising. But as we have no other leads to go on, we believe it might pay dividends if we were to have a look round the place where these motorhomes originated.'

The chief constable thought about it for a few moments. 'I agree,' she said eventually, 'however, I think we're moving into an area where it might be better to at least consult the specialists before we make a move. I think we'd have to proceed with extreme caution. By the sound of it, I don't for a minute believe the people running this show will have left the stuff lying about for us to find. Having rolled up the first two links in the chain of supply, we must be getting very close to the top. Before you do anything, I should have a word with the Drugs Intelligence Unit; it wouldn't do to have us gatecrash their party. This is first-class work, though, by both Viv and Lisa. Be sure to tell them both how pleased I am, will you, Clara? Now, is there anything else to discuss?'

'Just one other small matter, a bit of a puzzle we need to clear up with regard to Patrick Newsome. It may be of absolutely no significance, but when we arrested him he had a keyring on his person and we know for a fact that the keys on it don't fit any of the doors in his house. Or should I say houses' — Clara added with a grin — 'seeing we found him in bed with his mistress. Anyway, we asked him about the keys but he won't tell us anything, which we thought was suspicious. Actually' — her smile widened — 'he won't talk about anything, not since he discovered we'd told his wife about the other woman.'

'What an exciting life some members of our criminal fraternity lead,' O'Donnell commented. 'Didn't Mrs Newsome say anything? I thought once you'd let slip about her husband's infidelity she might have been only too anxious to drop him in it. A woman scorned and all that.'

'Oh, she's already trying to blame him for any crime she can think up,' Fleming interjected, 'but she knows nothing about the keys, nor does the other woman, Sharon. What Eileen Newsome did tell us was that she never knows where Patrick is for long periods of time. Of course, now she knows about Sharon she thinks he was with her all the time, but we believe if that had been the case, Patrick would have owned up to it. All Mrs Newsome said was he returned smelling of animal dung. Without finding the door those keys unlock though, we're none the wiser.'

'What about that dodgy friend of Nash's?' O'Donnell asked. She looked at Clara, 'You know, the little Scotsman, used to be a burglar — the one who rescued you from that quarry. Hasn't he got a locksmith's business nowadays? He might help you identify the mystery key. What was his name?'

'Jimmy Johnson! Of course, I never thought of him. I'll take them round to his shop as soon as I get back to Helmsdale.'

* * *

Shortly after Fleming and Mironova left, O'Donnell's phone rang. She listened for a long time, occasionally making notes on the pad in front of her. 'Say that again,' she said at one point, 'and spell the name out for me. OK, I've got that. I'll make sure it gets dealt with immediately. Is there anything else I should know?'

There was another long silence as O'Donnell listened to what was obviously a detailed explanation. 'My word,' she said eventually, 'you have been busy. What? There's more? Go on then.'

The caller spoke, and O'Donnell's face was a picture of incredulity. 'What did you say? What sort of . . . ? Oh, fish vans, right, I see.' She chuckled. 'Yes, I suppose it does make perfect sense, it just seemed so incongruous. And because it sounds so weird that makes it the perfect way of doing it. Who on earth would suspect one of them? I'll get the team on it. I've also got some information for you. It's to do with that woman's name you were given.'

* * *

The mild headache Clara was suffering, induced by her third whisky the previous evening, wasn't helped by the clamour that assailed her ears as she entered the premises of Helm Security. A succession of bells, whistles, sirens, and electronic wailing sounds of several different tones battered her eardrums into submission. Clara put both hands over her ears and waited for the racket to cease. It did so only when the man she had come to visit entered from the workshop at the rear and pressed a button underneath the counter.

'Sergeant Mironova!' He greeted her with a warm smile, not something he would have done for many police officers. 'Sorry aboot the din. I'm testing a new system fer a customer.'

'Well you can tell them from me that it works. How are you, Jimmy? Keeping busy?'

The Scotsman smiled again. 'Once upon a time I'd have had tae refuse tae answer that question on the grounds it could incriminate me. Nowadays, I'm happy tae say, I'm very busy. More than ever, wi' the recent spate o' burglaries. That's done wonders fer ma turnover.'

'Well, I hate to disappoint you, but we've arrested someone who was responsible for quite a few of them.'

'Spoilsport. Ah well, I'm no' that worried. With everyone being short o' money, there's bound tae be others willing tae nick stuff, just tae make ends meet. And judging by the reports I read, they were fairly amateurish. Anyway, what can I dae fer ye? Lost the keys tae the cells?'

'No, although it is about keys that I came to see you. These, to be precise.' She produced the keyring and laid it on the counter. 'I need to find out what they fit.'

Johnson pointed to the two bronze keys. 'I can tell ye what they are, or what they appear tae be.' He explained his idea.

Clara nodded agreement. 'Yes, that was what we thought. It's the steel one that we don't know about.'

He picked up the key and peered at it for several moments. 'Aye, I think I can tell ye what that fits. Bear wi' me a sec.'

He disappeared into the workshop and returned a few minutes later. 'Unit number twenty-one, Helmsdale Industrial Estate,' he told her as he dropped the keyring back in her hand.

Clara stared at him, as awestruck as a child who has seen her first magic trick. 'How on earth do you know that?'

Johnson smiled, enjoying the moment. 'Because I fitted the lock tae that door. In fact I fitted the locks tae all those units. When the industrial estate changed hands a couple o' years ago, the new owners wanted better security fer their tenants. Plus master keys for themsen in case any o' the tenants defaulted, an' because they have a habit o' losing 'em or needing extras.' He shook his head sadly. 'Ye've no idea how careless people are wi' keys. I've had tae provide three replacements already. That type o' key is a bit special, which was how I knew it was frae the industrial estate. All I had tae dae then was compare it wi' the numbers on the master copies in the workshop tae know which o' the units it fit.'

'Jimmy, I may have told you this before, but you're a genius. Thanks a lot.'

* * *

The male receptionist on the caravan park smiled at the man approaching the desk. 'Can I help you?'

'We're touring the area and don't have a booking. Is that a problem?'

'No problem at all. We've often got room for a few more vans,' he reassured him as he glanced through the window at the motorhome. He passed him the booking form. 'Would you fill that in, please? How many people are there in your party? We have to ask; health and safety, you understand.'

'Just three of us.'

'I'm afraid we have to take payment in advance, a credit card will be fine.'

'That's OK, it will be cash.'

He climbed back into the driving seat of the motorhome. 'Stand number thirty-four, courtesy of the youth on reception.'

As they drove slowly up the tarmac road, looking for the stand they had been allocated, he asked, 'What do we do now?'

'Do as before. Keep watching and behave normally.'

In the back Shakila was silent. She had trusted strangers once before, and the result had been dreadful. Now, she was with these people who had found her on the beach and were keeping her prisoner; but where else could she go? They had kept her safe, so far. They had supplied her with warm clothing and she supposed in a way they had been kind, even if they were drug runners. They had got her to tell them of the shooting on the boat and assured her she would be taken care of, but what reliance could she place on their promise, given the way they earned their living? Were they lying to her? If they were going to kill her they could have already done so. Might they not simply hand her over to those people she was most anxious to avoid, the gunman, or to the authorities, who would send her back to the place she had gone through so much to escape from?

CHAPTER TWENTY-TWO

Next morning, Lisa was alone in the CID suite.

Clara arrived. 'Any messages?' she asked, as she hung her jacket on a chair.

'Only one. God wants you to ring her; said it was urgent.'

'It usually is,' Clara remarked as she picked up the phone.

'I was right about the Drugs Intelligence Unit,' O'Donnell told her. 'They're very interested in the caravan park and are going to get someone to check it out when they can, and if they send word they will need us to be ready to go in. But more importantly, they've just got some intelligence about the other drug suppliers; how they bring them into the country and where they're based. At present they can't confirm any of this, so they need our team to investigate on their behalf — and our own, I hasten to add. I think we need to act speedily on this, so liaise with Jack Binns and traffic to help monitor the location. Have you got pen and paper?'

The chief constable gave her the details and chuckled at Clara's gasp of surprise. 'Pretty much my reaction when I heard it,' she agreed, 'but totally logical, when you think about it.'

'You're dead right, ma'am. We'll get on it straightaway, but I think we're going to need some help. Viv's giving evidence in court today, so there's only Lisa and me.'

'No he isn't. He's on his way to Helmsdale now along with Jackie Fleming. The defendant in the case changed his plea to guilty, which freed Viv up. I happened to see him when he popped in here and handed him over to Jackie. There are also four armed officers en route.'

'Brilliant. Thanks, ma'am. I also have to thank you for your idea about taking the key to Jimmy Johnson. He recognized it immediately. Coincidentally, it belongs to a unit on the same industrial estate as the address you've just given me. Jimmy fitted all of them, which helped. I was going to take a look around there today, but it will have to wait until we've dealt with this other job.'

Clara thought it was a strange coincidence that the site they had been directed to was only two streets away from the unit to which Patrick Newsome held a key.

The building, in the middle of a row of identical ones, was typical of many. Alongside the frosted glass door to one side of the unit, which usually led to a small office, was a larger roller-shutter door delivery entrance. Both of these were closed, there was no light on inside, no cars parked outside, no sign of life at all.

'They deserve to go to gaol, if only for their lousy puns,' Fleming commented.

Clara read the sign and laughed. 'Yes, they are pretty bad.'

The board, which had been fixed above the glass door, read, SOLE TRADERS, Fresh Fish Delivered Weekly from Our Plaice to Yours.

'Hmm, then it's appropriate that we're raiding them, because we suspect something fishy's going on,' Pearce commented.

'I wonder if customers have to pay C.O.D. for their fish?' Lisa joined in.

Fleming groaned. 'Don't you start! We've enough bother with Viv.'

Lisa turned to Fleming and asked, 'In that case, can you create a new rank for Viv? Defective Punstable perhaps?'

They were seated in Clara's car on the main road next to the side street where the unit was located. 'Hang on, one of the vans is coming,' she interrupted.

'Saved by the bell. I don't think I could have stood many more bad puns,' Fleming muttered, as Pearce radioed to the members of the ARU team in an unmarked Volvo estate car a few yards behind them. Pearce knew the innocent-looking vehicle contained a slide-out drawer below the parcel shelf that held a variety of weapons.

'Do we approach him outside, or wait until he's opened up?' Lisa asked.

'Let him get inside. Once he's on the premises, we'll be able to conduct a search and keep out of sight if any others turn up.'

The van driver was in a good mood. The business was flourishing. He and his boss hadn't expected the level of demand for their products as he and the others toured the villages. The lack of a fishmonger in the local towns and a natural dislike of supermarket produce was the reason for their success. He confidently expected them to be able to shift almost all the catch they had bought at the port by the weekend, and the free lobsters would make a healthy profit.

That, of course, was without taking the other stuff into account. Their employer paid handsomely for the small parcels he and his colleagues regularly collected along with the fish.

He parked the fish van in front of the delivery door, opened the office, stepped inside and operated the mechanism that controlled the roller-shutter. He turned to head back to his van, his intention to reverse into the building, when he became aware that he was being watched. His hand hovered close to the shutter button; then froze. His mood changed instantly. Two men were standing in the doorway, both pointing guns at him. For a moment, he thought that this was a hijack such as he had been warned against. One of the men shouted, 'Armed police. Stand still; put your hands where I can see them.'

Most of the speech was superfluous, for by then he had seen the flak jackets they were wearing which bore the logo 'police', and knew he wasn't about to be shot in cold blood. The realization didn't comfort him one little bit.

Having secured their prisoner and examined the contents of the van, the team concealed themselves in the warehouse. Their prisoner's vehicle was still parked outside, which should cause the other drivers to approach the unit in safety.

As they waited, Clara inspected the office and found only fish related invoices and paperwork, nothing to indicate who the gang leader was. In the warehouse she spotted a bank of large chest freezers, each labelled with the name of one of the drivers. A simple system adding credibility to the set-up should anyone in authority visit the premises.

Within the next two hours, the team had arrested all four drivers. Inspection of the vans revealed a compartment in the passenger footwell of each fish van, inside which a couple of small parcels had been secreted. These were removed for testing. The prisoners were ferried to the police station while Mironova, Andrews, and Pearce loaded the fish from the vans into the freezers. 'No point finding out that the packets contain flour and then facing a claim for damages because the fish has gone off,' Fleming told them.

As soon as they reached the station, one of the men requested that he be allowed to contact his solicitor for himself and the others. Their legal representative, following the call, immediately rang the mobile phone number that was permanently on his desk jotter, to inform Tony Hartley of the arrest of his men.

Hartley's instructions were clear. 'Activate the reserve fund and make sure they know the terms and conditions before the police start interviewing them.'

Sergeant Binns, who by now was beginning to think his job description had been changed to include the duties of a hotel receptionist, was thankful that all the other prisoners had been transferred to Netherdale to await their appearance at a preliminary hearing.

When the solicitor reached the station, he requested to speak to each of his clients alone prior to their interrogation. During which time, he passed on the message from Tony Hartley. Although they were only marginally cheered by the news that their families were to be cared for during their inevitable incarceration, they had no hesitation complying with the accompanying instruction. Thus, when they were questioned about the presence of the drugs in their vehicles, their suppliers, clients, and where they got the money to pay for the illicit produce, none of them said a word. The price of their silence could be calculated almost to the penny, but then Tony Hartley and his boss, the major, were careful planners.

The interviews and the accompanying paperwork took so long that there was no chance for the team to revisit the industrial estate that day. 'We'll have to look at Newsome's unit tomorrow,' Clara told them.

* * *

Mironova parked in front of her flat and got out of the car. Before turning to go inside, she glanced across the road. Her heart lurched and she felt an almost physical pain as she saw David's mother and father climb out of their car and begin crossing the road towards her. The inference that something terrible had happened was obvious; immediate and unbearable. She bit back a cry of anguish, but her look of distress was sufficient to cause David's mother to break into a run. She clasped Clara in a tight embrace. 'It's all right, it's all right,' she repeated again and again. 'David's OK. He's safe. He's been wounded, but he's safe.'

'He took a nasty wound in the shoulder,' David's father added as he joined them. 'I spoke to the medics, they're usually pretty cautious types, and they assured me he'll be fine, given time. We thought it better to come and tell you in person. Not the sort of thing you want to hear over the phone.'

'Come on, Clara, relax,' Mrs Sutton told her. 'They'll be flying him home as soon as he is fit enough to travel.'

'Is he . . . did you speak to him.'

'Very briefly, after they'd operated. He was pretty doped up as you can imagine, but he insisted we let you know as soon as we could. He said you'd already be worried, because he hadn't been able to phone.'

'I was. And you're certain it's nothing worse? No nasty complications?'

'Absolutely certain. He even made a joke, sent you a message. Something about it being the perfect excuse for him to get out of decorating — whatever that means.'

Clara laughed, albeit a little shakily. 'He's been threatening to redecorate the flat for ages, but something always seems to get in the way. I'm sorry I folded up like that, but I naturally thought, when I saw you . . . Look, where are my manners. You must come inside. Let me get you a drink or something.'

'No, not a chance,' David's father said. 'We're taking you out to dinner. That was something I had to promise we'd do. He said you'd probably be working far too hard and living off pizzas and whisky. I can't fault the whisky, but I detest pizzas. Like chewing cardboard.'

Clara managed a smile. 'He's wrong; it's quiches, not pizzas. This is ever so kind of you. Will you at least come in while I get changed?'

'Of course, Dear,' Mrs Sutton coughed delicately. 'And if you want time to have a shower . . .'

'Oh! Of course, I'd quite forgotten. We arrested some men today who deliver fish. We'd to transfer their stock from the vans to the freezers. I must stink like Billingsgate Fish Market.'

'It is a little noticeable,' Mrs Sutton agreed. 'We'll come in and wait for you.'

* * *

'I think we must hold a press conference,' O'Donnell told Fleming. 'We're being hounded by the media over the lack of progress, especially regarding the unsolved murders. Added to which the media must have got wind that we've made several arrests, and there's nothing worse than news reporters who are short of facts. They tend to make up their own. At least if we announce the results we do have, they'll know we're not sitting back, twiddling our thumbs.'

'I was on my way to see you. I've had a call about the drugs that were found in Lee Machin's motorhome and the home of the dealer Clara's been referring to as Greasy Palms. It's confirmed that only one batch was contaminated; so technically we've got our murderer of the addicts. I suppose we should be thankful that Greasy Palms had only just started distribution, and only a small amount at that, so there isn't much on the streets. Whether either of them will say anything more, remains to be seen. At least at the press conference we can be more positive. Do you want to set it up now, or wait until Clara and the team have had a look at the other unit on the industrial estate?'

'When are they going there?'

'It was scheduled for today, but then Clara rang in and requested the day off, and in the circumstances, it would have been churlish to refuse.'

O'Donnell raised an enquiring eyebrow.

'You've met her fiancé — Major Sutton? Well I'm afraid he's been wounded, fortunately not too seriously, and his family has arrived.'

'In that case we'll have to go ahead with the media conference in advance of any other activity. I can't hold off any longer. It would also be right to let Clara conduct the search on the other unit, so that can wait until she's back. We owe her that for the magnificent work she's put in while Nash has been away.'

'I still don't understand why you refused point blank to even allow me to contact him. Knowing Mike, I feel sure he would have returned, if only for a few days.'

'Which is exactly the reason that I didn't allow it. There are times when it's necessary to take the broader view, particularly in my job, and I've already told you, Mike needs a rest.'

CHAPTER TWENTY-THREE

The media conference was difficult, but at least the chief constable and Fleming were able to identify certain areas of success. O'Donnell began by giving a full account of the tragic deaths of the addicts found at the derelict house. 'The cause was adulterated heroin,' she told the assembled reporters. 'Sadly, with the chemical used to contaminate the drug, we believe this was a deliberate act. Although at this stage we can only speculate as to the motive, we believe it may possibly have been a particularly malicious part of a turf war between two competing drug gangs. I am pleased to say we have since recovered quantities of the drug. What we've seized has been similarly adulterated and, although it is too early to say that we have removed the threat completely, we are confident that there can be very little left out on the street.'

She continued by elaborating on the quantities of heroin the police had seized; an announcement that caused even some of the more experienced journalists to raise their eyebrows. 'I can also tell you that we have arrested several members of the two factions involved in bringing drugs into our region and we hope, in time, to stop the supply route they have been using.' O'Donnell then let Fleming take up the story of the arrests in detail.

A reporter from the *Gazette* positioned at the back of the room called out, 'Where's Inspector Nash? Why isn't he on this case?'

O'Donnell stared directly at him. 'Inspector Nash is on compassionate leave.'

Realizing the connection between his paper's former staff member and Nash, the reporter squirmed and looked at his feet.

'I am pleased to say that we also have a suspect in custody who has been charged with the recent spate of sneak-in burglaries and knife-point muggings in and around Helmsdale,' Fleming announced. 'A considerable amount of stolen property has been recovered from the man's home.'

The pressmen wanted to know what progress was being made on the murder cases and here both officers had to admit they didn't, at that point, have any good news to report.

'However, there still remain several lines of enquiry to follow up,' Fleming stated, 'lines that look promising.'

The vague nature of her remarks left the reporters baying for clarification. O'Donnell intervened. 'You will have to be patient a little while longer to avoid prejudicing the effectiveness of my officers' inquiries. I'm aware that you're all as keen as we are to see the guilty parties arrested, if only to enable you to serialize their partners' memoirs in your Sunday editions.'

The pressmen laughed at the chief constable's remarks, which signalled the end of the briefing. O'Donnell didn't consider herself to be any sort of prophet, but she was to remember her closing remarks when reading one of the more lurid Sunday tabloids several months later.

* * *

The next morning's edition of the *Netherdale Gazette* devoted several columns to the media conference and the background to the various aspects of both the chief constable and Fleming's statements, which was only natural, as these were the most important local news items they had covered in months. Their staff photographer's images of the derelict house and the sad procession of bodies being carried from it, together with smaller photos of the picnic site and the scene of PC Riley's murder were vivid reminders of what their reporter referred to as the surge in violent crime that had beset their normally tranquil region.

At Morag Caravan Park, Ivan Kovac was incandescent with rage. Stanley had presented him with a copy of the paper and although there was no mention of any of the arrested men by name, he knew from Stanley that Patrick Newsome and Lee Machin had been detained. Kovac also knew beyond doubt that his distribution network had been severely damaged, possibly beyond repair. His kneejerk reaction was unequivocal. 'Stanley, I want you visit each of our dealers, find out who hasn't landed in jail and find out who's been talking out of turn. In the meantime, I'm going to check everyone staying on the park. I need to know how the police suddenly got clever enough to start arresting our people. I want you back by lunchtime so get moving. Oh, and one other thing. If you find out someone has been talking out of turn, deal with them. If it's someone here, you can help me find out what else they know.'

* * *

For the people staying in the motorhome parked on stand thirty-four, early breakfast was a leisurely affair. A dinner plate piled high with croissants sat on the centre of the small table 'We need to visit the site shop today. Although I don't for one minute think they'll stock any of these.'

'You never know your luck.' He turned from watching through the window as the site came to life. 'These places must get a fair number of visitors from the continent. What else are we short of?'

'Milk, butter and fruit are the main items, although if we can't get croissants, we'll need bacon, eggs and bread. The milk is running out because you insist on coffee that's milkier than latte even.'

'Do you want me to go?'

'No, I'll take my time and have a scout about while I'm out.'

'How long will we stay here for?' Shakila looked from one to the other for a reply.

'That's not easy to say. As long as we need to be here, we just stay put. It might happen today. If a delivery arrives, that'll be it; we can leave. On the other hand, we could be here another week.'

'And what about afterwards? After we leave here? What will happen to me? Suppose the man on the boat saw me, he would know I can identify him. Suppose he comes looking for me, to shoot me like my friends.'

'I told you, it will be taken care of.'

She wasn't convinced. Why were they keeping her with them? Would they really let her go when their business here was over? She stared out of the window, her attention not really on the scene outside. A movement in her peripheral vision caused her to turn her head slightly. As she did, the man walking down the line of parked mobile and static caravans came into plain view. She stared at him in disbelief then gasped; a sound that was half-sigh, half-muted scream, all terror.

'What is it? What's wrong?'

'That man there!' The girl pointed. They all looked out of the window, but the man, if there had been one, had vanished behind a caravan. They waited, but no one reappeared. 'He was there, I tell you. He was walking that way.' She pointed towards the shop and the reception lodge. 'I wasn't dreaming. I did see him.'

'OK, so you saw someone you thought you recognized.'

'How could she? She doesn't know anyone in England.'

'You don't understand. It was him: the man from the boat. The man who shot my friends.'

The two looked at one another. 'I believe you,' one of the men said as he glanced up at his partner. 'The thing we have to decide is what we're going to do about it.'

'I'll text the boss. Let him know he's on site.'

* * *

Elsewhere, the article in the *Gazette* was scrutinized closely, but even more interest was taken in the local radio and TV bulletins that contained a report of bodies found in a cabin cruiser that had sunk off the North Yorkshire coast.

Tony Hartley had known his shipment of drugs would be hijacked, one of the benefits of having bugged the opposition's office. The news of the addicts' deaths at the squat following his arranging for the adulteration of the consignment was unfortunate, casualties of war, as was the murder of the couple on the boat who had carried the deadly cargo. What was more important was the continued escalation in the conflict between his group and the gang controlled by Kovac. The time had come to end all that. End it in the only way Hartley knew how. He called the sergeant into his office. 'Have you seen this?' He pointed to the newspaper.

Ron Mason glanced at the headline. 'I have. And I've heard the local radio. What are you going to do about it?'

Hartley knew it was more than a simple question; it was a challenge, a test of his determination. 'I was thinking, we ought to stop this once and for all.'

'How do you plan to do that? Sit round a table and draw lines on a map; launch a takeover bid perhaps?'

Hartley shook his head. 'I was thinking of something a little more direct, a little more radical. I've already got someone snooping around, now tell me, how much do you know about country life?'

Mason shrugged. 'About as much as the next bloke, I guess.'

'Do you know, for example, how you go about killing chickens?'

'You chop their heads off, and then . . . Oh, I get you.'

'Yes, once the head is chopped off, the chicken runs around a bit, if allowed to, then dies. Have you still got that pea-shooter of yours?'

Mason grinned at Hartley's description of his highly sophisticated and extremely expensive sniper's rifle. 'I do, and I've plenty of peas too.'

'Right, you know the targets, and you know their location. Execute!'

* * *

Stanley had finished his visits to the dealers. Apart from those now occupying cells provided for them by the local police, all their contacts were in place, and even when faced by the threat of Stanley's unique brand of persuasive tactics, could shed no light on how their organization might have been blown. As he returned to Broughton-Le-Helm, he was forced to the conclusion that the source of the information leak had to be from within the park.

He was so deep in thought that he failed to notice the vehicle that followed him up the little-used country lane that provided a short cut to the caravan park. Stanley took this route, although it was several miles longer than the main road, to avoid getting stuck behind caravans that would slow his progress.

He had almost reached the caravan park before the car behind his turned off, to take an even quieter road; one that circled the top side of the park, before wending its way across the head of the dale towards Black Fell.

If Stanley was oblivious to the presence of another vehicle, Ron Mason, who was driving close behind him, was just as ignorant of the identity of the driver ahead. His objective was to seek out the best place to position himself for the job he had been tasked with; to kill the two men heading up the gang that was causing them so much trouble. It was ironic that this would be the closest he would come to the man he had been told to eliminate.

Stanley reached the site, parked alongside the office, and walked in. 'I've checked everyone, all our contacts. Nobody knows anything more about the arrests,' he told Kovac. 'Two of our drivers have been nicked, a couple more I couldn't find, maybe they're in the cells. None of our dealers had the faintest idea how word got out, not even when I threatened them. So I think the leak must have come from here in the park. Which is interesting, because apart from us, there's nobody else here who could have told the police, or is there?'

'If you mean anyone resident or working here on a permanent basis, I agree. However, I've been talking to the receptionist. I asked him about visitors to the site, and he told me something I found very interesting. I was waiting for you to get back, I think you should come and look at the CCTV tape.'

* * *

Jackie Fleming was sitting with Clara in Nash's office, reviewing the evidence files they had compiled when the phone rang. She answered and listened for some time before replying. 'Very well, ma'am, Clara and Viv are here at the moment, we'll move out straightaway.'

She replaced the receiver. 'That was the chief. She's had an urgent call from the DIU. Their undercover officer is at Morag Caravan Park following up on the lead supplied by Viv and Lisa. Apparently the officer requires urgent assistance. There's a double ARU team already en route along with a Territorial Support Group from York, and the chief wants us to head there immediately. We've to expect extreme resistance as it's believed the people identified are extremely dangerous. I want everyone in flak jackets and you'd better have paramedics on standby.'

CHAPTER TWENTY-FOUR

Outside the entrance to the caravan park Fleming deployed the members of the various teams. 'I want one ARU team inside the park with me. Clara, I want you to take the other armed officers and secure the perimeter.'

Mironova looked disappointed, but Fleming insisted. 'From what little the chief told me, this could be extremely dangerous, so it would be rash to have both senior officers in close proximity. Now,' she turned to the TSG leader. 'I want you to leave one of your men on the gate with DC Pearce. Nobody enters or leaves — clear? Fortunately, most of the tourists will be off site at this time of day. The rest of you, inside the park with us. Armed officers go first, spread out, and the minute you see anyone acting remotely suspicious, detain and restrain, OK?'

The caravan park was on a hillside. That in itself was not remarkable, given the location of Broughton-Le-Helm at the head of the dale. Although this had severe disadvantages, these were outweighed by the spectacular views of some of the most picturesque scenery in the whole county.

One of the advantages the gradient provided was the excellent field of vision provided for a marksman. Settling down into the bracken overlooking the park, one such officer from the ARU team had a clear sight of anything and everything that moved. He wriggled a little to make himself more comfortable and used the telescopic sight on his weapon to get a closer view of the scene. For a few moments he noticed nothing of interest until a slight movement to one side, almost at the periphery of the lens, attracted his attention. He refocused on the place he had identified and stared at what was there for several moments.

'Well, well, well,' he said after a while, 'what's this all about, then?' The officer wasn't renowned for talking to himself, but with no one else within a quarter of a mile, this may have been an exception. As he continued his surveillance of the man he had seen, something about his posture struck him as unnatural. He adjusted the focus again, and this time was able to make out what the man was holding. A rifle! And he too was settled into an optimum position for firing, directly at one of the motor homes. This was certainly unexpected. The ability to react to rapidly changing situations had been an essential part of his training. He could almost hear his tutor's voice echoing in his ear, 'It's what marks the professional out from the amateur'.

That was all very well, in theory, and on a range where the targets were dummies, not living, breathing people. It was vastly different in practice, on a deserted hillside. Here, choosing the right course of action was essential. He waited for a moment, then pressed a button on his radio. He began to talk, his voice little more than a whisper. He prefaced his remarks with a warning. 'I don't want you to reply to or acknowledge this. Do nothing that would give my position away. I'm on the hill above the camp. I need backup; now!'

* * *

Inside the motorhome, a mobile rang. It was answered with protests at some of what the caller was saying. 'But we haven't finished here. It could still be tricky.' It seemed that the protests were falling on deaf ears for the call was ended with a reluctant statement of acceptance. At that moment the door burst open. The man framed by the doorway was a stranger — to two of them at least. The intruder quelled any protest at this invasion of privacy by waving a pistol at them as he stepped inside.

Hard on his heels, a second man entered. His appearance was less threatening, the only object he carried being a roll of duct tape. The holster on his belt and the tool therein hardly seemed dangerous, at that point.

'I own this site,' the gunman explained, 'and I make it my business to ensure all visitors to Morag Caravan Park have everything they need.' As Ivan Kovac spoke, he gestured to the man by the window to sit down.

Obedience was compulsory. He returned to his place; his arm slipped protectively around the young woman's shoulder.

'So when my receptionist told me someone had booked in, I thought I'd better come over and greet you. Especially after my colleague here' — he indicated Stanley — 'was able to confirm that someone he'd seen a few weeks ago was in the site shop this morning. I simply had to satisfy my curiosity about such a strange coincidence. By the way, I feel I ought to apologize for not introducing him earlier. This is Stanley. To be fair, that's only a nickname. Show them how you got the name.'

Stanley produced his trademark knife and laid it on the table, extending the blade as he did so. If the sight of the blade alarmed them, the expression on his face chilled them to the bone. All three stared at it. Their faces left no doubt they could guess that, however he used the knife, it wasn't going to be good news for them.

'Now, Stanley is going to bind your wrists and ankles with tape. He is also going to use it to gag two of you. Please don't attempt to resist, as a bullet often offends.'

* * *

On the hillside, Ron Mason had been watching for some time before he spotted the men he was after. He watched

Kovac and Stanley disappear round the side of a motorhome. Now, he was puzzled, had been since he saw Kovac striding across the caravan park carrying a pistol. Why did Kovac feel he needed to carry a gun on what was his home ground? If he felt safe anywhere, surely Kovac would be secure in the middle of his own property. Using his telescopic sight, Mason watched through the large side window that was directly facing him as the two men moved into the motorhome. He wondered what the owners had done to offend Kovac. Hartley had told him he had a man on site, the Soldier must be inside. No matter, from where Mason was he could relieve the occupants of at least one of their tormentors, possibly two. He was unable to see Kovac clearly, but he could take Stanley out and with luck that would force Kovac out into the open; then he could finish the job.

Behind him the officer was watching; saw the movement as Mason looked to be taking aim. He whispered into his radio again.

Jackie Fleming reacted; all the radios sprang to life. 'Our target is one of the motorhomes. Stand thirty-four!'

* * *

Mason's attention was totally focused on his field of fire, to the exclusion of all else. Nor did he bother to look behind him. He didn't for one minute think anyone else would be on that hillside. He lined up the shot. Sniping is, at best, an inexact science. Too many variables stand in the way of a higher success rate. The long-range accounts for most of these. Invariably, the target being human, their behaviour can influence the outcome drastically. A sudden movement would be all it took to render a perfect shot harmless. Then again, a sudden gust of wind can affect the bullet's trajectory. Windage, they call it, and it is the sniper's curse. Last, but not least, an obstacle in the bullet's path can ruin his attempt.

In this instance, the range was not a problem, nor was there even a slight breeze, but there was an obstacle; a window. All he could do was hope that the bullet's velocity would be sufficient for it to maintain its original trajectory, even after encountering the glass. He lined up Stanley's heart in the cross hairs and squeezed the trigger, not once, but twice.

Stanley had stepped forward, duct tape in hand, when the window alongside him exploded. Kovac watched in horrified shock as Stanley slumped forward, blood spurting from a wound somewhere on his upper body. The sound of the first shot was still echoing in their ears, when they heard a second report. Instinctively, they ducked.

Mason had got both shots off but was uncertain how successful they had been. He waited, hoping for a reaction. But before he could see if that was going to happen, his attention was claimed by a sound from behind him. It was that of a human voice; the message it conveyed was stark. 'Armed police; drop your weapon and place your hands on your head.'

Mason looked round, saw the marksman was only a few yards away, saw he was standing in the classic firing pose, and weighed up the chances of his rifle against the officer's automatic weapon. At that short range there was no chance of the officer missing. The only question would be how many times Mason would be shot before he could lay hands on his rifle. He decided the odds were too long for him to chance a bet. As he obeyed the instructions, another armed officer appeared from one side, underlining the wisdom of Mason's decision. Within seconds, he had been handcuffed.

* * *

Kovac was completely unnerved. For a second, his mind flashed back to his childhood, to the hazard of war-torn, shell-ruined streets of his native country where an unseen marksman could take down anyone bold enough to hazard venturing forth; even if their need was desperate. His sister had been cut down by one such, the precious loaf of bread she had secured for her family still clutched in her hand. He froze, unable to move, paralyzed by fear.

Shakila was not aware of the English phrase, 'the last straw', but this latest outbreak of violence was enough for her. Bullied by her family, threatened with death and forced to flee for her life; then an unwilling witness to her friends being cut down on the boat; and now, her rescuers were under threat. Shakila lashed out with her foot and kicked hard — hard and accurately, sending the pistol spinning from Kovac's hand. Panic-stricken, he turned and thrust his way out of the motorhome. Ignoring the step, he jumped clear and began to run. The man he had been threatening gave chase, ignoring the protests and warnings of his partner.

Kovac headed straight for his office. In his blind panic, he had no clear idea where he was aiming for, as long as it was beyond the range of the sniper who had shot his deputy. He had almost reached his safe haven when he halted abruptly. The risk from the hillside sniper forgotten as he faced the new, more immediate and far more potent threat facing him.

A few yards to the rear, Kovac's pursuer had also stopped running. The instructions issued by one of the two armed police officers were terse, and to the point. They were reinforced by the automatic weapons pointed at them. Obeying these instructions, Kovac knelt on the ground before lying spread-eagled, face down on the grass that was still wet from the overnight dew. His pursuer followed suit and within seconds both men had been handcuffed.

Fleming's radio crackled. 'Two suspects detained and secured,' one of the officers reported. 'Vehicle secure. One casualty.'

She gestured for the uniformed men around her to approach. As they got close to the motorhome a young woman emerged with her hands on her head; her expression one of terror. She was closely followed by a second adult clad in jeans, checked shirt, and baseball cap. An armed officer's instructions were being ignored.

'I said hands on head,' the officer ordered.

There was a loud sigh as the baseball cap was removed to reveal a woman. She looked across the caravan park towards the office, then glanced at the police officers surrounding the motorhome. 'Who's in charge here?' she demanded.

Fleming looked at the speaker. 'Detective Superintendent Fleming. I'm in charge, and you are under arrest. Do as the officer says.'

The woman ignored her. Instead she pointed to the man who had been chasing Kovac. 'Kindly instruct your officers to release my partner,' she told Fleming. 'He isn't one of the gang.'

Before Fleming could act she heard Mironova's voice over her radio. 'The perimeter is secure and we've detained the shooter, complete with his rifle. We're entering the park now. I've detailed a couple of men to investigate a suspect vehicle parked on the other side of the hill. We think it might be the sniper's car.'

'Meet us by the site office,' Fleming told her. She turned to the TSG leader. 'Have you ordered the paramedics to the injured man?'

'On their way,' he replied.

'Now—' She turned to the woman from the motorhome and was about to question her further when, to her annoyance, she saw the woman attempting to use her mobile. 'Put that away! And when you can spare me a moment of your valuable time I want some questions answered,' Fleming snapped. Her irritation deepened as the woman raised one hand, commanding Fleming's silence.

'Get the phone off that woman,' Fleming ordered one of the officers as she turned away, striding angrily towards the office and the detained men. As she did so, she saw Mironova approaching.

'What's going on?' Clara asked.

At that moment, they were interrupted. 'Will you take those handcuffs off my partner immediately?' It was more of a demand than a request.

'Nobody gets released until I know exactly what the hell's going on around here,' Fleming snarled angrily.

The woman reached for her jeans pocket and the ARU officer raised his weapon. 'Hands where I can see them,' he ordered.

The woman sighed, exasperated. 'OK then. You get my ID out. Let me be perfectly blunt, Superintendent whatever-your-name-is, you aren't in charge here. I am! And if you have any doubts about that I suggest you refer to Chief Constable O'Donnell. And do it now!'

'Jackie,' the man on the ground called out, 'do as she says. I'll explain everything.'

Fleming and Mironova looked at each other, astonished and more than a little apprehensive. The voice was familiar — very familiar. This wasn't going quite as they'd planned.

Clara walked over and peered down at the prisoner. She gestured to the armed officer standing alongside him. 'Do as he says. Let him go. He's a police officer. But what the hell he's doing here is another question entirely. He's supposed to be on leave in France with his son.'

CHAPTER TWENTY-FIVE

Once the handcuffs had been removed, Nash rolled over and got to his feet. 'Thank you.' He nodded to the officer, then, to Mironova and Fleming's further surprise, he walked past them without a sideways glance and went to where his companions were standing. 'Are you OK, Alisha?' they heard him ask. 'And how about you, Shakila? Are you all right?'

The younger woman looked even more terrified. 'You are police?'

'It's all right, these are friends of mine. You're safe now. We are all police officers. I promised you that we would help you and I meant it. It's all over now, you're quite safe.' He slipped a reassuring arm around Shakila's shoulders. 'Jackie, Clara, I'd like you to meet Shakila. This extremely brave young lady is our star witness in a shooting.'

The detectives watched; their bemusement furthered when they saw the older woman put her hand on Nash's arm in a gesture that was almost a caress. 'We're both fine, Mike, but that phone call I took before this blew up means I have to leave immediately. There should be a car arriving any minute now. The French police have identified some suspects and a possible location in Brest and they want me there to liaise.' She glanced around. 'Anyway, we're done here. Can I leave you to sort this lot out? All that needs doing is tidying up the odds and ends, doing the paperwork, and taking care of Shakila, of course.'

'No problem,' Nash assured her.

Alisha turned to Shakila and hugged her. 'I'm sorry I must leave, but Mike will look after you. I promise. Without you we wouldn't have solved the case so quickly.'

As she was speaking one of the officers on the gate came on the radio. 'There's a car here from the DIU. The driver says he has instructions to collect a Mrs Nash and drive her to the airport.'

'Tell them I'll be there in a minute after I grab my bag.' Alisha instructed him. 'Walk with me, Mike.'

Nash looked across at his colleagues and saw the astonished speculation in their eyes. He managed to suppress a smile, turning away to speak to Shakila. 'Don't worry; I'll be back in a minute.'

He turned to leave and missed the words Clara mouthed to Jackie. 'Mrs Nash?' Nor did he see the helpless shrug that Fleming gave by way of a reply.

As they walked to the car, Alisha saw Nash grin, the humour of the situation unable to be contained any longer. 'What are you laughing at?' she asked.

'My colleagues. They're consumed with curiosity now having heard you described as Mrs Nash.'

'Come to that, so am I. Did I sleep through the ceremony?' Alisha asked.

'Well I had to sign us in as a married couple, didn't I? I wasn't sure who we could trust.'

'But why should that intrigue your team so much? Surely they'll realize it was part of the act?'

'Possibly, possibly not. Besides, I haven't told them yet that we're not married! When I do, they'll probably be wondering how far we carried the husband and wife act.'

'Oh, I see.' They had reached the car, and Alisha turned to him. Nash could see her eyes were alight with mischief. She glanced back and, sure enough, the detectives were staring in their direction. 'It would be a shame to disappoint them,' she murmured. 'It was great fun working with you again, Mike. Almost like old times in the Met.' She reached forward and kissed him, long and passionately. 'That should get the rumours going nicely.' She patted his arm and got into the car. 'I'll be back to give a statement as soon as the job allows.'

Nash waited until the car had disappeared from view then turned to walk back up the hill. Clara, who knew Nash better than most, thought he looked sad. She glanced at Fleming. 'Yes, I agree,' Clara told her.

'I haven't said anything.'

'No, but you were thinking it.'

For once, Clara had read Mike wrong. His expression wasn't sad, merely thoughtful. Whatever he'd expected from Alisha it wasn't a teasing farewell kiss.

* * *

Fleming signalled to the ARU team leader, who was waiting to report. 'We've removed the sniper we arrested on the hill-side, together with his weapon. We've run a DVLA check on the car we found. It's registered to a man by the name of Ronald Mason. He has form, but not in this country. When we gave the car the once-over we found something very interesting in the boot, so we've left it for CSI.'

'What did you find?' Fleming asked.

'An Indian club, the sort used by fitness fanatics. It was covered in what looked like dried blood. I thought you'd be interested, given the report about the men killed at that picnic site. I've suggested that CSI liaise with the garage to pull the vehicle in for detailed examination.'

'Good work,' Fleming thanked him and turned to Nash. 'Well, go on then,' she demanded. 'I think you owe both of us an explanation. Not least about "Mrs Nash".'

Nash shrugged his shoulders. 'It was a deception operation. We were tasked with finding where the drugs coming into our area were entering the UK. DIU knew, from information received, that the North Yorkshire coast was the entry point, but weren't sure exactly where and how they were getting inland from the coast. I was co-opted to help Alisha. We posed as a married couple acting as tourists in the motorhome. That meant we could drive up and down the coast at will as information was passed to us and investigate without attracting suspicion.'

'Where did you get the vehicle from?' Clara asked.

'I borrowed it from a friend. The Range Rover's in their garage.'

'Friend?' Clara muttered acidly. 'I didn't know you had any.'

Nash ignored the barb and signalled Shakila to come and join them. 'What we didn't bargain on was this young lady. 'Clara, Jackie, I told you that Shakila is very brave, and I think you'll agree that she had to be in view of what happened. Shakila was on board the vessel, Blooming Rose, in the North Sea when the owners were shot. She was a witness to the murders *and* saw the killer. This morning she spotted Ivan Kovac on site here and identified him as the man who committed the murders; which is when Alisha texted for backup. You arrived in the nick of time.' Their eyes widened as Nash told them the rest of the youngster's story. 'Shakila's details and involvement have already been given to the chief; I had to spell it out for her — literally. She has arranged a protection order for her and is fully aware of what's been happening. In exchange for her evidence and, because of her special circumstances, the chief has already obtained the Home Secretary's permission to grant Shakila permanent asylum is England.'

'If the chief constable is fully aware of what's happening that is more than I am,' Clara muttered crossly.

Nash ignored her for a moment. 'We need to run a ballistics test on that pistol of Kovac's. It's inside the caravan; Shakila kicked it out of his hand. I told you she was brave. I think the weapon will prove to be the same one that was used in those shootings on the boat.'

‘So all this time when we thought you were on leave, you were working.’ Jackie smiled. ‘No wonder the chief wouldn’t let me ask you to come back.’

‘Yes, we thought you’d taken Daniel off to France on an extended holiday to get over the news about Becky,’ Clara added.

Nash looked from one to the other of them. ‘What date is it?’ he asked, suddenly looking alarmed. ‘You lose track of time in one of those things.’ He gestured to the motorhome.

Fleming glanced at her watch and told him. ‘I wonder,’ Nash said, ‘with a bit of luck I might just be able to save my reputation. Excuse me for a minute, will you?’ He wandered away and they could see he was using his mobile.

Fleming turned to Mironova. ‘I’m going to supervise the transfer of the arrested men. As the cells at Helmsdale are full, I’ll send them to Netherdale. That way, not only can I interview them, but I can also get the chief constable to give me a full briefing about what Nash and this DIU woman have been up to. It will be nice to find out exactly what’s been going on. Will you see to the crime scene? Once CSI have finished with the motorhome, get Pearce and the TSG to help you go through the office of that guy, Kovac. I understand he’s the park owner. From what little the chief told me, she believes the DIU think he’s the head of one of the drugs gangs, so you should ask CSI to do a chemical sweep as well. I want every building searched, shop, storerooms, everything. Get TSG to bag all the paperwork and you can take it back to Helmsdale. I want to know what else this guy is into and what contacts he has. The same with any mobiles you come across. I want names and addresses of everyone on this site. Nobody leaves or enters, until we’ve finished. I’ll get the team on the gate to ensure that.’ Fleming paused. For breath? Clara wondered.

‘Sorry,’ Jackie apologized. ‘I should know better. You know what to do just as well as I do. I’ve also got to sort out this bloke called Stanley. We’ll have to get some proper identification and charge him.’

Fleming was busy with the prisoners when Nash returned. 'What's going on?' he asked.

Clara told him.

'Oh, good.' He smiled. 'She can give me, I mean us, a lift.' He gestured to Shakila, who was waiting uncertainly nearby.

'Mike, will you please explain what's going on?'

Nash smiled. 'Tomorrow afternoon,' he told her. 'It will all become clear then. Now I really do have to go.'

Clara watched the vans containing the prisoners leave. The wounded man was already en route to hospital under guard and, with the departure of the escorting officers, her forces were depleted. The forensic officers and the TSG team were now tasked with searching Kovac's office; she and Viv, along with two uniformed officers, were the only ones left on site.

As they awaited the completion of the CSI search, the officers spoke to the residents of the static caravans and interviewed members of the caravan park staff. These were the receptionist, the employees in the shop and cafe, and a couple of cleaners whose principal task was to care for some of the vans that were hired out. None of the employees was able to add anything to their less than adequate store of knowledge about the park owner's activities.

It was well into the evening before the scientific officers had completed their initial work. The team leader, reporting to Clara, told her they had found no drugs on the premises, although there were traces that indicated heroin had been stored at some point in a cupboard within the caravan used as an office. Clara and Viv accepted the evidence bags containing all the paperwork and the laptop from the leader of the TSG team. 'You might be interested in this,' he said as he handed Clara a small evidence bag.

She squinted at the tiny object inside. 'What is it?'

'Some sort of bugging device, I think. But forensics will confirm it. It was secreted on the underside of the desk. Someone else must have been curious as to what was happening here as well as you,' he suggested, before he headed back to the team's van.

'Let's get this lot back to the office and then go home. You can drop that device in at Netherdale on your way, please, Viv.'

'No problem. It's a good job there wasn't too much paper to sort through,' Viv suggested as he watched Clara lock the door. 'This guy obviously didn't trust people around him enough to commit himself to hard copies. There was a shredder in there too, and it looked to have been very well used.'

Clara handed the key to the uniformed officer charged with guarding the caravan overnight, and the detectives set off back to Helmsdale where they got a pleasant surprise. At Jackie's urgent request, Lisa Andrews had been called in from her day off. She had already begun preparing and collating reports.

'Jackie said to tell you neither Kovac nor Mason will say anything, beyond giving their names. Apparently, according to what Jackie said, they're not called Kovac or Mason. They're both called "no comment", which Jackie wasn't happy about. The other thing she mentioned was about Mr "No Comment" Mason. His driving licence shows he lives in Nottingham and to the best of our knowledge he has absolutely no connection with anyone from this part of the country, and yet, as soon as he got to Netherdale he demanded to speak to his solicitor. He gave the name and recited the local phone number without being prompted or needing a phone book. It transpires he uses the same practice as our fishermen friends.'

As with the earlier arrests of the drivers of the fish vans, as soon as Ron Mason had spoken to his solicitor, news of his detention reached Tony Hartley only minutes after the call. But Hartley already knew this from his man employed as a seasonal worker on site. Within half an hour of hearing this, just as Mason was greeting his legal representative, Hartley was locking the door to his operational premises for the final time. As he walked over to his car, the only evidence of his involvement lay inside the laptop he was carrying.

Leaving the premises hadn't been a panic measure, more the action of a well-trained and careful man. Tony Hartley was certain Ron Mason wouldn't talk and his men, playing the part of the fish salesmen who handled distribution, had been well paid to keep silent, but he still felt the move to be a wise precaution. Later that night at a pre-arranged time, he reported the development in a series of text messages to his boss, Major Simon Wardle. In the privacy of his solitary confinement cell at Felling Prison, Wardle read the messages, then deleted them. News of the collapse of the drugs business was softened by the profit Hartley reported.

The money Hartley had amassed was now sufficient to put into operation the next stage towards their ultimate objective; managing Wardle's escape from prison. Another text message indicated that plans for this were reaching an advanced stage, and that Hartley should be able to report developments within the next couple of days. He hoped he would be able to put the plan into operation in three weeks time.

CHAPTER TWENTY-SIX

It was turned midnight by the time Clara got home; she was exhausted. The message light was flashing on her phone and her spirits lifted when she listened to her voicemail and the news conveyed by the cheerful voice of David's father. The reports were encouraging; David should be flown home in three days time when the next transport was available. Although he would be in hospital for a while and might need a reconstructive procedure on his shoulder, at least they would all be able to visit him.

Early next morning, on her arrival at Helmsdale, Lisa and Pearce asked her where Nash was.

'How should I know? Probably in France, where he ought to have been in the first place.'

The others thought it wise to keep quiet and asked instead what she had planned for them to do that day.

'We ought to make a start logging the evidence we removed from the caravan park, I suppose.' The lack of enthusiasm in her voice was obvious.

'What about that industrial unit?' Lisa asked. 'Shouldn't we take a look at that?'

Clara's expression grew instantly more cheerful. 'Of course we should, and thanks for reminding me, Lisa. The paperwork can wait. That job has been delayed long enough.'

The key on Patrick Newsome's key ring turned easily in the lock, confirming Jimmy the locksmith's assertion that this was the unit. Clara pushed the frosted glass door open, reflecting that she felt as if she was acting out a scene from Groundhog Day. It had only been days since they had entered just such a unit albeit, this one was much larger.

She waited, but no alarm sounded so she stepped over the threshold. She was inside a miniscule reception area, on one side of which was an equally tiny office. The other side led to the warehouse, or storage area, or whatever went on in the main body of the building. She signalled to the others that, before opening the inner door, she was going to check the office first.

The office barely lived up to its name. Apart from the counter below the sliding glass reception window, under which was a double deck of shelves, the room was completely empty. Lisa had joined her in the small room, leaving Pearce watching from the doorway. 'Look there.' Lisa pointed to the shelves. 'Was Newsome running a used car dealership?'

On the upper shelf was a series of sets of vehicle number plates, with alternating background colours of white and yellow. 'Nothing so upright and honest,' Clara replied. 'Viv?' She signalled Pearce to join them.

He squeezed apologetically past Lisa and looked at the display. 'What do you reckon? Ringers, perhaps?' he suggested. 'Do you want me to check them out?'

He pulled his mobile from his pocket. 'Do so,' Clara told him, 'and while you're doing that, we'll see what's through here.'

With Lisa watching over her shoulder, she opened the door into the warehouse. Both of them blinked in surprise. 'That's about the last thing I thought we'd find,' Clara muttered.

The vast majority of the space was occupied by a large commercial vehicle. The livery and signage proclaimed it to be the property of a well-known local firm of livestock transporters. In common with the firm's other vehicles, the body had been adapted to carry sheep or cattle. 'There's another van, behind it.' Lisa pointed to the rear of the wagon.

As Clara looked across, she recalled the expression, 'domino effect'. She had never experienced it before. However, as she looked from the wagon to the Transit van she recalled something in Pearce's report from the Patrick Newsome arrest and ideas tumbled into one another in her brain, leading to a solution. 'A cattle truck and a van. And Newsome owns a dog,' she muttered.

Lisa was mystified to begin with. 'What?'

'Viv, can you come through here a minute,' Clara called out.

'You rang, m'lady,' he intoned in the manner of a butler.

'In your report on the Newsome arrest you mentioned a dog. What breed was it, do you remember?'

'A Border Collie. Why, is it important?'

As he spoke, he looked past Mironova, to the wagon, the van, and the significance of the question hit him, at about the same time as Lisa made the connection. 'Hell's Bells!'

Lisa walked to the back of the unit and peered down the side of the van. She could just make out a tall oblong shape in the far corner. Standing about five feet high, it's grey metal surface contrasting sharply with the whitewashed wall against which it was fixed. She recognized it immediately. 'There's something here you ought to see.'

The others joined her. If further proof was needed, this was it. Although they had no definite facts to support their theory, the circumstantial evidence was overwhelming. The presence of a gun cabinet was the last link. 'Patrick,' Clara muttered, 'I think you've got some explaining to do.'

She turned to Lisa and Viv. 'We'd better leave here immediately. Try not to touch anything on your way out. I'll phone Jackie as soon as we get outside and ask her to get a CSI team here as fast as possible. If that gun cabinet contains what I think it does, Mr Newsome senior will have a whole new charge sheet dedicated to him, ranging from murder downwards.'

As they waited, Clara instructed Pearce to check with the haulier whose logo was on the cattle wagon.

'It's a ringer, sure enough,' he reported. 'The real one is a Scania, not a Volvo *and* I spoke to the driver. He's on the outskirts of Kelso at the moment, having collected a dozen Highland cattle from somewhere unpronounceable and is ferrying them to a farm at the far side of York. He seemed to take it as a personal insult that his wagon had been cloned.'

As he was speaking, Jackie Fleming's car pulled into the car park, closely followed by a van marked 'CSI'.

'I didn't want to miss the fun,' Jackie commented as she got out.

After they had instructed the team leader, Pearce told them the result of his check into the van's registration details. 'That's an even more radical change. The number actually belongs to a double-decker bus that, according to the company's route manager, should be approaching Leeds city centre at the moment.'

'They're not short of imagination, you have to give them that,' Clara commented. She explained to Fleming what Pearce was referring to, and added, 'the vehicle identification number, can't be changed though, so once our specialists get their hands on them we'll be able to find their true identity.'

They watched the CSI team at work with interest. Jackie indicated the wagon. 'When you look at it closely, the paint job isn't brilliant, nor is the signwriting.'

'True, but close enough to pass at a casual glance, especially at night, which is the only time I suspect this wagon was on the road.'

'I suppose it makes more sense to use a vehicle with some sort of livery than an unmarked one. And you'd expect livestock transporters to be transporting livestock.'

'I've asked Viv to make a note of all the other numbers on the plates in the office and check them out later. It'll be interesting to see what he comes up with.'

'We're ready to move the wagon,' the team leader informed them. 'Do you want to know what we've found so far, or wait until we've finished on the Transit?'

‘I think we’ll have it all in one go,’ Fleming told him. They watched the forensic officers descend on the van and then Jackie turned to Mironova. ‘The chief wanted to hold a media conference today, but in the end I persuaded her to hold off until we knew what you’d found in here. It was a gamble, there might have been nothing of any importance, but it’s beginning to look like a wise decision. The impact of passing all the news in one go will be far greater.’

It was a good hour before the forensic team announced that they were ready to move the van. ‘Here’s what we have so far. There were two sets of prints in the Scania, identified by our magic machines, as belonging to Patrick and Dwayne Newsome. The same prints are in the cab of the Transit. We also collected what we believe to be dog hairs from the cabs of both vehicles. There was also some animal hair in the back of the Transit, but from what I could tell without a microscope, I’d guess it isn’t canine. Considerable amounts of it, some of which was stuck to what we think are dried bloodstains. We may even be able to match the tyre prints. And that’s about the size of it; apart from a few sweet wrappers and a sandwich carton. Oh, there was also a piece of sticky paper on the foot-well of the van, driver’s side that might be of interest. I think it may be a label of some sort, although it could just as easily be a parking ticket, or the price sticker off the sandwiches. Again, we’ll know more when we get back to the lab. Now, we’re going to have a look at the cabinet.’

Clara frowned, something the officer had mentioned rang a bell with her, but she couldn’t remember why at that moment.

Of the two bronze keys on the ring, the first wouldn’t go into the upper lock and Jackie looked sharply at Lisa, who had maintained all along that these were keys from a gun cabinet. ‘Try the other one,’ Lisa said. ‘The locks have to be different to comply with firearms regulations.’ She smiled at Clara who acknowledged that Lisa living the country life with forester Alan Marshall had its advantages.

Seconds later the officers were staring at the contents. The shelf near the top was stacked with ammunition boxes.

The rack below held two twelve-bore over-and-under shotguns, but the weapon that gripped their attention was a large calibre hunting rifle. Ideal for bringing down a deer: or an equally defenceless police officer.

'I want to know whose fingerprints are on that weapon and I want a ballistics test carried out, using the ammunition on that shelf,' Jackie told the officer. 'If it was the weapon used to kill PC Riley, I want there to be absolutely no chance of the evidence being challenged by some smart-arsed defence counsel. And I want all the reports from in here ASAP.'

'That could take a while.'

'In that case' — Fleming smiled at him, sweetly — 'don't let me detain you. The sooner you get started, the better.'

'I just wish we'd found something to show where Newsome took the livestock. It would be nice to nail the receivers as well,' Clara said.

'Patience, Clara. Let's be fair, we've made enormous progress today. If the tests come back positive, we've got Patrick and Dwayne Newsome in the frame for murder. Apart from the clear-up rate and the PR benefit, that will be a huge morale boost for the force. And, who knows, if we get lucky some more evidence will turn up, or one of the Newsomes will talk.'

As there was little they could do about the discoveries at the industrial unit until they had word back from forensics, the detectives returned to Helmsdale station and started to collate the evidence retrieved from the caravan park. There was only one message, which was from Nash, to tell them he'd been delayed, and wouldn't be able to get back to the office until the following day.

* * *

When Clara arrived at the station next morning the phone in the CID suite was ringing. The caller was Jackie Fleming and Clara could tell by the excited tone in her voice that the news was good.

'CSI have just been on. The hairs in both vehicle cabs are canine. Those in the back of the Transit and the bloodstains are from deer. The rifle has been tested and the ballistics officer confirms a definite match. That is the rifle that was used to kill PC Riley, and Patrick Newsome's prints are all over it. In addition, the hair we removed from Dwayne Newsome's hoodie when he was arrested has been identified as being from a fallow deer.'

She paused and then added, 'I've also had news about our shot man from the caravan park.'

'Stanley?' Clara asked.

'Yes, his fingerprints have been matched to one, Terrence Blake. Vanished off the radar years ago. Wanted by several forces in connection with some of the ugliest knife work around. Many of his victims were lucky to survive, if lucky is the right word when you see the mess he made of their faces.'

'That sounds like game, set, and match.'

'I agree; the only thing we haven't resolved is that piece of paper. You remember, the one off the floor of the van? Apparently it's some sort of packing label. The initials on it are KMP, but what that stands for, I've no idea.

'KMP? No, it means nothing to me either.'

Clara was in the general office and as she spoke Lisa Andrews looked up from the report she was typing. 'Did you say KMP?' Lisa asked.

Clara nodded. 'Hang on, Jackie; I think Lisa wants to tell me something.'

'Could it be Kovac Meat Packers? I found some invoices with their letterhead in amongst the stuff from the caravan park. They're based in Leeds, but I couldn't see any connection to the drugs business.'

'Maybe not, but there is a connection to the theft of sheep, the poaching of deer and the murder of PC Riley.' Clara relayed Lisa's comments. 'I think we might need even more charge sheets for Patrick Newsome and Ivan Kovac.'

'Dwayne Newsome as well,' Jackie told her. 'His prints were also found in both vehicles. We now have that hair sample *and* it would take two men to lift a fully grown deer into that van.'

It was strange, Clara thought. Of the two men being charged, she would have believed Dwayne far more capable of committing a cold-blooded murder than Patrick. And yet the evidence pointed clearly to the father's guilt . . .

Anyone less murderous in appearance, Clara couldn't imagine. Patrick looked so ordinary. Then she remembered something Nash had said a long time ago. 'How many times have you heard friends or neighbours being interviewed and saying, what a nice man he was, polite, quiet, considerate and helpful? As if they expect all murderers to have fangs, two heads and to go around with blood dripping from their clothing.'

At this moment, Patrick Newsome looked downcast; more than that, he looked thoroughly miserable. He nodded acceptance of the charges and turned away to confront his son, who was awaiting his turn. The sight of Dwayne seemed to depress Patrick all the more. It was no part of Clara's job description to cheer up accused men, but she was unable to restrain herself on this occasion. 'About the only good news to come out of this whole sorry mess, Patrick, is that if you're found guilty of all the charges against you, the sentence will be so long that by the time you're released from jail, Eileen might have got around to forgiving you for sleeping with Sharon.'

Newsome gave her a sour look. 'You think so? You really believe that Eileen will forgive me? Where's the good news in that?'

Clara headed back to CID reflecting on the Newsome family who had turned out to be more than a mere nuisance and the satisfaction Maureen Riley would feel in knowing she had helped to catch her husband's killers.

CHAPTER TWENTY-SEVEN

Clara asked Jackie if she could take a week's leave with effect from the following Monday. She explained about David's return and the likelihood that he would be in a Birmingham hospital for some time. Having received a conditional acceptance from Fleming, Clara walked back into Nash's office to attempt more paperwork.

It was lunchtime and once more it was Pearce's turn to collect the sandwiches. He was walking back across the car park when Nash's car pulled in. Pearce watched Nash get out. He was surprised when the second occupant of the car emerged and, when the third climbed out, only a smart piece of fielding on his part saved Lisa's egg mayonnaise sandwich from disaster. Pearce stared at the trio in astonishment.

Clara was in the kitchen making coffee. She carried the brew into the CID suite and set it down on Lisa's desk. It was as well she did, for at that moment, a small tornado in the shape of Daniel Nash burst into the room and, with cries of 'Aunt Clara', rushed across and hugged her tight.

'Daniel,' she exclaimed, 'where have you come from? I thought you were in France?'

'Yes, I was. But when Papa phoned yesterday, we caught a flight and he picked us up from the airport this morning. Now we can go to the test match.'

Clara looked up to see Nash walk in. He was accompanied by an extremely attractive woman. A woman Clara recognized immediately, although her hair had been quite different in the photograph Clara had seen recently. The photograph in the *Netherdale Gazette* that accompanied the announcement of her 'presumed death by drowning'.

Clara stared at her, dumbfounded. 'Becky? Becky Pollard? What's going on?'

Nash answered for her. 'Sorry, Clara, everything that happened at the caravan park was such a rush that I didn't have chance to explain. I hope it isn't too big a shock.'

As he was speaking, the chief constable entered, followed by Jackie Fleming. Pearce was dispatched to organize more coffee and when they had all been supplied, chairs were dragged up for everyone.

Nash excused himself and took Daniel downstairs to reception. 'Can you lock this young villain up, Jack' — he grinned — 'in one of those nice new patrol cars? Show him how all the sirens and things work while I tell the others what's been happening.'

'No problem, Mike, leave him with me and if he gets bored, I know where the ice cream is; just across the road in the sweet shop.'

Nash returned to CID as O'Donnell answered her mobile. As soon as she had finished, she looked across at Nash. 'Before we explain to everyone what's been going on, that call was from the DI investigating what I understand is being referred to in the press as the "lobsterpot murder". He said that thanks to the information you and Alisha supplied about what boats were missing from the harbour that night, they've arrested two fishermen. One of them has confessed. He's identified the man we have in custody, Ronald Mason, as the one who struck the blow that killed the fisherman. So that seems to have been cleared up satisfactorily.'

She turned to the assembled team. 'And now, I guess you're looking for some explanations. I know the strain this inquiry has put you all under, but once you know the facts I think you will appreciate why you were kept in the dark about certain facets of the investigation. Becky, I think you should tell everyone how this all started.'

Becky took a deep breath and began. 'An old school friend of mine, Aimee, turned up in London at the offices of the newspaper. To be honest, I didn't recognize her at first. We joined school on the same day and became friends, but she left before I did. She was a lovely girl but frail.' Becky paused. 'No, frail isn't the right word, perhaps fragile would be more like it, both mentally and physically. We shared a dorm for years, sat next to one another in class; visited each other during school holidays, all the usual things. But although Aimee was a good, close friend, I wasn't blind to her weaknesses. I could spot good and bad in people, but Aimee was easily led, sometimes with disastrous consequences. Boys were one of Aimee's weaknesses and a lack of will power was another. Sometimes, I thought she was too afraid of offending someone to say no to them.

'Aimee wasn't academically inclined. I went on to university, so we more or less lost touch. I hadn't heard from her for years, but then, she turned up out of the blue. She was pitifully thin; the cotton dress she wore was hanging off her. With gaunt, hollow cheeks she looked haggard, and her posture was like an old woman's.'

They all waited, shocked by Becky's distress, which spoke even louder than her words. 'I took her to the nearest coffee shop and began to drag her story out of her. It wasn't easy. She'd spotted my name on an article in the paper and came to London specifically to see me. Now that she'd arrived, she was reluctant to tell me what was wrong. I think she had some romantic notion that I could make everything right for her. If she could just see her friend maybe that would bring her the justice she was seeking. Or maybe she believed I could wave a magic wand. All she would tell me was that she was broke and in the power of an evil man, a drug baron who had become her boyfriend. He'd seduced her with his fancy lifestyle, got her hooked on heroin and then pimped her to all his friends and business acquaintances.'

Becky smiled sadly. 'Not an uncommon story. But doubly shocking when it happens to someone you know and you see the pitiful wreck they have become; comparing it to the lovely, vibrant person you remember.'

She paused and looked at each of them in turn. 'What shocked me the most was when she was complaining about how much it had cost her to get from Leeds to see me. It wasn't the price; it was how she earned the money to pay for the ticket.'

'Did she tell you the name of this man, the alleged boyfriend?' Clara asked.

'She did, and she didn't. All I knew was he was European. She referred to him, but she was terrified, said it wouldn't be safe for me if she gave me his real name because he could come after me as he'd done with others who had crossed him. She told me about one man he'd ordered to be killed by his creepy sidekick. Disposed of, was the expression he used. A week later this man's body was found in a burnt-out car on the outskirts of Leeds.'

'She really believed he would come after you?' Lisa asked.

'She did, and with good reason as it turned out. But fortunately, by the time that happened I'd learned enough about him to take evasive action, so to speak. What I didn't know was his English identity.'

'Sorry, I'm not with you?' Clara was mystified.

'All I knew was a foreign name and where he came from before he arrived in this country. That was all she would say. So I took a few days leave from work and put her up at my flat. Gradually, the whole sorry story came out. How she knew he had at least one other woman, a Scotswoman she heard him mention, by the name of Morag, who was in charge of distributing the drugs. All Aimee knew about Morag was that she lived in Yorkshire because of something he'd said, something about more drugs being brought inland so it was time to send someone to collect them from Morag.

'You have to understand that what I've just told you only came out in dribs and drabs as she remembered it and when she was lucid enough to talk — which to be fair wasn't very often. After three days I had to go shopping; I was running out of food. I promised I'd be back within an hour. When I got back, she had gone. I assumed she'd changed her mind and gone back to him, and I spent the rest of the evening cursing her selfishness.' Becky shook her head sadly. 'I should have known better. It was almost a fortnight later when I got a phone call from the police. I met with a detective sergeant who asked me if I'd given my business card to anyone recently. I hadn't. So he asked me to take a look at a body.'

Becky's face became even grimmer, if that was possible.

'If I'd had trouble recognizing Aimee before, when I saw her in the mortuary, it was well nigh impossible. If it hadn't been for the dress and shoes I don't think I would have known her. Apparently her body had been found floating in the Thames. Her face . . .' Becky was too distressed to go on for a moment, but with a supreme effort of will she regained her composure. 'Her face had been cut to ribbons. Not cut; but sliced by someone who knew exactly what they were doing. The police had phoned me because they found my business card in her pocket. The detective asked me if I'd drawn anything on it. I said not, and he produced it. Someone had drawn a skull and crossbones on the back in indelible pencil. Obviously knowing it was going to be immersed in water, equally obviously intending it to be seen by me.

'I decided to follow up on Aimee's story. After all, it is my job. So I began to try and find out what I could about her supposed boyfriend, which wasn't easy. Bear in mind, I was working from a name and background, neither of which was English, but after a while I started to get fragments.

'For a while I'd been under the impression that someone was following me, but I believed it was my imagination, or nerves. Then I realized I was seeing the same man. In the meantime, my flat was broken into. Almost everything I had of value got smashed up and my laptop and a few files that I had at home were stolen.

'A couple of days later I was turning into a side street when a van coming towards me slammed the brakes on, all I could do was jump and pray. I tripped and a passing jogger caught me as I fell. I got off lightly with only a badly bruised knee, a pair of ruined tights and a broken heel. I got the impression someone wasn't trying to mow me down, but to grab me. If that jogger hadn't run round that corner who knows what could have happened.'

Becky looked across at Nash. 'That was when I decided to cut and run. I went to my parents' house in Bournemouth but even there I knew I wasn't safe. I spotted the same man following me again.' She looked at the chief constable and smiled. 'I knew my investigation must have upset someone. That was when I phoned Aunt Gloria and told her everything that I'd discovered. We needed a plan. She consulted Mike and he came up with the idea of pretending I had drowned. The weather in the Bay of Biscay is never good, but luckily for me there were some particularly bad storms at the time. It took some doing but we persuaded my friends at the newspaper to put the drowning story out; I thought that might buy me time.'

'But what about your family?' Clara was shocked. 'Surely they would have been grief stricken.'

'Clara,' Nash said, 'how many times do missing persons turn up safe and well? The press report said feared drowned — it didn't say she was dead.'

'And besides,' Becky continued, 'by then I was already hiding out in Netherdale. I'd rung my parents before the report went out and suggested they took a holiday, away from the possible press questions. Aunt Gloria called on Mike not only to help me, but to liaise with the drugs team to break up the suppliers. He decided the only way I'd be safe in the long-term, would be if they could get to grips with the people threatening me.'

'I assume the man you identified from what your friend Aimee told you is Ivan Kovac?' Clara asked.

'Yes, she told me his name was Todor, and that he came from Serbia. I came up with lots of people called Todor, but one seemed a likely candidate. His name was Todor Nikolic.'

Nash interrupted. 'Then I suggest we charge him under the name Nikolic and threaten to apply for a deportation order against him. If he's the man Becky thinks he is and he believes there's a chance of him being extradited, I think he'll talk.'

'So where have you been, Becky, and what have you been doing for the last few weeks?' Clara asked.

'In France as a house guest of Master Daniel. As for what I've been doing, most of my time has been spent bowling leg breaks at him, over, after over, after over. Some days I'd wake up and be unable to move my arm.' Becky smiled at the memory 'He says I'm not a bad spin bowler — for a girl.'

Clara rounded on Nash. 'Why didn't you tell me? Surely you knew you could trust me.'

'Of course I did, in fact I pressed for it. But I was under orders. Not from within, I feel sure the chief would have agreed. It was Alisha's boss who made the rules. And as DIU was running the show I couldn't argue. There wasn't time, either. I'd to get Becky to safety as fast as possible, and as soon as I returned, I was off on the search. You have to appreciate how quickly all this happened. All we knew was that someone was bringing drugs in via the North Yorkshire coast and we believed they were the same ones who were trying to silence Becky. The idea was that if we could discover how the drugs came into the country, then find out how they brought them here, we could block the operation. In the end, you did most of the work for us.'

'So how come you were the one who had to go with the DIU agent?' Clara asked.

'Because everyone would think I was away on compassionate grounds because of Becky's accident. And let's face it, the plan worked didn't it? Besides, it was thought that a couple were more likely to go unnoticed.'

'OK, I'll give you that. But you seemed to be getting on extremely well,' Clara added, giving Jackie Fleming a sidelong glance.

'Alisha and I go back a long way. We worked together in London.'

'Yes, we thought you seemed to know each other well,' Jackie added.

A while later, once Nash had told them about Shakila's part in the enquiry and answered the team's many questions, he stood up. 'Now I am going on leave,' he told them, but I'll be back in the office on Monday.'

Before leaving, he had a quiet word with Clara. 'I heard the news about David, how is he?'

She explained, adding, 'I'm hoping for a week's leave, depending on how we go with staff.'

'I know, Gloria told me, that's why I'm coming back on Monday as long as Daniel is looked after, which I think he will be once I've phoned the childminder. Right, we'd better be off. I'll drive Becky back to Gloria's and then I've got a test match to go to, otherwise, Daniel will never forgive me.'

As they walked back across the car park, Mike asked Becky, 'What now?'

'I need to get back to London as soon as I can. I've had my holidays' — she grinned at Daniel — 'but I need to get back to work. I've got a story to write — one hell of a story! Then it's time I came home. I was only supposed to go to London for a year — that was over five years ago.'

'There is one more thing I'd like to know.'

'What's that?'

'Where did you learn to bowl such good leg breaks?'

CHAPTER TWENTY-EIGHT

On Monday morning Nash was surprised to find Clara already in his office tidying his desk. 'What are you doing here?'

'As someone once said to me, these are outstanding case files. I've been through all of them and made notes for action wherever possible. Then I'm on leave.'

'Ouch! That sounds familiar. I'm sorry, Clara. I have explained.'

'I know, but I couldn't resist it,' she said with a grin. 'I've only come in to hand over. These aren't outstanding cases, they're all the reports. I thought you'd want to see them and there's bound to be something you need to ask that's not in there.' She pointed at the pile of files. 'How was the cricket?' she asked as she handed him the stack.

'Fine, just don't ask Daniel about it. Not unless you've a couple of hours to spare.'

They moved into the CID room where Viv and Lisa joined them. Nash studied the files with Clara supplying additional background. 'You've done a terrific job, all of you. I think I should go away more often.' He was about to add something more when his eyes narrowed as he looked at one of the reports.

'This Mason character, the one who used to be a mercenary, it gives his service details here. I think it would be worth checking a bit deeper, but from memory I've got a feeling his regiment was the same as Simon Wardle's.'

'Aren't you being a bit paranoid? I know you have special reasons for thinking Wardle is wholly evil after what happened in the past, but he can't be behind every crime in the area.'

Nash shrugged. 'Possibly, but I still think it's worth a look. Viv, get Tom to dig Wardle's file out.'

'And if it does happen to be the same regiment?' Clara continued.

'Then I think we ought to take a look at the fish van drivers and see if they were members of that unit. Birds of a feather, if you get my point. And they have done it before, more than once.'

As she was leaving she commented, 'By the way, I got the shock of my life when that woman from the DIU was referred to as Mrs Nash. I thought you'd gone and tied the knot. Then, after I heard everything you'd done to help Becky, I wondered if that was on again.'

Nash's expression changed, became sombre. He shook his head. 'No in both cases, and I think you know the reason for that, Clara. Now off you go, give our regards to David, and don't worry about us here, we'll do our best to manage without you.'

As Clara walked across to her car she recalled the sadness in Nash's eyes when she'd asked about his personal life. It was clear nothing had changed.

* * *

The plane leaving Leeds/Bradford airport for Corfu was packed. Tony Hartley and his family had obtained the last available seats, but only courtesy of a cancellation. A few weeks in the sun at his villa was just what he needed. As they queued for check-in, Hartley thought about all that had happened and what he had to do following their return. He knew he was secure now. He had never dealt directly with the drug dealers on the street, so there was no likelihood of them giving him away. His men were being taken care of and although they knew his identity they wouldn't talk, there was too much at risk for their families' financial security. Only Ron Mason knew the location of his island hideout; and he certainly wouldn't talk.

When Hartley got back it wouldn't matter anyway, not with the intended escape of his boss, Simon Wardle, from Felling Prison well in hand. Even the planning of that had reached an advanced stage. So much so, that he was confident that within days of his return to England, it could be put into operation.

It had taken Hartley eighteen months, a lot of criminal activity of varying degrees and some lives lost, to amass the funds required to finance the scheme. But now the plan was close to being activated. It needed a certain set of events to coincide *and* it relied on the unique design of Felling Prison. Hartley had sent Wardle a covert text message the previous night warning him to be ready.

* * *

The next morning, as Tony Hartley was watching his children playing in the sea while he enjoyed a drink in a local taverna, back in England an officer entered Simon Wardle's cell. He was carrying some large, clear plastic bags which he handed to the prisoner.

'Start packing, Wardle. Put all your possessions in there. Time for a change of scene. You're being moved. From tomorrow, the inmates of Durham Gaol can delight in your company.'

THE END

ABOUT THE AUTHOR

Having taken early retirement from the finance industry, prolific writer Bill Kitson enjoys the challenge of writing both crime and general fiction, often with a twist of humour. Both his series, the DI Mike Nash crime thrillers and his Eden House Mysteries, are set in North Yorkshire, the county of his birth.

He also writes Greek Island Romances under the pseudonym William Gordon.

Living and working throughout most of the North of England he is now settled on the east coast of England, along with his wife.

His writing never stops, and when he isn't seeking inspiration from the surrounding countryside he can be found in a small fishing village on one of the Greek Islands, staring out to sea — laptop at the ready!

For further details go to:
www.billkitson.com
www.billkitsonblog.wordpress.com

ALSO BY BILL KITSON

THE DI MIKE NASH SERIES
Book 1: WHAT LIES BENEATH
Book 2: VANISH WITHOUT TRACE
Book 3: PLAYING WITH FIRE
Book 4: KILLING CHRISTMAS
Book 5: SLASH KILLER
Book 6: ALONE WITH A KILLER
Book 7: BLOOD DIAMOND
Book 8: DEAD & GONE
Book 9: HIDE & SEEK
Book 10: RUNNING SCARED

Join our mailing list to be the first to hear about the next book in the series:
www.joffebooks.com/contact

finger

Tues 8.45

Blood Test

Printed in Great Britain
by Amazon

46736033R00142